SHIFTER GOD

SHIFTER WAR, VAMPIRE ORDERS BOOK 1

MEG XUEMEI X

First Edition
ISBN: 9798763251739
Printed in the United States of America

❀ Created with Vellum

Book 4: Blood Fae

THE WAR OF GODS SERIES

A Court of Blood and Void

A Court of Fire and Metal

A Court of Ice and Wind

A Court of Earth and Ether

OF SHADOWS AND FIRE SERIES

The Burn of the Underworld

The Rise of the Underworld

The Dragonian's Witch

The Witch's Consort

SHIFTER'S WITCH

NEWSLETTER SIGN-UP

Did you enjoy this novel and want more? Sign up to Meg's mailing list to receive new release notifications. In addition, you will receive an exclusive bonus scene and a special gift—my way of saying "thank you" for sharing this journey with me.

You can also join Meg's Legion of Hellions on Facebook to chat about all of Meg's books.

SHIFTER GOD

~ About the Book ~

A wild band of smoking-hot shifters rescue me from the hunters.

I want to be grateful, but the shifters turn out to be assholes as well, especially Jared, the Alpha Heir and apparently my fated mate.

He's chosen another, a powerful shifter princess, over a nobody like me. Even worse? He claims I'm a spy for the vampires and drags me to the fortified Shifter City.

After dumping me at a shifter military academy, he thinks he can forget about me. Only he underestimates his hot and heavy lust for me.

And I listen to his sweet, vicious lies and let him act on his urges. Afterwards he goes back to his fiancée, who wants me dead more than the air she breathes.

When I try to escape, Jared punishes me and locks me up. But there's something he doesn't know, that not even I know. A formidable Vampire God has been hunting for his destined **Bride** for over a century.

Me.

And Marlowe kills anyone who gets in his way.

*H*er stunning golden eyes burned like liquid fire and widened in shock. Her soft lips parted in pain then ecstasy, which excited me more.

My fangs pierced her creamy skin. The veins in her neck pulsed against my mouth. Her rich blood, sweet and pungent, coated my tongue. For the first time in my long, lonely existence as a Vampire God, I tasted unveiled sunshine and a piece of heaven that had been denied to my kind since the dawn of time.

She'd once fought me with every ounce of her fiery strength. Now, she finally surrendered to me.

"I'll protect you with my last breath, my *Bride*," I whispered the promise into her ear. "I'll hand you the world and pluck the distant stars for you."

"Will you, Marlowe?" she purred between

moans of pleasure. Her feminine, magical scent drove me out of my mind.

My large hand cupped her breast. She arched her back, her need becoming mine, echoing in my veins.

My Bride was ripe for me to take.

I growled in approval and pushed the thick crown of my hard shaft between her plump folds. My cock found home as it plunged through my female's narrow passage and sheathed deep within her. She gasped in pleasure, her eyes shifting to a color between honey and fire.

Ophelia pressed her hands against my face, wanting to hold on to me with everything she had. My control slipped. My primal male need roared for me to claim her. To make her mine.

I'd never wanted any woman more than I wanted her. My cock had never been so hard and throbbed so painfully. I thrust into her tight, pink pussy wildly. I would fuck her to eternity. I would never stop…

The dream or vision had been ripped from me, and it never returned again.

But I knew what I had to do.

Those who hunted her called her Death's daughter.

She'd been hunted like a wild beast for a long time. And now, she was being held captive and tortured. Her mind shattered, no longer able to tell day from night, in order to escape the memory of her true nightmares and the ugly reality of unholy abuse.

Those beings wanted her hidden power yet claimed that they did it for the greater good and the survival of humanity.

All living things would tremble in front of her once her wrath awoke along with her power.

She might be Death, but she was more than life to me.

She'd been born, become a woman, and come to our world.

My Bride.

My eternal sunshine.

I'd waited for her for an eon and hunted for her for centuries. And now I had finally learned where she'd been taken and held and tormented.

So, I set out to find my Bride, bring her home, and kill all those motherfuckers who damaged her.

CHAPTER ONE

PIP

*I*n one heartbeat, I was trapped within a nightmare I couldn't escape from, but in the next, blood pumped into my ears as I ran for my life, chased by dangerous men and women.

"Don't let the Death bitch get away!" a man shouted.

Panic filled my lungs. My bare feet pounded on the leaves, twigs, and old pine seeds. A tiny, sharp rock stuck in the bottom of my left foot and hurt like a bitch, but I dared not slow down.

I had no freaking idea who those people were and why they had to hunt me with torches, archers, big guns, and spells, but my instincts told me they were bad news, and if I got caught, I'd rather beg for death.

I couldn't help but curse myself for not grabbing a pair of shoes before running. Maybe I didn't have time? I had no memory until this point, but I knew I was terrified.

A gunshot rang through the night air, so loud that I grimaced, but no one considered my feelings. A series of shots followed, exploding beside my ears. Bullets bit into the tree trunks around me, but none hit my person. I'd ducked my head earlier, and now I ran in a zigzag fashion, as if my senses could tell where the next bullets would land. I didn't know how I could tell, but I was glad to have this ability, yet it couldn't predict the direction of the exploding tree bark and flying bits of wood—the result of being bombarded by a barrage of shrapnel—when they grazed my arms and shoulders.

It hurt, but it would be worse if I got pierced by a bullet.

My heart nearly blasted out of my tightened chest and my blood chilled when I heard a pair of hounds yowling with bloodlust. Someone had brought them along to hunt me.

What had I done to deserve this?

Had I stolen something from those people? I didn't feel like a thief, though. I had no time to figure it out as a fireball erupted in front of me between the trees, narrowly missing me and lighting up half of the dark forest.

A wave of scorching heat slammed into my face.

My heart pounding and my pulse skyrocketing, I made a mad dash to the side path and charged into another sector. Another fireball ignited behind me, scorching a patch of land.

The stench of sulfur and dark magic hit my nostrils. The hounds' snarling and galloping closing in on me sent icy water coursing through my veins.

I plunged ahead in panic while leaping over a broken branch and alighted on a bed of sharp pine needles. I dared not groan, for fear of giving away my exact location.

"Hurry!" a woman barked. "We can't let the abomination get away!"

Oh my gods, I was the abomination she was referring to, and she was spurring the hounds to go faster in order to capture me.

As soon as I got out of this hot shit, I would find a mirror to inspect myself. I couldn't remember how I looked, but I was damn sure that I didn't have two heads or three eyes.

The hounds' howling sent a wave of dismay into my bones. They were gaining on me. The rapid thuds of their powerful paws hitting the undergrowth jarred my thinning nerves. I pictured their massive jaws clamping down upon my neck and shuddered.

In blind panic, I willed something bad to happen to my pursuers, to slow them down. Then

I heard a loud clashing sound followed by vicious swearing. It seemed that at least two members of the mob had fallen on their faces and probably eaten a mouthful of dirt.

"Watch out, Sara!" an older man snarled. "I'm right behind you!"

"It's not me, Guy," Sara protested in a scratchy voice. She might have smoked too much. "That little bitch made the branches swing at us. You know she can do that."

They knew me better than I did. And if I'd made those trees hit them, I could probably do more.

Concentrating hard, I pictured the wind, imagined it blowing and summoning it to come to me. A strong gust rose, hurling a load of dead leaves, dirt, and pine needles at the hunters.

They halted to fend off the elemental attack and cursed at me.

"I twisted my ankle," a younger man's mean voice whined. "That bitch will pay!"

"Counter spells!" Guy yelled with harsh authority.

A chorus of chanting filled the night, chilling the air and turning the forest even more ominous.

The wind I'd conjured fell silent, and the air stagnated and smelled like dead water.

This time, when I willed a storm to come to my aid and to sweep away my foes, nothing happened.

These hunters were clearly powerful users of magic. Their combined magic and spells had countered my will.

So far, I'd only slowed them down a little. They were a horde, one I couldn't stop.

Dread weighing upon my chest like lead, I stumbled ahead without seeing what was in front of me. A thorny branch from a shrub tore the hem of my gown at my knees.

While running, I glanced down to check the damage as a throbbing pain radiated from my right thigh. For the first time, I noticed I was wearing a white sleeping gown. Thorns had torn open the fabric and left a faint trace of blood across my leg.

The hounds' bloodcurdling howls growing closer iced me over. The scent of my blood must have driven them into a frenzy. I ran faster, willing my strides to be longer. One of the hounds had gotten so close to me I could feel its horrid breath steaming my neck.

Fear seizing me, I looked over my shoulder to see how close the beast actually was, hoping I'd imagined the closeness. My foot rammed into a fallen branch, and I tripped. The momentum sent me flying headfirst into a clearing.

It might've been a quiet, nice night in the dark forest if this hunting scene hadn't happened. And now even big animals didn't dare to make a sound as they hunkered beneath thick undergrowth. Owls had stopped hooting a while ago.

It was just the hunters, hounds, and me disturbing the night, with my nose pressed into the earth and my tears flowing down my dirty face.

Before I could scramble to my feet, a hound lunged toward me. Its yellow eyes glowed in the dark as they fixed on me with hunger, its jaws wide open, its serrated fangs glinting in the moonlight and dripping with saliva.

"The hound got her!" Sara shrieked enthusiastically.

A few men shouted in harsh excitement.

Howling in rage and fear, I pushed myself up and thrust my hand toward the hound in midair. In front of my eyes, my hand turned to claws with five blades at lightning speed.

The blades sank into the beast's belly, slashing all the way through to his heart. The hound screamed horribly, and I rolled out from under it before it toppled over on me. I wasn't fast enough. Its forepaw battered my shoulder. Gore and blood splashed across my face and half my body.

I scrambled to my feet and dove into a row of trees ahead for better cover. An idea hit me. Maybe I should stay and fight since I wasn't as helpless and powerless as I'd thought. I had claws made of blades. I stared at them. My gods, I was a freak.

Maybe I could hide behind trees, darting here

and there, and pick off the hunters one by one. I'd keep the last one alive and get answers from him/her about who I was and why they hunted me.

Before I turned back to fight them, my claws receded. I willed them to come out again, but they wouldn't budge. I threw my hands forward forcefully, yet my blades still didn't appear.

It was as if I'd imagined I had them, but the dead hound testified otherwise.

"That abomination bitch slaughtered my hound!" Sara wailed behind me as if she'd lost a child.

Bolts of light and fire shot toward me like a rain of comets. None of them hit me, but only because my senses had told me where they were going to crash, giving me time to dive away from the magical assaults a second before they hit.

Yet I didn't come out completely unscathed from the magical show. A few strands of my long hair were singed as they flew behind me. The stench of burning filled my nostrils.

I didn't need any further encouragement to scratch my plan of staying to fight. Instead, I ran.

Another streak of fiery bolts whooshed by my ears, disappearing into the darkness. A barrage of spells chased me, making my ears ring. As I wondered if they'd ever stop, a spell crashed into my middle.

The pain was harsh but manageable. I dared not slow down. Low branches ahead slammed into my face, but I kept on sprinting.

Fatigue caught up with me, making my limbs feel heavier. At some point, I didn't care anymore. I just wanted to curl up and sleep.

Only a rush of adrenaline and fear kept me pounding my bloody feet against the forest floor and zigzagging between trees to avoid bullets and spells that continued to shoot toward me.

While my wild heartbeat and laborious breathing filled my ears, I heard the sound of water not far away.

A spark of hope surged inside me. I could lose my pursuers if there was a river. I picked up my speed, pumping my arms back and forth and sped toward what I hoped would be my freedom.

The shouting behind me grew louder. It was followed by a downpour of arrows attempting to block my path, but I didn't stop. An arrow sank into my thigh. I cried out in pain, nearly stumbled, but managed to keep going in an awkward limping run. The sound of water grew closer, maybe less than half a mile away.

Moonlight shone through a clearing fifty feet ahead. I inhaled a lungful of air that tasted of earth, spice, and burned sugar.

It must be autumn.

A wave of sadness washed over me. How many seasons had I missed?

I tore into the clearing. Without the trees blocking my view, I could see that ahead wasn't a river but a cliff, and the roaring sound came from a waterfall.

I didn't stop.

I sprinted toward the cliff with all the strength I had left. The hunters and their hound charged out of the forest behind me, shouting angrily and desperately.

A volley of arrows zipped toward me, and I dodged them to the best of my ability, which was hard to do, considering I had no cover.

When I reached the edge of the cliff, a bullet got me, which wasn't too bad, as it went right through me under my right shoulder. The wound wouldn't be fatal.

I wheeled toward the hunters, grinning savagely while flipping them the bird.

"Fuck you!" I roared and jumped backward into the thundering waterfall.

CHAPTER TWO

*T*he roaring rapids eventually slowed and brought me to grasslands dotted with shrubs, probably five miles from where I'd jumped.

If I stayed in the water any longer, my skin might just peel off. I swam against the current toward the bank, trying not to black out. I'd lost a lot of blood from all my injuries. Eventually, I made it and sprawled along the riverbank to catch my breath.

Slowly, I sat up, my head pounding from blood loss and fatigue. But it was a nice surprise to see that the bullet wound in my shoulder had already sealed. The only indication that I'd been hit by a bullet was a red, angry mark on my skin.

So, I healed fast, which was fantastic. Was that why the hunters wanted me, so they could study me and steal my power?

I scanned my surroundings one more time to make sure I was the only one in the wilderness and temporarily safe, then I took a more thorough inventory of myself, specifically the damn arrow which was still embedded into my thigh.

I inched back toward the river until half of my ass was on the edge of the lapping water. I held the hem of my sleep gown and tore four long strips to make a makeshift bandage.

I snatched up a twig and inserted it between my teeth before gripping the shaft of the arrow, which had snapped in two while I was in the churning pool of the waterfall. I yanked the arrow out with all my might and bravery. The sound of flesh tearing filled my ears, but was quickly drowned out by my screams of agony.

Blood gushed up from the ragged wound. My shaking hands grabbed the strips of fabric and wrapped them tightly around the gash. I groaned in agony, all while telling myself I had to live through this nightmare, if only to find out who I was and where I came from.

I spat the twig out of my mouth and washed the remaining blood from my skin. With the last of my strength, I dragged myself across a grassy field, shivering uncontrollably. The moon had faded, leaving me in complete darkness, and a breeze had grown chillier.

Just up ahead I spotted a place to hide. I

crawled to the large shrub, flattened its woody stems, and curled into a ball on the stem bed and wet grass. Then I tried to make sense of what had happened.

Did I have a name? I tried to recall it, but my memory abandoned me. So I focused on the people hunting me instead. Who were they and why did they want me dead? When I couldn't come up with an answer for those questions either, I cried until there was nothing left. The release couldn't erase my exhaustion, pain, hunger, and apprehension, but I felt a little better after crying.

I'd gotten away, and that was a big win. This small comfort soothed me as I fell asleep with the hopes of a better tomorrow.

Much too soon, a splash of sunlight spilled across my face. My eyes flashed open, my head jerked, and I stared into a hard, handsome, and masculine face.

CHAPTER THREE

*S*uspicious shouts rose outside the tall, thick shrub where I lay hiding, sending a wave of blind panic through my system.

My first thought was that the hunters had found me, but the three men who stared down at me through the branches didn't seem to be from that lot. They had clean-cut appearance and carried the air of disciplined warriors. They also dressed differently.

The hunters had worn robes, like from some kind of cult, which was probably true. But the men in front of me—two of them brushing aside the long stems on either side while giving the taller one the center position—wore blue-and-gray military uniforms.

Their garb stretched nicely across their broad chests, showing off their taut muscles. The taller one had more decorative stars on his uniform that also bore extra golden strips, which meant he ranked higher than the other two hotshots. How could I remember those seemingly insignificant details yet couldn't remember my own name?

I returned the men's quizzical stares while shifting my position into a crouch. It would be stupid to stand up; it'd only make it easier for the intruders to grab me.

It would also be stupid to open my mouth first and give away my vulnerable condition, so I resorted to quietly taking inventory of the trio while reevaluating my situation.

My guarded gaze trained on their leader, and I tried not to show that his handsomeness had an effect on me. His eyes were a distinct gray, like the sharp winter sky before it went dark. His nose was straight, his jaw was stubborn and strong, and his lips looked so carnal that one might connect him to a beast.

Though all three men had razor-cut hair, the ringleader had neatly trimmed sideburns, mutton chops style.

"Don't hiss, Catnip," the younger man to the left of Sideburns crooned with a disarming smile, like he was trying to calm a cornered feline. "We won't hurt you, I promise. But if you bolt, I'll catch you. I love to chase. My name is Shade."

Shade had boyish good looks, like Romeo. I

blinked, frustrated that I could remember Romeo's name and other useless information.

My memory may be junk right now, but at least I wasn't a fool.

I knew when people promised that they wouldn't hurt you, they were usually lying. However, I kind of believed this guy. I could tell by his aura that he was more of the lover type than a killer.

Tall and muscled, he bore a resemblance to Sideburns, but Shade's complexion was more golden, with deep blue eyes and stylish, short blond hair. I wanted to call him Canary, a fitting name for him.

Canary could be a hot underwear model even wearing such a uniform, but Sideburns was hotter for some reason. But he looked too serious about himself, as if he was the owner of all the lands.

The third man to the right of Sideburns looked like he could be Sideburns' uncle. The sides of his hair were peppered with grey, and his brown eyes that regarded me uncompromisingly were hard yet clear, like a man who held no secrets.

Sideburns turned to glare at the men outside our little circle and barked, "Lower your voices. We have a traumatized girl here!"

I could imagine how I looked to them. Home-made bandages wrapped around my wounded leg, tainted by dried blood. My tattered sleeping gown barely covered my thighs. My hair was wild, full of grass and twigs, and some strands still stuck to my dirty face. Even though I'd washed myself by the river, some residual blood still stained my clothes and skin.

And no normal girl would sleep in a shrub in the wilderness.

The men outside our circle quieted down, and Sideburns returned his stern attention to me.

"Who are you?"

All three men narrowed their eyes on me as if I were an exotic animal that had just escaped the zoo.

That was the worst question they could throw at me.

The fuck I know, I almost blurted in annoyance while I glared back at them. Turns out I also have a bad attitude.

An idea swirled into my mind. I needed to send this lot on their way as soon as possible, and I must get on the road before the hunters caught up with me.

I looked like a beggar and a wild thing. And the men were high and mighty, literally. It wouldn't be hard to persuade them to fucking leave me alone.

A tactic formed. No one would be interested in a mentally challenged girl if I took advantage of my unkempt and undesirable appearance and the situation of being in the wrong place at the wrong time.

I cowered back and grabbed my hair with a hiss. "Boo-booo! Boo!" I thrust a hand at them to fend them off, demanding they go away. "Wahdudd!"

Sideburns frowned at me, his brows creasing together. "Are you deaf?"

"Duddub! Boo!" I shouted, dragging my hair a bit harder for better effect.

Sideburns shook his head in disappointment. "The girl doesn't understand English, and I think her brain's scrambled."

I inserted two fingers into my mouth and whistled, then pulled them out to fling a string of saliva at Sideburns. He jumped back, but not that fast, and my spittle fell upon his shiny leather shoe.

It was gross, but it had to be done and done right.

"Fuck," he cursed, glancing at his shoe then at me, a look of disgust in his gray eyes.

"Poopooo!" I yelled louder to get them out of my little world and kicked out my good leg at Canary, since he was closer to me.

He sidestepped swiftly and grinned at me.

"The girl is crazy, Alpha Heir." Going-gray darted a glance at Sideburns. My heart stuttered. I was right about Sideburns being their leader. "She isn't worth our time, no matter how odd the situation seems to be. We should get going. If we hurry up, we can get back to our city by tomorrow night. I want to sleep in my own bed sooner rather than later."

Sideburns stared down at me uncertainly.

"Boo-boo!" I barked to prove that his second was right about me. I was thinking of spitting at him again to help him make up his mind, even though it would double hurt my image. But my dignity had gone down the drain as soon as they'd discovered me.

Sideburns seemed to read that I'd spit on him again, and he stepped back another half pace. Irritation crept over his face. He was a powerful man, and powerful men always got what they wanted. But he wouldn't get a damn thing from a crazy chick who spat and kicked and talked nonsense.

It satisfied me to frustrate him.

"Do you have any other words than boob and poop, Catnip?" Canary asked with undying interest.

"Fuckooo!" I spat at him, my eyes glinting in anger while I struck out my good leg in his direction.

All three men jumped back.

Canary laughed.

"What's so funny?" Going-gray, the one who looked like Sideburns' uncle, asked gruffly. "I say let's leave her be. We've wasted enough time on a crackpot."

"You aren't the sharpest tool in the shed if you missed all the hints, Jay," Canary said. "If we leave without this girl, our mission will be a complete bust. We'll end up going home empty-handed."

"How will our mission be accomplished if we bring a fruitcake with us to the city?" Going-gray sneered. "We shouldn't have trusted a vampire's oracle anyway. This little cuckoo will only be a burden to us. And you know the rules. No outsider is allowed to live within Shifter City." He gave my bird's nest of lilac-blue hair a meaningful glance. "I can even see lice there. But if you're interested in washing her, Prince Shade, by all means do so. However, I'd caution you not to stick your dick—"

"That's enough, Cousin Jay," Sideburns said. "My brother is no longer that man."

Going-gray flung a string of insults my way, but in the meanwhile, he'd also unwittingly provided me with a lot of intel.

So, Canary was Sideburns' brother. He wasn't an heir, but he was still a prince. Going-gray was their older cousin. I also pocketed several keywords they'd mentioned in their banter: vampire's oracle, Shifter City. No outsiders.

But none of them made any sense to me other than Canary had been a notorious womanizer.

Well, his pretty dick wouldn't get anywhere near me if he wanted to keep it in one piece.

"Let's roll out," Sideburns called and turned away from me, heeding his cousin's advice.

Going-gray shot Canary a smug look before he let go of the tall stems. I jerked my foot back, concealing a gloating smirk. I'd outwitted all three princes. I should flip them the middle finger after they all turned their backs on me.

Like a flash of lightning, Canary bent down, his arm around my waist, and snatched me out of the shrub.

I shoved at him and kicked, but his vise-like grip wouldn't budge.

Sideburns and Going-gray stopped in their tracks and wheeled toward us, an identical look of annoyance flitting across their faces.

"What are you doing, Shade?" Sideburns scolded. "We don't have fucking time for this!"

"Oh, we'll make time for this, my dear brother," Canary crooned. "My gut feeling says this girl is very important. Think of the odds of a gorgeous young girl getting lost in the middle of nowhere, like a wounded bird. Obviously, she's been hunted, or she wouldn't have hidden in the shrub for the night, which was clever of her. She also left no trace of blood. If we weren't shifters, we wouldn't have sniffed her out. Call it fate or something else, but it was our destiny to find her. No offense, guys, but all of you missed the details staring you in the face. If you'd caught that conniving glint in the girl's golden eyes when you were about to leave her alone, you would never have dismissed her as the Mad Hatter. She's more cunning than all of us. And finally, I've sensed a beast in her. She's like us."

I sucked in a breath.

Many of his points were valid, except that I didn't know how I looked. But being called beautiful didn't hurt my case. However, his last opinion made me want to punch him in the throat. I wasn't a beast girl. But then, I stopped cold as I thought of my claws coming out and slashing open the hound.

Was I like them?

Could I really be a shifter?

No matter; I wasn't going with this lot either. I'd escaped hunters who could throw fireballs. I could get away from the shifters as well. While the asshole Canary held me in his iron grip, I took the opportunity to count his company and map out an escape route.

There were two dozen men scattered about. I could tear through the space between the bushes. Unlike the hunters, who would be happy to put me in a body bag if they couldn't have me, this lot would want to catch me alive because of their prince's stupid interest in me and because they wanted answers.

All I needed was to outrun them, rush to the

river, jump in, and let the current take me further down. The basic rule of Escaping 101 was to flee at the first chance, or you might never get a second chance.

I opened my mouth and bit into Canary's forearm. He yelped and gazed down at my teeth in his skin. The soldiers all around were about to surge forward to stop me, but Canary put up a hand to stop them.

The skin between my teeth suddenly hardened, and golden fur sprouted, tickling my throat and nearly choking me.

What the fuck?

Canary let out a low chuckle, utterly amused. "I can partially shift. I can also change into my warrior form at leisure. Would you care to see it, Catnip? My foes find it frightening, but women who like to walk on the wild side find it irresistible and attractive."

I heard some soldiers' barks of laughter.

This fucking Canary thought he was funny, and his team members thought he was hilarious.

My teeth abandoned his furry arm, and I spat out a few golden hairs that I'd torn from his fur.

"You think you're cute, Canary?" I seethed. "You're far from it." I spat one last remaining hair from my mouth. "This is fucking disgusting!"

"Canary?" He scowled before he laughed again, peering down at my beet-red, angry face. "Sorry,

Catnip, I forgot to warn you, but it's worth it to hear you talk like this. You have a lovely voice, and it'd be a waste if you kept shouting something like 'fuckooo'."

Sideburns and Going-gray wheeled around to stare at me. Yeah, I could talk. I wasn't the Mad Hatter either. At this point, it was useless to pretend further, since Canary, the ultimate man whore, had busted me irrevocably.

"Don't feel bad," Canary continued, in a perky mood. "Your act earlier was impressive. You nearly fooled me as well. Now quit being mad. I think we can be friends, if you can keep from holding a grudge. But I have a feeling you're the kind of girl who never offers the other cheek when someone slaps you."

"Which fucking idiot would let both her cheeks be slapped?" I hissed at him.

Canary grinned. "Fierce and foul-mouthed, just my type."

Before I could demand he let me down, a strong wind blew over, throwing up my gown and letting my ass feel its cold kiss.

"Quit flirting—" Sideburns' mouth clamped close, and he inhaled.

He happened to be downwind. Something shifted in his eyes. Shock and confusion wrestled for control over his expression. He sniffed again, his handsome face nearly morphing into a wolf's.

A blink later, he seemed to regain control, but his eyes started to glow silver.

He stalked toward me, suddenly in a hurry, as if his butt was on fire.

Canary stared at him, looking stunned. Sideburns clearly wasn't acting normally. The Alpha Heir stared at me with strange intensity, which sent my heart pumping.

What was he going to do to me? I took a step back. Not in fear, however. He didn't look like he wanted to hurt me. He looked more like he wanted me, and he wasn't going to take no for an answer.

Fuck!

Somehow, I knew men didn't take rejection well, and he was no ordinary man. He was a privileged, powerful man. Even so, if he thought he could force me, he'd have another thing coming.

My heart fluttered like nervous wings, and I struggled in Canary's grip, ready to defend myself. While he held me, I'd stolen a small dagger from the sheath strapped on his left thigh.

The younger prince wasn't as smart as he thought.

"Put her down! Now!" Sideburns shouted before he reached me. "And don't ever touch her again!"

That sounded unnecessarily possessive.

He shoved Canary away, grabbed me to him, and put me gently on the ground. Well, he'd done the job for me, so I didn't need to wrestle with Canary or issue harsher demands.

My eyes darted wildly as I estimated how far I could get from my new captors if I bolted now. But then Sideburns' scent of pure male musk and honeysuckle hit my nostrils.

A spark of fire leapt within my belly, warming and waking up something within me. A lick of liquid flames materialized out of nowhere and caressed the tender flesh between my thighs. Lust swirled to life, coursing through my veins.

My pussy was suddenly slick, and Sideburns suddenly appeared to be the most attractive man on Earth.

I parted my lips in surprise.

What the fuck?

I stared back at Sideburns. Lust stormed in his glowing eyes. If I didn't run or stop him, he might just mount me right there in front of everyone. At least, he looked like he wanted to.

My body urged me toward him, but my will pushed me to stagger back a step.

"Fuck me. How can it be?" Canary murmured to himself, his eyes widening in shock and bitterness.

"Fuck me indeed." Going-gray echoed his younger cousin's opinion as he darted his gloomy gaze between Sideburns and me.

A realization bloomed in me.

Sideburns and I had a connection. It was more than a physical link. It was biological. I didn't want to admit it, but I knew what it meant.

He was my fated mate.

Sideburns sniffed again, inhaling my scent. His gray eyes never left me, then he nodded as if to confirm what he already knew.

"What happened here stays here." He lowered his deep voice and said in a curt, commanding tone, "No one shall know about it."

Canary and Going-gray traded a glance, hesitated for a beat, and nodded solemnly.

Okay, so everyone thought this connection and chemistry thing between Sideburns and me was bad. It wasn't difficult to draw a conclusion that Sideburns might feel attracted to me, but he wasn't going to follow his urge, or even acknowledge it.

He was basically a stranger to me, no matter how Fate wanted to link me to him, and I didn't even like him that much, so his subtle rejection shouldn't hurt.

But hell, I still felt the sting.

I turned my face in the direction of the river. The shifters milled around, packing their stuff and getting ready to depart.

To get past them would be difficult. Or I could just leave like a normal person, peeling off from a group I didn't belong in.

Act normal and get the hell out of here.

I turned on my heels and restrained myself from running.

"Where are you going, Catnip?" Canary called and jogged after me. "You're heading in the wrong direction."

"No, I'm heading in the right direction," I said, waving a hand at them without turning. "Bye, guys. It was nice to meet you."

Moving faster than a flash, Sideburns blocked my path. "You're not leaving."

I arched an eyebrow mockingly. "Really? Who says so?"

"I say so," he said. "You're staying with us. I have questions for you."

Despite him being a jerk, and despite the fact that I wanted to shove him out of my way, the attraction between us rippled like rays of sunshine.

I snickered as I put a hand on my hip. "You're not the lord of me, and you have no right to detain me."

Sideburns gazed down at me. This close, I could feel his intoxicating heat, his lust crashing into me like bricks.

Fire twirled between my thighs, licking my perky bundle of nerves. I had to fight not to squeeze my legs to stop the aching need within me.

He sniffed again, and his eyes turned bright silver.

"I can smell your wolf, girl," he said, inhaling deeply as if he couldn't get enough of my scent.

But then he caught himself the next second and held his breath. His fists clenched at his sides. The Alpha Heir was trying hard to rein himself in.

His body wanted me, but it wasn't his will to desire me.

I got it. Look at him, and then look at me. Anyone would understand why it was a wrong fit.

"You're a shifter," he said in a hard voice while heat simmered in his eyes. "Every shifter in North America is the Shifter King's subject, whether you like it or not. You're probably a rogue wolf, yet you're still under the king's jurisdiction. I'm the Alpha Heir, who speaks for my father in his absence. And thus, you're my subject and you'll do exactly what I tell you."

I was tempted to show him a vulgar gesture and tell him to fuck off. I also wanted to tell him he was mistaken about me being a wolf girl, but then, I had no idea what I was.

I knew it wasn't wise to provoke him, but it didn't stop me from stepping back and kicking a cloud of dust and dirt into his eyes. He yelped in surprise and brought a hand up to rub at them.

I made a mad dash toward the river.

* * *

SHIFTER GOD

I JUMPED OVER A BUSH. All hell broke loose as the shifter soldiers surged toward me from three sides, shouting like fiends.

Why had I chosen to hide inside that shrub? Now I had to cross over fifty yards to reach the river.

"Don't hurt her!" Sideburns barked, joining the chase. "Block her only!"

Canary shouted behind me, "Catnip, stop. We can talk about this and sort it out."

Growls rose behind me. Fuck, they'd brought hounds too? I looked over my shoulder and saw a pack of wolves. The soldiers had shifted to their animal forms for speed.

A blink, and a massive black wolf cut in front of me. I nearly rammed into him and hurt myself. As I skidded to a halt, I fell backward on my ass.

Before I could pull my outraged ass up, a dozen wolves surrounded me.

"Shoo! Assholes!" I shouted, brandishing the knife at the wolf pack. "Gang up on me? Come closer and you'll see that I'm good at stabbing."

I was bluffing, of course. I hoped I didn't need to test whether I was good at knifing people or not. I needed to have a better exit plan, like talking my way out of this instead of fighting my way out.

The black wolf snarled at the others, and they backed off a few steps, yet he had no intention of stepping out of my way.

33

The beast regarded me and inhaled, affection brimming in his gray eyes. I instantly recognized him as Sideburns' wolf. His beast seemed to like me better.

Something dark stirred in me, and it wanted to crawl out. Was it the she-wolf Sideburns and Canary had sensed inside me?

The black wolf growled in encouragement, wanting my beast to come out to play with him. But I didn't know how to turn into a wolf, and I didn't want to try to shift in front of everyone, in case I made a fool of myself by doing it wrong.

The hunters had called me Death bitch and abomination. My hand had turned into blade-like claws. I didn't want to give this pack any more reasons to think of me as a freak that needed to be put down.

I reined in whatever was inside me, and the moment passed.

The black wolf stepped toward me, friendliness in his every move and gesture. I stretched out the hand that didn't hold the knife, ready to scratch the space behind his ear or simply sink my fingers into his silky fur, but the beast halted in mid-stride, as if a force restrained him. He growled and shook his fur as if struggling to break free.

It dawned on me that the man inside the wolf was taking control, and he didn't want his beast to get too close to me.

A gust of wind passed, and where the black wolf had been now stood Sideburns in his glorious nudity. His every muscle and line spelled masculine power.

I flushed and tore my gaze from him, yet I couldn't expel the low hum of heat in my belly.

I bet a lot of women drooled over him. Maybe he already had a few women. Maybe that's why he acted hesitant toward me despite lusting after me.

Fate had put him in my path. But I had this nagging feeling that we were wrong for each other, not in a biological sense but in other ways.

A young shifter soldier brought the Alpha Heir a set of casual clothes, and Sideburns stepped aside to pull on his attire quickly while barking at me, "Put down the knife before you hurt yourself, girl."

I bet giving orders was the only way he knew how to talk to people.

Two wolves were about to lunge to disarm me, but Canary blocked the aggressive wolves.

"Catnip," he said, flashing me a charming smile. "That small knife is a toothpick against a shifter, so you might as well return it. It was a gift from a nice lady."

I glanced down at it. It was a decorated knife with rubies on the hilt. I could sell it for good money if I had to.

"I'm not returning it," I said. "Finders, keepers. Call it and see if it answers you."

Canary arched an eyebrow.

I surveyed the growling shifters around me. It was time to pretend to be meek, withdraw, and bargain.

"I wasn't running away." I swept a hand around. "Where could I run? It's dozens of big grown men and wolves against one lone girl."

The wolves growled as if I'd insulted them.

"I just wanted to wash my face, and you all got your hackles up." I smiled at Canary. He had tried to use his bright smile to stun me, and I didn't mind returning the favor. He stared at my face, momentarily lost for words. "I'll go with you if I get to keep this dagger that a nice lady gave you. I can be a nice lady too. And you said yourself that it's a toothpick, so you needn't worry about me carrying a toothpick in my pocket. Besides, in a camp full of big, bad males, I'll feel a bit safer sleeping with a sharp toothpick under my pillow."

"No one in my camp will harm you." Sideburns pushed through the wolves' formation and faced me again. "Come. We have wasted enough time."

He said it as if the delay was my fault. Wasn't he a charmer? But it wasn't smart to give him a piece of my mind now, especially in front of his men. I still had some sense of self-preservation.

"Let's have Cadmus take a look at Catnip first," Canary said, gesturing at the bandage around my thigh.

This Cadmus must be a healer.

Sideburns frowned, yet a flash of concern flitted by his eyes. "She kicked hard and ran fast, so I thought— Yeah, have Cadmus inspect her." He gave me another once-over. "Find the girl a set of new clothes." His gaze lingered on my bare thighs longer than appropriate before he remembered his manners and self-control. He jerked his gaze up and turned away from me, trying his best not to look at this dirty, forbidden fruit. "After that, we'll leave right away. We'll camp at the neutral zone in a human city tonight."

"What human city?" I asked. I didn't mean to expose my ignorance or vulnerability, but it couldn't be helped. I needed to know where I was. I needed to know more of the world. Any information would help me decide my next course of action.

I wouldn't want to be at the shifters' mercy for long.

"Now she wants answers." Canary chuckled. "I'll tell ya, but you'll have to tell me your name first."

"Shade, I told you not to flirt with the girl," Sideburns said menacingly.

"You're ordering a dog not to bark," Going-gray sighed, as if he was the one who suffered.

I couldn't remember my name even if I had

one, but I wasn't a fan of being called "the girl" or "Catnip." A name popped into my head.

"Call me Pip," I said.

"Pip, I like it," Canary said.

"Glad you approve, Highness Canary."

Sideburns glared at his brother. "What did I just say, Shade?"

"Yeah, yeah, it's your territory. I got it," Canary said, rolling his eyes. "I was just talking to Pip, like a friend. What harm can I cause? It's you who needs to make a decision."

Sideburns thinned his lips. "That's none of your business."

Canary looked somber and walked away, but I followed him. He seemed to be a safety net for me at the moment. Maybe I'd stop calling him Canary.

"Stop, Pip," Sideburns ordered.

"Why?" I may not know my name, but I knew I wasn't the timid type. I felt the Alpha Heir's power, but I didn't cower. "I have a couple questions for the man-whore—sorry, I mean Prince Canary, and I absolutely meant no disrespect." Over Canary's narrowed eyes, I hurried to point at Going-gray. "I'm super bad at remembering names, so I call him Going-gray."

Going-gray glared at me. "I ain't going gray. I'm not even forty yet."

"You *are* going gray, sir. No offense. You might want to pay attention to your diet and not drink too much," I said, then swept three fingers toward Jared as if he deserved more of my fingers due to his higher ranking. "And he's Sideburns or Mutton Chops."

Now Sideburns glared at me. "This is childish and unacceptable. You'll always address me as Alpha Heir or Prince Side—Prince Jared."

"Yes, I will, with all due respect," I said, flipping my wild hair. "But I'll call you Sideburns on a good day and Mutton Chops on a bad day inside my mind."

Canary roared with laughter. The soldiers nearby turned around to conceal the laughter on their faces. A couple of them coughed into their fists. No one dared laugh except for Canary. I decided right then and there that I liked Canary. I'd call him Shade from now on most of the time.

"Alpha and Beta teams, get ready to move out!" Sideburns yelled, ignoring Shade and me.

"Should we run as wolves, Alpha Heir?" Going-gray asked.

Sideburns gave me a measured look. "Can you shift?"

"Uh? Me?" I spread my arms.

Why did he keep asking ridiculous questions? But I knew better than to tell him so. I hadn't had time to put myself together or even acquaint myself with my new name. Considering what I'd been through, I'd say I was doing pretty well so far.

"I might consider it if you have snacks or something," I offered and cleverly brushed off the question.

My stomach chose that very moment to growl. I didn't feel embarrassed, though. No one should be embarrassed for things that were natural, especially as I had no memory of when I'd eaten last. Hunger wasn't a joke.

"See what I mean, Highness?" I grinned at Sideburns while he frowned at me, probably not expecting me to be so unladylike. But who was he to judge? Shifters ate raw meat in their animal forms, right?

"Here." Shade reached into his pocket and removed a snack bar with "Chocolate Protein Bar" written across it. He was a godsend.

Unexpected relief washed over me. It wasn't that I finally got to eat, but that I could read. If I were illiterate, there'd be more obstacles in the way of my survival.

I grinned at Shade as I took his offer and bit off half of the bar. I barely chewed it before I swallowed it, and then I regretted it and stared at the rest of the protein bar.

"Take it easy, Catnip," Shade said, laughter in his bright blue eyes. "I have more for you."

My eyes lit up. "You do?"

"Of course," he said. "Now let's get you checked out before we get on the road."

Sideburns growled at him, but Shade pretended not to see his brother's scowl and led me away to see a healer.

It turned out that my wounds had all healed after the healer removed my bandages. The only indication was a faint, red star on my skin.

The healer looked a bit puzzled. "You can heal even faster than the Alpha Heir."

"Pip is more than meets the eye," Shade said, then whisked me away to get a clean outfit.

I was happy to see that it wasn't a uniform like the shifters wore. I managed to get a man's shirt and casual pants to fit me with a belt, though I had to roll up the long sleeves and pant legs.

When I came out of the bush, Shade beamed at me. Sideburns' heated gaze roved over me before he barked harsh orders at the men. Except for the three princes, all the shifters had changed into their animal forms or forms in between.

They were triple the size of their animal counterparts. The shifters in their warrior forms, half-animal and half-human, carried the equipment.

"You can't shift?" Sideburns asked me again with a critical tone.

What the fuck do you expect? I almost shouted at him.

Shade saw a flash of anger in my eyes, even though I tried to rein in my short, hot temper.

"A virgin shifter?" His lips tilted up. "I can show you—"

Sideburns glared at him. "Do not keep testing me, Shade. Remember your place."

He really didn't like the idea of Shade and me getting cozy.

"I was about to offer Pip a service," Shade said, a smile still ghosting his lips. "I can carry her—"

"Not a chance," Sideburns said in an unnecessarily harsh tone. "Jay will carry the girl." He gave me a decided look and added, "Pip."

Going-gray looked very unhappy, but he nodded and shifted into a big brown wolf.

Sideburns, my supposed fated mate, wasn't planning to act on that role and was shedding his supposed responsibility for me, which was fine. I preferred no one to carry me anyway, but I didn't want to get into the middle of their arguments.

Sideburns came to help me get on the back of the brown wolf, but I leapt onto the back of the wolf just fine before he touched me. Then Sideburns and Shade also shifted, one massive black wolf and one smaller golden beast.

Going-gray shot forward like an arrow, and I had to grab his fur tightly to stay on. At some point, I thought of leaping off the brown wolf's back and running away again, but the river was too far away now.

I guess I'd just have to stick around and play it

by ear. I had nowhere to go anyway. Plus, Shade might look after me for a while. He seemed to have taken a liking to me.

As for Sideburns, I would shove my attraction to him aside, pretend that he didn't exist, and stay out of his sight as best I could.

And he was out of my sight at the moment, as he led the pack in a race at the front.

Shade ran beside the brown wolf and me for a while before his wolf turned into his warrior form, which was half-beast and half-man in his eight-foot-tall glory. I didn't shudder one bit but grinned at the golden monster.

"What's the plan, Canary?"

I leaned forward and clung tightly to the brown wolf like a tough cowgirl.

The warrior wolf narrowed his corn-blue eyes in displeasure.

"Don't call me Canary. It's a horrible name," **he said gruffly. His pronunciation sounded a bit off with fangs filling his mouth.**

"You prefer me to call you Man Whore?" I asked sincerely, arching an eyebrow.

Going-gray grunted. Maybe it was a wolf version of a chuckle?

"You haven't told me which human city we'll stay in," I pursued.

"Do you even know where you are?" he asked.

"No idea. I feel like I dropped onto Earth from the stars and met you."

"I feel like that all the time, Catnip." Shade chortled. "We'll stay in California for the night. You do know that we've just passed the border of Mage Town in Oregon and will head toward Shifter City in Nevada?"

CHAPTER FOUR

*T*hose city names sounded vaguely familiar, but none of them struck a chord. I had the ability of weighing my predicament and coming up with the best solution. I believed that I had a sound mind instead of a damaged one. But why could I remember the feel of a spring rain on my eyelids but not any events or faces of the people from my past?

I took inventory of all the names Shade had mentioned and gathered intel for later use as we trotted through the expanse of grass blades and colorful shrubs. They'd placed me in the middle of their formation.

"No shit, we're in California!" I cheered, though I had no idea what I had to cheer about, only that I was doing this smokescreen thing. I had to be careful what I asked, so I wouldn't raise any suspicion. "Humans. Can't live with them, can't live without them."

That statement was a safe bet, since I bet no one got along with each other.

Shade snorted. "We couldn't live without them when they had the technology, but now that they've lost it? They don't even know what to do with their own toes other than going to war with each other. It's painful to see their civilization crumble."

I bit my tongue before asking what had happened. It seemed the world had passed me by while I had no idea what had happened to myself.

"Yep," I echoed. "They aren't number one anymore, are they? Those good old days of policing the Earth are long gone. Fuckers."

I had nothing against humans. I was just making conversation to fish for more information. But somehow, I knew humans were non-magical and mortal. Those who hunted me clearly weren't humans since they'd thrown magical fireballs at me singing a few strands of my lilac-blue hair.

Shade sent me a non-committal look. "No one expected the arrival of the second horseman when things were all great and humans were all excited about stepping toward the quantum age. All of a sudden, War came, clad in his armor, riding a red horse, blowing the war horn, and raising his sword into the sky. Then global wars swept over

Earth. It was before my time, but the horror he struck into mankind and every species half a century ago is still raw. Humans haven't been able to get themselves together in the wake of War's destruction. The mass slaughter not only devastated human society but also crippled their entire civilization."

What? Horseman? And War had come? The name sounded awfully familiar. A series of images spiked through my head like a flood of lightning piercing though a corner of darkness, outlining a formidable figure in red armor on a crimson horse. I could see his flashing clover-green eyes staring straight into my soul, and I shivered in front of such a being, not due to fear but an uncanny connection between us that was buried deeply in my genetic memory.

While I was still unnerved, the brown wolf beneath me suddenly grew in size and height.

"Hey!" I shouted a warning and was about to slip off his back.

Shade snatched me from the brown wolf's back and placed me on the massive shoulder of his warrior form. I quickly wrapped an arm around Shade's corded, furry neck to keep from falling. I didn't need to see myself to picture the ridiculous image of me learning against a monster like a doll.

Going-gray turned to us. "Humans going backwards works fine for us. They still outnumber us, but without their technology, the playing field has been leveled. They're no longer our biggest threat."

He wanted to join the conversation, so he had shifted to his warrior form. He also wanted to use this opportunity to get rid of me riding him, especially since Sideburns wasn't around and his younger cousin was more than happy to oblige and make me his burden.

"Humans aren't our enemies, vampires are," Shade explained. "And you forget that even before the human global wars ended, the supernatural war had already started."

"Everyone wants power." Going-gray shook his head. "Without War, the second horseman, paving the path for us, the supernaturals would never have dared come into the light. The Feds would still have control of the fifty states, and we'd never have been able to claim Nevada as Shifter City."

"The bloodsuckers got Washington State, which has richer soil," Shade said ruefully.

"There's always good and bad." Going-gray shrugged one of his massive shoulders. "And they don't come to our land of sun and heat."

"California still belongs to humans, though," I chimed in after I had safely deduced that I could throw in a question. "Shouldn't we take it?"

"It's best if California remains independent and neutral," Going-gray said. "It's our cushion."

"It's dangerous to be complacent, cousin,"

Shade said. "War might have done us a favor, but it was not out of the kindness of his heart. When Death, the next horseman, comes, he'll have no discrimination toward any species. The prophecy said that even if we can delay him, as every power on Earth has been trying to do, his daughter will still come to finish the job. In fact, she's probably already here."

My heart rammed into my ribcage and nearly burst with panic.

The hunters had called me "Death bitch."

But it couldn't be me. I couldn't be Death's daughter who came to finish everyone off. I wasn't that kind of person.

Was that why the hunters had tried to put me down, as they deemed I was horror and death incarnate? I didn't believe those assholes who would go after a lone girl like me, but then why had my limbs gone ice cold?

Shade glanced at me sideways. "So what was a pretty girl like you doing in a sexy sleep gown in the wilderness anyway, Pip?"

He wasn't calling me Catnip, which meant he wasn't trying to make a joke. He only used the light tone to disguise his serious concern.

Going-gray snapped his eyes toward me with undisguised suspicion. This one always thought the worst of people. That was why he was Sideburns' second-in-command.

"I don't remember," I half-lied. "I might have been sleepwalking, and then I fell from the waterfall and hurt my head. Then the river brought me here."

Shade regarded me steadily. "Be careful next time."

I knew he didn't believe me, but he was kind enough not to call me out on my half-truths. What he didn't know was that it was simply too hard to explain what had happened to me. Plus, I didn't want the shifters to know about the hunters.

What if they were associates? The shifters might just hand me over to—

Wait a second. Shade had mentioned that Mage Town bordered both Shifter City and California. We were heading to the inner city of California now, and from there, we'd cross to Shifter City in Nevada.

That meant I had escaped Mage Town, and the hunters had to have been mostly mages.

I swallowed hard, and reminded myself to tread carefully to get answers as to not draw unwanted attention to myself. My survival depended on my smarts and discretion.

It didn't take long for the pack of shifters to run across the grasslands, bypass some rolling hills, and enter a thick forest. We ran for hours, and the sun finally set.

We struck up a conversation now and then, and

I learned more about the world and gained some insight into current events without showing my ignorance. Of course, I often goaded Going-gray into heated debates against Shade, so I could glean intel without raising suspicions. The duo loved to have an ardent audience who sometimes presented as cheerleaders and sometimes as merciless critics.

Things were starting to look up.

I raised my face toward the canopy, feeling the last golden ray of sun sifting through the leaves and glimmering across my skin.

I hoped I'd be safe with the shifters for a while.

Suddenly, Sideburns appeared beside us in his warrior form. He towered over Shade and Going-gray by half a head and looked intimidating. I wondered what his royal parents had fed him when he was a child.

"I asked you to run, not to chat and flirt, Shade!" he growled at his brother. He'd been a jerk to Shade just because the younger prince had been nice to me.

While he didn't want to get close to me, he couldn't stand watching Shade and me hit it off.

Shade had shifted me to his back, a more comfortable position for both of us. I heaved myself up, my arms around his neck, my legs wrapped around his waist, to glare at Sideburns on Shade's behalf.

It was so potent that Sideburns snapped his

harsh gaze toward me. His eyes glowed silver again. My instincts told me to lower my head and drop my gaze while trembling, but I held his alpha stare instead. He might be an Alpha Heir, but he wasn't my alpha. Plus, regarding my shifter status, the jury was still out. I could be something else.

And what was he going to do? Beat me up because I glared instead of cowered? Hitting a defenseless girl would only make him look bad.

Only weak leaders preyed on the weak and small. I wasn't weak, I knew that, but I was much smaller than him. And in the eyes of his pack, I was both.

An odd expression lit his gray eyes. If I didn't know better, I'd say he was surprised and proud that I could hold my own. However, he wouldn't acknowledge how he really felt about me, just like he wouldn't acknowledge what I was to him. So the Alpha Heir did what he was best at—he scowled at me.

Going-gray had long since dropped his gaze and displayed his submission, but not before he'd caught me getting into a glaring match with the Alpha Heir. A shocked expression parked itself across his face.

Yeah, I knew that a potent alpha stare could make weaker beings piss their pants, but I'd just learned that my inner bitch could be more dominant than an alpha's when she was challenged.

Even Shade's warrior body tensed beneath me. He probably knew what his brother and I had gotten into, and he was trying not to get in the middle.

Sideburns sniffed again, his eyes bright. He was definitely trying to get more of my scent. He was such a contradictory creature. He desired me and he acted like he didn't want me. I had no time for hypocrites.

But my body still felt hot and heavy for him. Whenever he was close, my core tightened in need, and I grew wet.

I could tell that he wasn't happy that his brother carried me. But if he snatched me into his arms, I wouldn't fight him. Disappointment and bitterness brewed in my middle when he turned away.

For a moment, I sincerely thought there was something wrong with me, terribly wrong. The hunters had called me Death and abomination, and now, by some one-in-a-million chance, I had bumped into my fated mate, but he kept me at arm's length.

Before I allowed myself to further wallow in my misfortune, a wolf from the very front howled an alarm. The rest of the pack followed, howling ferociously. We stopped moving.

A war song vibrated in the air and resonated in my veins, as if I'd known that song since birth.

"Bloodsuckers!" Sideburns snarled, looking deep into the forest for the looming threat. "We've run right into their fucking ambush."

"We tried to keep this mission top secret," Shade hissed. "But with a pack of two dozen shifters, we're bound to be noticed."

Sideburns nodded my direction. "Your job is to protect her, brother."

He couldn't even bring himself to call me by my name most of the time, even though Pip might not be my name. However, he didn't know that.

"I can protect myself just fine," I said, sliding off Shade's back. "And my name is Pip. P-I-P."

The Alpha Heir ignored me.

I flexed my legs while doing a few stretches. After being on Shade's shoulder, then his back, for so long, my legs were asleep.

"Battle ready!" Sideburns roared. "Alpha Team up front. Beta Team back up."

He didn't seem very creative.

The pack howled their battle cries.

The horrible feeling of being hunted swirled back into me. Cold sweat gathered under my armpits. I prayed this bunch of vampires weren't another group of hunters targeting me. But I knew that even if they weren't coming for me, I still didn't want to be caught in the crossfire.

CHAPTER FIVE

*I*n the blink of an eye, shifter soldiers had formed a ring in the clearing with Shade and me at the center. They had dumped their tent equipment and bedding, among other supplies, in two large piles near me. Without a word, I dove toward the bigger pile at high speed and wiggled myself inside to hide.

Shade sent me a disapproving glance for the first time since our encounter. Right, shifters weren't about hiding. They were all brazen and charged into the enemies' ranks, snarling, tearing, and biting. The younger prince was trying to tell me that I didn't need to cower while he was there to protect me.

I was only being practical. There was no shame in skulking when the situation called for it. I wasn't going to risk myself if I didn't have to. The bloodsuckers were lurking behind the trees outside the clearing while closing in on the shifters from all directions.

From what I could count, there were at least fifty vampires coming at us, which was two to one against the shifters. Plus the vamps carried long swords, which indicated that they were cold-hearted killers. I was being smart cowering here.

Luckily, I found a ball cap amid the supplies. I threw it over my head and hid my hair inside. The vampires would have a hard time recognizing me if they happened to be hunting me.

I could never fault myself for being careful. Settling myself nicely, I peeked out of the pile of equipment, my heart pounding in my throat.

Shade stood near me, his disappointment in me switching to rage as his eyes trained on a horde of vampires coming toward us like a surge of shadows.

A black wind picked up. Trees trembled. Bushes shuffled. A flock of mockingbirds let out rasps and trills, flapped their wings, and flew away.

Violence pulsed in the air.

The shifters waited, ready to burst into action. A dozen or so soldiers were in their warrior forms, their clawed hands grasping a sword, an ax, or a spear; the other dozen remained in their animal forms. I saw a colossal bear, a leopard, and twin panthers mixed among the wolves. Each soldier in his warrior form paired with a shifter in his animal form.

The vampires, on the other hand, weren't as bulky as the shifters. They were mostly tall and lean and looked refined. All of them wore dark trench coats. It was impossible to tell whether they hid nasty weapons inside them or not.

The lead vampire, who carried himself with regal poise and icy beauty, strode toward Sideburns but stopped at a certain distance. He also didn't draw his weapon, the long sword strapped behind his back.

Suddenly, a flash of images pierced through my skull with a blinding pain.

Agony filled my every fiber.

Cold steel pressed against my back.

I was lying on a table, masked faces hovering above me. I couldn't move, icy lead in my limbs, terror drenching my mind.

Who were those people? What were they going to do to me? A needle pricked my skin. A moment later, my blood pumped into a syringe. It was dark red and thick.

I tried to scream. I tried to kick, but I was bound and drugged. My eyes slowly rolled to the side and spotted a display of sharp surgical tools.

They were going to open me up. A second later, I felt a cut on my skin. Pain hit my nerve endings. I whimpered, trying to call for help, but no sound came out. Tears flowed from the corners of my eyes.

I was a lamb in a slaughterhouse. I didn't know why they had me here or why they hurt me so.

An ear-splitting alarm sounded on the ceiling, followed by a thunderous cracking. The thick door tumbled from its hinges.

A giant man stepped through the door in a dark trench coat. His rich brown hair flowed to his chin. Even in great pain and terror, I still recognized his dark, icy beauty that took my pained breath away. To some beings, he might be a nightmare come to life, but to me, as if my soul just knew, he was my dark angel and shining knight.

Our gazes held for a heartbeat but felt like an eternity to me. He drew me in like a moth to his dark flame, even though I couldn't move. His sapphire eyes brimmed with ancient power, loneliness, aching need, and terrifying rage.

A shiver passed over me.

No one and nothing mattered anymore. Not even my agony or my tormentors in the room.

I'd known this man before, even though I couldn't recall it. And now, he had finally come for me when no one else would. My ordeal and nightmare would be over soon.

'Take me away', my eyes pleaded. I hoped I could speak to him, but when I tried to move my mouth, I found that my vocal cords had also been bound.

My tormentors shuddered, but for a very different reason than I.

The immortal trained on them, crimson rage flashing in his wrathful eyes.

"The Vampire God! He's come for her!" one of the beings in the room hissed, fear drenching his voice. I grinned inwardly at their terror.

When I could move again, I would strike them down.

Shouts rang out everywhere. The blaring alarm grew louder and more urgent. Armed guards and men in robes rushed the lone vampire. Fire and light exploded around him, and a jet of fireballs shot toward him.

My heart pounded in fear for him. My skin was both hot and cold.

"We have to finish her off now!" a woman's voice called, jerking me back to the room. "The plan has changed. We can't let him take her. We can't let anyone else have her if we want to stop doomsday!"

Everything happened at once.

The group of masked men and women no longer cowered away from the vampire but rushed to me, scalpels, scissors, and saws in their hands.

The vampire produced a machine gun, and roaring bullets cut through the people in the room. My tormentors dropped around me before they could saw me apart. I watched in dread as a ball of fire hit the vampire in the chest.

My heart squeezed in pain, yet I could not help him,

as I was still immobile. I struggled to no avail, just like before.

An explosion sounded to my right, and the wall behind me came tumbling down. Fire erupted, bringing with it thick smoke. A cloud of dust filled the air and bits of concrete rained down on me. A shard of broken wood scratched my cheek.

A young brunette rushed through the hole in the wall and came into view.

My gaze turned to her in fear for I knew my vampire knight was busy fighting his own fierce battle outside, trying to prevent anyone from getting in to harm me. He wouldn't get to me before the woman.

"I came to get you out, Ophelia," the young woman said, surprising me. "You were drugged, and the spells bound your power. This potion will help."

Ophelia. Was that my true name?

The woman raised a syringe and stabbed it into my heart. I wasn't sure if I could trust her, so I waited for death to come.

But it didn't come. Instead, a shot of new energy raced through me. I sucked in a great breath as the numbing and binding inside me vanished.

I let out a cry and bolted up like I'd been held under murky water for too damn long. I wiggled my toes to try to wake up other muscles.

A blade burst from the woman's chest, and an old man in a robe appeared behind her with a hiss. "Traitor!"

My eyes widened in shock, and sorrow bloomed inside me as I stared at the blood pooling on my rescuer's white blouse.

"Run," she mouthed, blood dripping from the corner of her lips.

I couldn't help her now. I could feel the light and life slipping out of her.

The old man raised his hand, a dark spell forming and darting toward me. I had no defense against him. And it was too late for me to snatch a weapon from the surgical side table. So, instinctively, I threw my hand toward him in a roar. A flash of dark light blasted from me and slammed into the old man's face. His spell dissolved a few inches from me. He opened his mouth, but no scream escaped. Only terror and hatred filled his milky eyes.

He turned to dust the next instant. I stared down at my hand, unable to comprehend what I'd just done. But when I called for the dark light to come again and show me that I did indeed possess its power, it didn't do my bidding.

I turned to search for the vampire, but I didn't see him. It was chaos all around.

The sound of footfalls heading toward the room ricocheted off the remaining walls. I couldn't stay here one second longer. I couldn't be caught again.

I grabbed a gown hanging from the ruptured wall, pulled it over my head to cover my nakedness, and leapt though the hole in the wall.

I ran with everything I had.

Shade laid a massive beast claw on my shoulder, jerking me back to here and now. He'd seen my devastated expression and the tears streaming down my face.

"Don't worry, Catnip," he said. "I'm here. I won't let anyone get you."

I nodded and wiped away the tears with the folded sleeve of the shirt I'd borrowed.

My emotions were still raw after I'd glimpsed the horror of that portion of my past. My body felt cold, and my heart raced a mile a second. But I forced myself to stay in the present. I wouldn't allow myself to get lost in the past.

I'd escaped. I was a survivor, and I'd remain so, with my strength, cunning, deception, and determination.

I shrugged Shade's claw from my shoulder so I could focus.

My gaze homed in on the horde of vampires, searching for the one my former tormentors called the Vampire God. He was like a godly being, so he should have survived, right, even with fireballs raining down on him? He'd drawn all the fire to him so I could make it out.

Now that I'd seen that part of my memory, a sharp feeling of guilt and shame punctured me. I should have looked for him or tried to help, but that might have made me a liability. And under the circumstances, filled with icy panic, I just couldn't stand staying in that place of horror a nanosecond longer.

When I didn't find that vampire amid the horde, an unreasonable ache bloomed in my chest. The world called vampires unholy creatures, but that one giant, gorgeous, and formidable vampire had saved me that day and given me an opening to escape the horror of my life.

The silver-haired, dark-eyed lead vampire nodded curtly at Alpha Heir, who was fuming.

"What's your business ambushing us, bloodsucker?" Sideburns snarled in his warrior form. "If you want a war now, it'll happen."

The lead vampire sneered. I'd regarded him as beautiful, but after I'd had that glimpse of the memory of the Vampire God, I'd say the current vampire couldn't hold a lick of flame to his god.

"Alpha Heir, I meant no disrespect," the vampire said in a silky voice. "The final war between our species will eventually happen, but if it's your desire to avoid a bloodbath today, I'm willing to do the same. We outnumber you more than two to one, and Lord Lucian believes you might have taken something that belongs to him."

"Did you just call me a thief?" Sideburns snarled.

"Well, every party has been hunting a girl whom the Seer said has come," the lead vampire said. "My informant saw you intercept a parchment that the Seer delivered to my lord. When we reached the location, the building had been leveled. My source said that you and your force had visited there around the same time."

My heart skipped a beat, then pounded in my ears. This horde of vampires was a second group of hunters. Was Lord Lucian the one who had come for me in that demolished lab building? Maybe I should sneak out, grab a vampire, and get some answers. However, I wasn't sure I could overpower a vampire. If I failed, I could put myself in a worse situation by handing my ass to the enemies.

Before I could be sure whom to trust, I shouldn't let any bloodsuckers discover me. I lowered my hat over my face and cowered lower.

"What the fuck are you talking about?" Sideburns spat.

A tall female vampire stepped up and whispered in the lead vampire's ear. Even with my superior hearing, I couldn't hear what she was saying.

She stepped back.

The lead vampire sneered again, his eyes glued to the Alpha Heir the entire time. "Oh, you know exactly what I'm talking about, especially about the girl."

From what I'd seen, shifters relied on brute

SHIFTER GOD

force, but vampires were more into playing games to get what they wanted.

Sideburns retorted, "What's so special about this girl?"

"Let's just say she belongs to my lord," the vampire said. "She's his lost pet. If you don't have the girl, you have nothing to worry about. And if you allow us to take a look around your camp, you need not fear a battle."

Ice clogged my veins, and terror slithered up my spine.

The vampire said that I belonged to his lord. Did it mean Lucian was the mastermind behind me being locked up for who knew how long? Had my tormentors in that lab been working for him? Or was Lucian the Vampire God? If so, he'd have been here instead of having his minions fetch me.

He'd come for me in that lab building, which meant this lot had nothing to do with him.

It would be equally bad if the vampires broke through the shifters' ranks and came for me, or if the Alpha Heir handed me over. I had to flee now. I couldn't go back to the slaughterhouse. I'd rather die.

I was about to rise and bolt, but Shade pushed me down. He held my panicked gaze, his own steadfast, with the promise of protecting me with his last breath. He wouldn't let anyone, not even his brother, harm me.

65

"Like hell I'll let your filthy bloodsuckers touch anything of mine," Sideburns roared and charged without another word.

The lead vampire drew his sword from behind his back at lightning speed. His long sword and Sideburns' broad one clashed with a harsh sound. Then all around the forest, steel crashed against steel, claws tore into flesh. The vampires hissed. The shifters snarled.

The beasts and the vampires charged each other in a brutal battle. Blood splashed everywhere, the stench of copper and gore permeating the air.

A bear dragged down a vampire, but another vampire skewered the bear's hind leg with a blade. The bear bellowed in pain and rage. A shifter in his warrior form slammed his claws into the vampire's chest before the vampire could finish off the bear with a follow-up blow.

The bear tore out the throat of the vampire that he'd pinned down and lurched at another one. The shifters fought in pairs and went against four vamps.

A beastly sound rumbled out of Shade's throat. He was guarding me, but he couldn't stand watching his pack members be slaughtered, as they were outnumbered.

"Go," I told him.

I'd sided with the shifters, since I considered

Shade my new friend, and also I didn't trust this lot of vampires. There was only one vampire I'd go with, and unless I saw his face, I wouldn't go near any vampires.

"Promise me you won't run unless we're about to lose," Shade said. "Even so, I'll come back for you and get you to safety."

"Fine," I said. "Just go help your pack."

Shade leapt into the heated battle, his sword rising and falling as he beheaded a vampire that buried a blade into a gray wolf's belly.

Sideburns was still crossing blades with the lead vampire. They were both excellent swordsmen. Sideburns swung his sword up to meet the vampire's in another strike. With a snarl, he pushed the lead vampire back with his brutal strength. The vampire feigned a strike, wheeled away, and slashed a cut along the Alpha Heir's thigh.

The vampire's speed was amazing. His movements blurred as he brandished his long sword, yet my eyes could see all of his moves in every detail. It didn't take me long to predict where his sword would land next. Sideburns was a bit slower compared to the vamp warrior, but his strength was admirable. Somehow, he didn't let the vamp get the upper hand.

Their swords locked again. Sideburns found an

opening and kicked the vampire in the middle, sending him flying into a tree.

I thought about jumping into the mayhem and helping the shifters, but I was worried that I might do the opposite. I was tired and hungry, and the lingering pain or drugs hadn't completely left my body.

While I watched the battle, I had a sudden eerie feeling that I was being watched.

I wheeled around. A petite female vampire stared at me with a hungry grin.

Crap! Creep!

Then, everything about vampires slammed into the forefront of my brain, like a spark coming alive in my genetic map. In that instant, I knew she was only a halfling—half-vampire and half something else.

I pulled out my dagger and wielded it in front of me, but her grin only grew bigger and hungrier. I bared my teeth and hissed, as if that could scare her away.

Suddenly, a pair of blue wings whooshed out of her back.

That was wicked. If I had those wings, I wouldn't be here, running and hiding like a fugitive. She might have read the undying envy on my face and winked at me.

I mimicked how Shade snarled and hacked my blade in front of me, kung fu style.

Just as I thought she was going to lunge for me and snatch me up, while I posed viciously for battle, the vampire girl shot into the air and whistled sharply.

Shade made a mad dash toward me, face paling. I didn't blame him. No one had seen the half-breed vampire girl get inside the shifters' defensive ring, but it was too late. She was leaving.

The rest of the vampires suddenly disengaged from the battle and withdrew in the direction the petite vampire girl had gone, away from me. In an instant, they cleared, leaving their dead-again peers behind.

The shifters howled as one, but they didn't pursue their enemies. I bet they were all exhausted. Besides, the vamps still outnumbered them.

"You okay, Pip?" Shade asked me in concern, residual fear flashing in his blue eyes. He thought he'd almost let that vampire girl get me.

I nodded, though my hand shook a little as I slid the dagger back into the sheath.

Sideburns was checking on his wounded soldiers. Five shifters dead, and those who had been badly wounded received attention from their healer. As for anyone else injured, they healed themselves, and they remained in their animal forms to regenerate faster.

In total, seven vampires had been killed. The battle had been brief.

"What did that vampire girl say to you, Pip?" Shade asked carefully after I took a long swig from the bottle of water he handed me.

"She didn't say anything," I said defensively. "I thought she was going to attack me, but then she just flew away."

"And the others all followed her just left like that," Sideburns added. I hadn't even noticed that he was suddenly by my side. "And it was all after she saw you. That was strange behavior, even for bloodsuckers."

I shrugged, my face hard, as I didn't like what he was insinuating. He regarded me, his expression blank, which was even worse than when he looked at me with suspicion.

"I have no idea how vamps behave," I said. "I have no idea how shifters act either."

"They were looking for a girl," Sideburns drawled.

"Yeah? And you thought I was that girl?" I didn't hide the sarcasm from my voice. "Then why didn't you just hand my sorry ass over to them?"

He flashed me a hard look, not liking my language.

"We guarded you. Some of my men died," he bit back. "Learn to be grateful."

I was very sorry that a few shifters had died, but they hadn't exactly died defending me. Shifters and vampires were natural mortal enemies, and they'd go to war with or without me. This was just the way things were.

However, I was grateful the Alpha Heir hadn't given me away to the vampire hunters, but I didn't appreciate that he made out like it was all about me and that I owed him a debt.

"Sure," I said. "Everything points to me, including the prophecy, just because I got lost in the wilderness."

"Which was very unusual," Sideburns said, his eyes pinning me like a hunting eagle's.

"I'm more trouble than I'm worth then," I concluded. "Why don't we part ways from here?"

I straightened my shirt and patted my pants. They wouldn't be so petty as to ask me to give back the clothes, right?

Shade grabbed me, his hands on my shoulders. He'd shifted back to his normal form, but he still towered over me.

"Pip, you're a shifter," he said. "Even though you haven't learned how to shift. You're one of us, and you're our responsibility."

"I'm not your responsibility," I countered. "And I can take care of myself super well."

That lie sent a wave of misery rippling over me. I didn't know if I had a home. Other than the Vampire God and the hunters, I didn't know if anyone had ever looked for me or missed me.

"You'll be coming with us, Pip," Sideburns

insisted with authority. "That's my final decision, but I'll get some answers later." His gaze shifted to Shade. "Get your hands off her!"

Shade let go of me while rolling his eyes.

Sideburns walked off, and then came back to hand me a plate of dried fruit, meat, and a half-roll of bread along with a new bottle of water.

"We'll leave as soon as our wounded soldiers can walk," he said sternly, then left to check with the healer.

I watched him go, wishing I didn't feel burning heat for him simmering inside my core.

CHAPTER SIX

*W*e camped in a valley between the forest and the desert. We were far from the ocean and deeper inland now, near the border of North California and Nevada, according to Shade.

The shifters bustled around, setting up beds and tents. A few of them roasted game they had hunted en route over hot flames. I was excited, thinking of a hearty dinner and a good night's rest beneath the starlit sky.

Shade and I huddled around the campfire, chatting easily and sharing snacks. Going-gray came toward us.

"Alpha Heir requests your presence," he said gruffly.

"For what?" I asked, my heart suddenly thundering.

I wasn't up for questions when I myself didn't have answers. I also didn't want anyone to know that I'd lost my memory and that Pip wasn't my real name.

Going-gray stared hard at me. He wasn't used to anyone questioning his superior's orders. He stepped forward, ready to grab me and drag me to his boss. If he touched me, I'd kick him in the nuts really hard, and he wouldn't like it.

But Shade shot to his feet first and stepped between us with an easy, bright smile.

"C'mon, Catnip. Let's do something instead of being lazy." He glanced at me over his shoulder. "My brother will only ask you a few questions so let's get it over with. The roasted rabbit isn't going anywhere. I promise."

My stomach grumbled. For the sake of a full belly, I rose and walked after Going-gray. Besides, if I refused to go, I might not get dinner tonight.

No one was too nice these days, and they all wanted a piece of ol' Pip. I had nothing to give, though they didn't have to know that. When you had nothing to offer, everyone treated you like trash.

I followed Going-gray into a large tent that must belong to Sideburns. Before I disappeared altogether within thick, canvas material, I glanced back once at Shade to make sure he was still with me. I felt better knowing he was here, stronger even.

Witch-light crystals lit the interior of the tent, casting a golden glow in all directions. A makeshift bed lay in the corner, neatly made. Three folding chairs and a folding table had been set up and placed upon an ornate, thick rug.

Sideburns occupied the most comfortable chair on the other side of the wooden table. He studied me, trying his best to put on a poker face, but heat radiated from him. I didn't know if others could sense it, but I could see his desire for me, even now.

He gestured at the empty chair across from him with the table between us. "Sit, Miss Pip."

So my status had been upgraded from the girl, Pip, to Miss.

I perched on the edge of the seat, trying not to make myself too comfortable. This wasn't the place for that, plus I couldn't really relax around Sideburns.

Going-gray walked around me and stood behind Sideburns, folding his beefy arms across his chest, and stared at me like a bulldog. He'd been wounded in the battle against the vampires, just like Sideburns. By now, both of them had mostly recovered. The Alpha Heir had also changed into a clean, fitted uniform that accentuated every hill and valley of his muscular body.

He was a very handsome man, sexy even. My pulse spiked, despite my best efforts to remain calm, breathe evenly, but it was impossible not to stare at him with desire.

Sideburns glanced over my shoulder. "Your presence isn't required, Shade."

I turned to look at Shade near the entrance of the tent, pleading. I didn't want him to leave. He was my only ally.

"I think I'll stay, brother," Shade said in a mild, yet firm voice.

Sideburns' expression darkened. "You know I can have you removed. When Father isn't around, my word is law."

"Yes," Shade said. "But I ask you to allow me to stay, please. I'm here for Pip."

Sideburns gave him another hard look before he sighed. "Just don't get in my way."

Don't get in his way? What's he going to do? I didn't have a good feeling about this. It seemed like getting dinner from these shifters required too much work, and I wasn't sure I was up to the task.

I kept my expression even and waited.

Be calm and friendly, I reminded myself. *Answer a few questions, get it over with, and then have dinner with Canary.*

The delicious smell of roasted rabbit with spices already permeated the air, making my mouth water. The shifters could eat raw meat, and a lot of them preferred their dinner bloody and raw, but they still cooked a quarter of their game for a variety of flavors.

"Why did the vampires want you, Pip?" Sideburns asked.

"The fuck I know." I hadn't meant to blurt it like that, but my temper flared. We'd covered the topic already, so I wasn't thrilled he kept asking me the same question when no one could provide him with an answer. Certainly not me.

"Watch your tone and your language, girl," Going-gray snarled. "You'll show respect to the Alpha Heir as his subject, or I'll throw you out."

"You can throw me out. I don't mind." I narrowed my eyes at him. "I'm not anyone's subject, unlike you, you mean guard dog."

Going-gray's face turned somewhere between angry red and angry purple.

"How dare you!" he barked as he moved toward me.

Was he going to strike me down?

Shade moved to stand by me. Sideburns raised a hand to stop grandpa from grabbing me.

"Cut her some slack," Shade said, his voice always calm. "Pip has never lived in our city so she doesn't know our shifter rules. Hell, she might have never met a shifter before."

I smiled. His words gave me an idea.

"That's right," I said, trying to match the tone of

Shade's voice. "I'm a small-town girl. I'm not in the same league as you big boys."

"That's not what I meant," Shade said, pinching the bridge of his nose.

"Of course, you aren't in our league," Going-gray growled. "But when you refer to the Alpha Heir or any of your betters, you don't use the word 'boy'! You need to learn some shifter etiquette."

I grinned at him. "Will you teach me, sir?"

Going-gray clenched his teeth.

"Let's not get sidetracked," Sideburns interrupted. "The girl has a tendency to get everyone off track."

"I don't want to get anyone off," I offered him a smirk. "And my name is Pip not girl."

If he kept avoiding saying my name as if it'd bite him in the ass, then why did he even bother bringing me here?

Going-gray glared at me. "You'll not speak unless spoken to." He rubbed at the back of his head as if I'd given him a severe headache. "We should send this girl to Shifters Academy, but it might be too advanced for her. However, we can't drop her in the middle school either. She's too old to be put there and too crass. Consider the bad influence she'll be for our youth."

"What kind of bad influence are you talking about?" I asked in a sweet voice to irk him more.

Sideburns raised a hand to shut me up.

"Lucian's vampires are clearly hunting you," he growled, studying me closely to see if a muscle or two twitched under my eyes. If I had that kind of nervous reaction, he'd call me out as a liar. I almost wanted to do just that.

But when he referred to Lucian, my mind instantly remembered my vampire savior. Even now, sitting across from Sideburns and feeling the high sexual tension between us, my mind still worried about that specific vampire, and it wasn't because he was burning hot and gorgeous.

"Could you tell me more about this Lucian?" I asked, leaning forward, interest sparking in my eyes. "How does he look? I need details, like the color and style of his hair, the color of his eyes, basic skin tone, his height, build, manners, and what kind of clothes he usually wears."

A sudden possessive and angry look flitted in Sideburns' eyes, turning their color to gunmetal gray.

"Why do you want to know all about him?" he demanded, his expression hard.

"And don't play games, Pip girl," Going-gray barked.

"I'm not the one playing games here," I said. "You just told me that Lucian's vampires were hunting me, so don't blame me for being a little bit curious about my potential kidnapper."

"So you admit you're the one he wants?" Side-burns asked.

"Don't put words in my mouth. It won't help either one of us."

"I don't think her animal is a wolf," Going-gray murmured. "She must be a fox."

"You know that there are two rival vampire sects, right, Pip?" Shade chimed in. "One sect is under the thumb of Lucian, a primordial vampire, and the other sect is ruled by Marlowe, the Vampire God."

My heart nearly burst. "The Vampire God?"

"Marlowe is more of a legend," Shade explained. "He barely steps onto the continent of North America, though he has influences here too, but Lucian is the enemy we focus on."

My face grew hot, then cold. Marlowe was the one I needed to find. The vampire horde we'd encountered wasn't his. Just as my instincts had told me, the Vampire God wouldn't have had his minions fetch me. He had come for me in person in an even more dangerous situation.

Sideburns shot Shade a warning look. "We aren't here to discuss the vampires or their politics, even though Marlowe is a future threat. You can be certain of that." His hard gaze snapped back to me and roamed over my face. For a second, he even checked out my boobs, but he quickly moved his eyes up, trying to disguise the heat simmering within them. He really didn't like his attraction to me.

Another thought came to me, one I didn't like. He was ashamed of his attraction toward me. We weren't equals. He was the most high-ranking shifter, next to the king, and I was probably the lowest, if I even proved to be a shifter. We were mismatched in every aspect, except in biology.

My face suddenly burned with humiliation and anger, as I could feel his disdain toward me. I could also feel what was on his mind—bending me over and having his way with me.

Sideburns cleared his throat to rein himself in; the heat in his eyes cooled.

"Another group was also hunting you other than vampires," he said. "You were wounded before we found you in that shrub. Our healer said you had an arrow and a bullet wound, along with the remains of some potent black spells."

"I'm one hell of an unlucky chick," I said with a sigh. "The strangest things keep happening to me ever since I left home."

I frowned and decided to tell them some half-truths. I had to give them something, a story, before I could figure out the truth for myself. "You're damn right about there being another group. Some gangsters or satanic cultists were chasing me in the woods for no reason. I didn't even know them, and yet, they were calling me horrible names. There was no way I was going to let them capture me so they could probably rape and kill me, so I ran and jumped from the water-fall. I survived and hid, and then you guys showed up and dragged me out here."

"What did the gangsters or cultists look like?" Shade asked in concern, warmth and sympathy shining oddly in his brilliant blue eyes.

I shook my head. "It was dark in the forest, and I was running for my life so I didn't get the best look."

"I'm sorry you had to go through that, Catnip," Shade said. "But you're with us now. You have our protection."

"What were you doing alone in the forest?" Sideburns pressed. He didn't seem to buy my story. That dude wasn't as softhearted as his younger brother. "No normal girl would wander alone in the forest in just a sleeping gown."

He irked me. I hated it even more that my body craved him, even now, after all his sharp judgments.

"I might have been sleepwalking for all I know," I answered curtly.

"Your pursuers might have been a group of witches, sorcerers, and mages from Mage Town," Shade offered, trying to diffuse the rising tension. "Witches are into all kinds of cults and black magic, and they've been growing bolder lately."

"Oh my gods," I blurted. "Do you think they wanted me for a virgin sacrifice?"

All three men blinked, their mouths open, but no words fell from their lips. Heat rose in Sideburns' and Shade's eyes. The word "virgin" seemed to have a magical power over red-blooded males. I'd thrown them off track.

Excellent.

I should be a virgin, right, if I hadn't— I shook off the image of me lying naked, unable to move on that operating table, surrounded by a group of men and women in white coats. My mind refused to go back to that place.

"I must have slipped from my small town in the human city to the mages' realm without realizing it," I said, still flushing and shaking my head in dismay. "Talk about being in the wrong place at the wrong time."

Shade cleared his throat. "There have been a lot of illegal and suspicious activities on the border with the mages."

Sideburns looked thoughtful, heat still radiating from him. Perhaps he was still thinking about me being a virgin. He might not like it, but his body responded to mine. It was like we were both engaged in this battle of wills. Our wills and minds said we weren't good for each other, but our bodies were attracted to each other like two magnets.

"Let's not speculate," Sideburns said, trying to shake off whatever image was in his head. "Everything must be based on facts. But, rest assured, I'll get to the bottom of this."

Then he started asking the same questions again. It was an interrogation trick, but I was in no mood to keep playing this game. Anger boiled within me. If anyone else tried to do this to me, I could be more understanding and even pretend to accommodate them.

But this man was supposed to be my mate, by big fat Fate's design, even though he was grumpy about being paired up with a girl who had no social status. In his big head, he refused to believe a "bottom feeder" like me could have sharp intelligence that rivaled his own.

As my supposed mate, he should want to protect me. It was a primal instinct, but he mostly fought against it. He'd done nothing to make my life easier other than that one time he'd told Shade to guard me.

All this time, it was his brother who took care of me.

"Thanks for the talk, which was amazing and utterly inspiring, but I'm done here," I said and rose.

Sideburns' eyes burned silver as his anger bled through. Power rippled off him and slammed into me.

"Sit," he ordered.

An invisible force slammed into me, and I tumbled back onto the chair.

He'd used his alpha power on me.

Prick.

I might be able to counter him, though I wasn't entirely sure. So far, my own powers were a wild card, but it wasn't worth it to test them against this asshole for a small matter and possibly reveal more of myself to him.

So I sat there and stared at him, my face blank.

I didn't show any submission, but I didn't rebel against him either. I was trying a new strategy. Let's give him a zombie and see how this jerk dealt with it.

He didn't gloat but sighed.

"Why must you fight me at every turn, Pip?" he asked wearily.

"I wasn't fighting you. I'm tired and hungry," I said, anger shimmering in me. "You keep asking me the same pointless questions that I have no answers for. Why torment me like this? Either you take me in as I am or kick me out."

I paused. "In fact, I'd prefer it if you kicked me the hell out so I can go my own way. But if you want info, here's all I can give you." I raised a finger, readying myself to be a better liar. "I am from rural North California. As a girl who was raised in a small, isolated human town, I don't know much about the world, let alone you super-naturals. Two, I was lost when I ventured into the mages' territory, not knowing anything about them. That was when misfortune struck. It seemed everyone was looking for young women, for what purpose is beyond me. Since I happen to be one of those, they gave chase. Fate really must hate me because she keeps putting me in the path of all the wrong kinds of people."

I was surprised that the words had just flowed from me like that, which proved once again that I didn't have a broken mind, despite the fact that I had no memories other than a glimpse of my tormented past.

"We aren't the wrong crowd, Catnip," Shade protested, appearing hurt.

"I didn't mean you, Canary," I said. "I meant everyone else." I purposefully brushed off Side-burns' displeased scowl, though he also looked surprised, as if he hadn't expected me to be so eloquent.

I waved a hand as if to dismiss a thought. "I can't remember more. I probably suffered a concussion and memory loss after I fell from the waterfall. So, sir, I'll be forever grateful if you release me and let me find my way back to my rural home."

Sideburns studied me in an unnerving way. "Though I'm less than satisfied with this interview,

I'll let it go for now. However, we're still going to take you with us into our city, for your own safety. But understand this: we haven't been able to check out your story yet, and since we can't validate it yet, you'll be under supervision. When we reach Nevada, you'll have to stay in the retaining center until we can clear you. That's the law, as we're on the brink of war with vampires."

The retaining center sounded very much like jail.

Rage shot through me. So far, almost everyone who came across my path had tried to dominate me, capture me, jail me, or kill me. One day, they'd all be sorry when I was no longer powerless and helpless and lost.

"Retaining center?" Shade cried. "Jared, you can't be serious—"

Sideburns' glare stopped the younger prince's protest.

I shrugged. There was no point in persuading or arguing with the Alpha Heir anymore. His words were law to the shifters. But I could undermine him from the sidelines. I'd slip away tonight after I had a full stomach and after everyone went to sleep.

"Go eat," the Alpha Heir ordered, hearing my stomach growl again. The rich aroma of roasted meat suffused the air. "In our society, no shifter goes hungry."

CHAPTER SEVEN

The wind blew open the flap of the tent where I slept, letting in a chilly current along with a ray of moonlight across my face. I hadn't expected to be among the four high-ranking shifters who enjoyed the privilege of sleeping indoors instead of on the hard ground under the moon and stars.

Two soldiers were parked outside the entrance of my tent, either to guard me or to prevent me from escaping. Or they might be worried that I'd walk around slitting shifters' throats.

I lay on a fur bed, my ears pricking as I ignored the background noises to tune in on the conversation between Sideburns, Shade, and Going-gray in a tent not too far from mine.

The trio hadn't gone to bed at midnight.

Shifters must be nocturnal, though they weren't as bad as vampires.

"That Pip girl isn't what she claims to be." Going-gray's accusing words drifted over to me. "She's playing dumb."

Grandpa hadn't warmed up to me one little bit even after he'd carried me for probably five minutes along the road. Most shifters didn't warm up to outsiders, but I didn't blame them. It was a dangerous world. All the more reason that Shade had my gratitude. He wasn't as jaded or stuck up as the others.

"Could you guys at least show some sympathy toward her situation?" Shade said. "Pip is lost, just as she said. Even if she isn't what she said she is, what harm can she do? She's but a lone wolf, almost a pup. It's our responsibility to guide and protect her. Yes, she doesn't understand any shifter rules, but she's got the spark. All the more reason why we should be patient toward her. You two have been jerks."

"We're on the brink of a new war, Prince," explained Going-gray. "And we're still suffering from the devastating aftereffects of the century-long war caused by second horseman. The twenty-year truce is going to end soon. When war breaks out again, it'll mean the extinction of one race or several. It'll be either us or them. We can't afford to be soft right now."

"Have you deployed a sound barrier spell, Jay?" Sideburns asked.

"Yes, Alpha Heir; no one can hear us," Going-gray answered. "We need to purchase more spells from the mages. Maybe we should find some new spell makers. Violet raised her prices last month, saying her ingredients were getting more expensive because of the looming war. Fucking greedy witch."

"Just pay her more and make sure she stays exclusive to us," Sideburns ordered.

Interesting. Their spells hadn't stopped me from listening in. Maybe they should hire a better mage, but then most spells didn't seem to have an effect on me, except the rare and powerful ones.

"The vampires confirmed our suspicions that the site we reached had been burned down two days ago," Sideburns said in a gravelly voice. "Whatever object we were looking for was either taken by someone else or burned to ashes. If the vampires hadn't ambushed us, I would've let the matter rest."

"You think the god-killing weapon could be a person?" Going-gray asked, almost carefully. "That vampire mentioned about looking for a young woman and not just an object. Could that Pip girl be it?" He then chuckled to himself, as if realizing how stupid he sounded, but Sideburns didn't laugh with him.

"I doubt she just appeared in the wrong place at the wrong time like that," said the Alpha Heir. "And she wasn't that far from the burning site when we found her."

Shade groaned. "C'mon, brother, will you ever stop suspecting her? Besides, a vampire saw her. If Pip is the one they've been looking for, the blood-suckers wouldn't have withdrawn right after the winged female vampire spotted her. They would've taken her right then."

"But don't you find that odd?" Going-gray countered.

My heart pounded. They would never really accept me, especially after that strange encounter, which meant they weren't taking me with them out of the kindness of their hearts, unlike Shade. They had an agenda, as they wanted to figure out my role in the great scheme of things, while I didn't even have a fucking clue what that great scheme was.

One thing was certain. War was coming. But what did it have to do with me? I had my own problems and didn't want to be caught in the crossfire between shifters and vampires.

"I understand you have a soft spot for the girl, Shade," Sideburns said. "You've always had a soft spot for stray animals. So be her friend, gain her trust, and find out what she really knows."

"Are you seriously sending me to spy on her for you?" Shade asked incredulously.

"Just don't cross the line. Don't go beyond that friendship thing that you've been doing." Sideburns lowered his voice. "You all know what she is to me. And that will never leave this tent."

"So you don't plan to acknowledge her?" Shade asked quietly.

"You know I can't," Sideburns said. "I'll soon be engaged to Princess Viviane after our father and her father reach an agreement in favor of the throne. Viviane is the heir to the Great European Shifters Kingdom. She's the key to our expansion—"

"Are you listening to yourself, Jared?" Shade cut in. "What happened to you? I know you've always been a hardass, as you've been destined to be the heir since before you were born. But you weren't always this bad. It's like your ambition is making you lose your head." He paused. "Do you know how hard it is to find a fated mate? You've got that one gift every shifter is willing to fight to the death over, and you're going to throw it away?"

"You think this is fucking easy for me?" Sideburns snarled. I could picture his veins throbbing angrily in his temples. "I don't expect you to understand this sacrifice! I've always been the one who shoulders every duty and burden, and all you've ever done is fool around and chase women.

I've even been helping you get rid of the title of 'Prince Playboy.'"

"Really?" Shade sounded hurt and angry too. "That's how you think of me?"

"Alpha Heir didn't exactly mean that," Going-gray said, trying to be the buffer between the brothers. "And Prince Shade has been working hard on every assignment these past few months to meet the challenge."

"Fine, he's trying," Sideburns said curtly.

"I'm only going to say this one more time," Shade said. "You decide to sacrifice your happiness for power, your loss. But if you don't want her, release her."

"So she can choose you?" Sideburns snarled. The unexpected, fierce possessiveness in his voice made me jump on the fur bed. "Never! Do not touch her. She's my prize! I'll kill anyone who tries to lay claim to her." He paused, surprised by his own vehemence. He lowered his voice a notch and sounded more controlled now. "It's not that I don't want to claim my fated mate. My wolf has set his eyes on her. She's his mate too. I know better than to alienate my beast too much. I just have to balance it all for everyone's benefit. I can't have her the way I want or in a conventional way, as I'm in the center of politics. On one side of the scale is a powerful princess who will inherit the entire European shifter territory. On the opposite side is a lost wolf girl who has no ties and no social standing. I don't know why, but Fate chose her for me and put her in my path, so I won't waste the opportunity. She might still have something to offer as she can bear my children on the side."

"You'll make her your mistress and a broodmare?" Shade asked incredulously.

"I wouldn't say broodmare," Sideburns grated. "After I wed Princess Viviane, she won't be able to dictate what I can or can't do, since I will become her alpha. It's the best course for everyone. Pip won't have a thing to worry about. She'll have shelter and food. I'll take care of her. But first, she must attend Shifters Academy and learn all the rules, etiquette, and some fighting skills. She needs to have a good education and be primed if she wants a future with me."

Silence stretched long until Shade kicked something. A chair made a scratching sound across the ground.

"You're one selfish bastard, Jared," Shade said furiously. "I'm sorry that I ever looked up to you as a kid."

"Careful, Shade," Sideburns said. "Even though you're a prince, I can still banish you if you step out of line. I might not be fair to that girl, but it's the way it is. We're living in a dangerous time, and my situation is more difficult than you can ever imagine. I'm letting you in on the plan, and I expect you to follow it accordingly."

"Alpha Heir is right," Going-gray said. "He has to look at the big picture instead of being ruled by emotions. We don't live in a perfect world. So, Shade, you'll need to pull your head out of your naïve ass and follow in your brother's footsteps."

No one could kiss ass better and faster than him.

"Pip won't hear a word of this," Sideburns warned. "You can never tell her, Shade."

Shade sneered. "You're afraid that once she knows she's actually the fated mate to the Alpha Heir, she'll cling to you like those gold-diggers and social climbers you used to date?"

"It's a possibility," Sideburns said in a rough voice, ignoring the sarcasm dripping from his brother's words. "But I can't take the chance. That girl is a wild card, and the last thing I want is for her to make a scene." He paused for a second. "Also, it's for her safety that no one else knows what she is to me."

Motherfucker really regarded me as dirt.

"You think Viviane will make a move to get rid of Pip if this leaks out?" Shade now sounded concerned.

Sideburns sighed. "You know she's spoiled, powerful, and vicious. What she wants, she gets."

"You know what's at stake, Shade," Going-gray

said. "We need Princess Viviane's shifter army if we want to win this war against the vampires. And that Pip girl has nothing to offer other than her good looks, foul mouth, and bad manners."

"She's too good for you anyway, Jared," Shade said coldly. "You're playing with fate, and it'll bite you hard in the ass."

"I know what I'm doing," Sideburns answered icily.

A riot of negative emotions twirled in my middle. Ice settled in the pit of my stomach. My fated mate had made his intentions clear. He didn't want me, yet he wouldn't allow anyone else to have me. He'd hang me high and dry for his own selfish needs.

For a full half minute, I felt utterly sorry for myself and cursed fate. There were millions of dicks, and the meddling, mean hag had to pick this asshole for me. She wanted to have a good laugh by seeing me heartbroken and losing any little hope I had.

But I didn't need to follow her program. I wouldn't commit to a jerk.

Fortunately, I didn't feel emotionally attached to Sideburns, even though the physical attraction between us felt like a live wire.

I had to escape him and the situation—the sooner the better. Once we reached Shifter City, he might lock me up. Shade would try to help me, but he wasn't the Alpha Heir, the second most powerful man in the shifter world.

Before I could get the fuck out of here, however, I'd like to teach Sideburns a lesson. I wasn't sure if I could do what I was about to do, but it didn't hurt to try.

With a mental push, I called a violent wind upon Sideburns. Surprisingly, the magic obeyed and blew open the tent in a small, swirling tornado that carried dried grass, dead bugs, and dirt. It twirled straight for him, then blew into his face before he could raise his hand to fend it off or cover his mouth.

While he let out a yelp of surprise at being bitch-slapped by nature, the legs of the chair he was sitting upon snapped. Sideburns fell on his ass at an awkward angle. But it wasn't over. The table flew up and tumbled on top of him. A mug of cold coffee dropped onto him too, pouring its content all over his dirty face.

Exactly how I imagined it. I smiled and stifled a laugh in the fur beneath me.

Sideburns cursed, Going-gray shouted calls for alarm, and Shade chuckled low.

"Karma couldn't wait, brother," Shade said. "The universe isn't a big place after all. It watches us closely. You might want to revise how you treat your fated mate."

I smirked as I wiped at a stream of tears from

my face. I didn't know when I'd cried or why, since I didn't cry for assholes.

But it was wicked cool that I could use magic to pull pranks.

My magic wasn't finished, however. With one final gust, it blew the posts over holding up their section of the tent. Half of the canvassed roof collapsed on top of them. I felt a little bad that Shade had to be collateral damage.

The entire camp stirred. The shifters were on the move and shouting. The guards posted outside the tent rushed in to see what had happened to their Alpha Heir's tent. More followed until the whole area became crowded with shifters.

I bolted upright, then rearranged my bedroll to make it appear like I was still sleeping inside. I put on the ball cap and slipped out of the tent.

No one looked my direction as I scurried away and darted into the shadows. Bathed in darkness, I sprinted as fast as I could away from the camp.

I'd go to California, lie low, and plan my next steps. When I was ready, I'd look for the Vampire God. For I knew in my gut, he was the only one who truly wouldn't harm me.

I only hoped he had answers for me.

CHAPTER EIGHT

I ran up the hill, only pausing to look at the shifters' camp far behind me. I regretted that I couldn't say goodbye to Shade. For all I knew, he was the only friend I had.

With tears in my eyes, I scrambled down the other side of the hill and plunged into the dark woods. After I put more distance between the shifters and me, I'd need to seek out a stream or a river to make sure they couldn't pick up my trail.

I doubted Sideburns would come for me in person, but he'd send a couple of shifters to hunt me.

Focusing all my senses, I glanced around trying to decide which direction to go, when a dark shape emerged from the foliage. I yelped, nearly jumping out of my skin.

I produced Shade's dagger and brandished it in front of me to keep the beast at bay.

"Shoo, beast, go away now. If you're smart, you'll let me pass."

My eyes darted wildly to the trees around me to see if I could leap and climb up one of them.

The beast halted and let out a low chuckle.

Just then, the moon came out from behind a cloud. Its faint light shined on the wolf's golden fur. He'd been so stealthy that I hadn't sensed him trailing me. I also didn't have a shifter's ability of detecting scent a mile away.

My heartbeat returned to normal, and I slid the dagger back into the sheath.

The wolf shifted back into a naked Shade, all hard muscles and defined lines.

I lifted my ball cap and threw it at him.

"Cover your junk, Canary," I said with irritation, but relief washed over me. I was glad it was him and no one else.

He laughed. The sound no longer held the same seductive purr as it had before he knew I was his brother's fated mate.

"There're worse things out here than me and my junk," he said.

"So you say." I tried to hide my smile at seeing my friend again.

At least I would get to say goodbye to him as long as he didn't try to stop me from leaving.

"How did you know to ambush me right here?"

And he'd gotten here before me, since he'd been running in his wolf form.

"It didn't take a genius to figure it out, Catnip," he said, putting my ball cap on his head instead of covering himself. Shifters didn't mind their nudity. I bet it was because they had good, firm bodies. "You've been trying to run away since day one."

"So what are you going to do? Drag me back to your brother and let him lock me up?"

"You know I don't approve of how he treats you," he sighed, "but he outranks me. But do not underestimate me, Pip. I promised to protect you when I got you out of that bush, and I won't break my promise."

"I appreciate it, Shade. I really do," I said. "But it's not in my nature to trust in anyone's promises."

"I get it. But if you leave now, there'll be many more hunting parties going after you, including my brother's men. You won't end up in a better situation, no matter which party catches up with you. Alone, you can't fend them off. Before you find your footing, the right course of action is to have shelter, even if it's only temporary. Come with me, and I'll guard you to the best of my ability. Shifter City might not be a forever home for you—I hope it is—but no one can get inside the walls. I don't know what exactly happened to you, but I know you don't remember a thing about your past. Someone did something bad to you, and it wasn't jumping into the waterfall that erased your memory."

My throat dried up and my chest tightened at his revelation.

"What gave me away?" I asked quietly.

"The arrow wound told me that you were being hunted," he said carefully and coolly. "Your stalkers weren't chasing a random young girl as you tried to lead us to believe. The burn marks and surgical cuts on your body also indicate that you've been tortured."

His eyes were on fire as righteous rage poured off him. "When I know who did this to you, those bastards will be dead." He paused for a second to pull himself together, as he was no longer calm. "The scars on you were faint, but I caught enough of them. There's also the residual effect of powerful dark spells on you, like some force tried to bind you. Our healer said the same.

"Not only that, but when I would ask you casual questions, you looked like you were trying to recall the information. You also watched every-one, eager to absorb anything we said. The hungry and confused look you tried to hide told me that you probably didn't remember anything. Lastly, en route, you drove Jay to argue with me to get your information. You wanted to understand the world quickly to aid your survival. But from now on, anything you want to know, just ask me in private."

My mouth fell open. He was the first one who had figured it all out. He was smarter than anyone gave him credit for. Under his carefree playboy exterior was a man with sharp intelligence and compassion. Another thought clicked in my mind. Maybe he was using his playboy attitude and reputation to disguise his smarts so he wouldn't be perceived as a threat to the Alpha Heir.

He knew the truth about me, yet he hadn't told a soul. He would never betray me. I knew that now.

I felt a sting of tears in my eyes, and warmth swell in my chest. It felt damn good not to have to keep lying, especially to the one I considered a friend.

"I won't force you to come back with me," Shade continued. "You'll have my blessing if you still decide to leave. But just in case," he dropped a backpack to the ground, "I've brought some supplies you'll need for your journey. But I do hope you'll come back with me and let a friend help you. I won't ask you anything that you aren't ready to share."

I laughed through a hitched breath. Why didn't Fate pair me up with him?

I threw myself into his arms, regardless of his naked state. I might have used too much force. The two of us ended up falling to the forest floor with me on top.

He laughed. "I didn't ask for this. Are you sure, Catnip?"

"Shut up, Canary," I said. "At least I'm on top."

I rolled up swiftly and offered him a hand while he remained lying lazily on dew-coated leaves.

CHAPTER NINE

*A*fter returning with Shade and packing up camp, we crossed to the other side of the valley and reached the desert in East California, where shifters had parked their big vans and open-roof army jeeps.

I rode with Shade and two others in a jeep, and we drove all the way to Nevada. I was more excited than anyone else at seeing colorful mountains and the landscape of endless sagebrush.

"The air is dry in this part of the country," I remarked, squinting at the blue and orange sky that looked like a painting. I loved the burning sunlight on my pale skin, especially as I felt like I'd never seen so much sunlight in all my life. I didn't mind overcompensating. "There's a lot of sun in Nevada."

"Shifter City is the opposite of the vampire lairs

in Washington State, which is all rain and cold," Shade said. "We picked the sunny state for a reason. No vampires like to venture into Nevada. Only a few very powerful vampires can survive the brilliant sun in our mountainous region."

My heart stuttered. "What about the Vampire God? Can he come here? He's powerful, right?"

"As I said, he's more like a myth," Shade said. "No one has seen him on this continent for a century. Though rumors say he was sighted in North America recently." He lowered his voice to a hushed whisper. "Even if he's hunting you, he won't get to you. We'll make sure of it."

"We're home," the driver, who was a bear in his animal form, announced happily.

A fenced city with high-rise buildings loomed ahead. Sparks jumped from barbed wire fences at its top, and a legion of shifter soldiers patrolled the walls.

"Are those watch towers?" I asked, pointing at one of the towers inside the gate. Four armed soldiers stood on the top platform beside a mounted machine gun.

"We have eight of those towers in the city," Shade said with pride. "We now have to rely on old-fashioned watch towers since the satellite era was over a century ago."

When War, the second horseman, had come to Earth, I wondered what had happened to him. Had he died, retired to his Heavenly home, or simply disappeared?

A chorus of howls from the city jerked me out of my trance. The shifter soldiers were acknowledging the return of their Alpha Heir and his team.

The leading jeep braked before the gate, as did the rest of the fleet. Sideburns jumped off the second vehicle and strode toward us. The strange thing was I hadn't missed him one bit, but as soon as he was in close proximity, my core tightened, needing him and wanting him in a shameful way.

From the sudden heat rising in his hard gray eyes, I could tell he felt exactly the same and he didn't like it either.

The Alpha Heir tilted his chin toward the two other shifters sharing the jeep with Shade and me. The shifters bowed to him, left our jeep, and filed into a black van.

My heart pounded erratically, and my hand reached out to grab Shade's sleeve. The younger prince had convinced me that his older brother had promised not to put me in the retaining center, but what if the Alpha Heir changed his mind?

Sideburns glanced at my hand as it landed on Shade's arm, and his face darkened.

"I'll escort Pip to the Academy and make sure she settles in," Shade offered, his eyes on his brother.

"That's where I'm going too," Sideburns said. "You drive."

Shade flashed me a comforting smile before he moved behind the wheel. Sideburns slid into the jeep and took the seat beside me. I wanted to scoot away and put some distance between us, but I didn't want to be that obvious and get further on his bad side. Who knew how he would take it? It wasn't exactly a smart move to give him the wrong impression or even let him know about his effect on me. He'd warned his inner circle not to reveal that I was his fated mate, and I was more than happy to pretend I was ignorant about it after how he'd treated me.

I might have nothing, but I wore my dignity like armor.

The fleet rolled forward and entered the city through the vast, heavy gate. Soldiers saluted their princes, and some curious eyes lingered on me. I regretted not putting the ball cap back on. My lilac-blue hair stood out from the others with us. Other than that, I didn't even know how I looked or how old I was.

As we drove, I sat quietly beside Sideburns. Neither he nor Shade talked to each other. I was also glad Sideburns hadn't interrogated me again after that night. The silence was heavy and awkward between us, yet the heat and desire that radiated off the Alpha Heir was thick and undeniable.

He might have decided that I wasn't good enough for him, but the mating call harassed him just the same. It would almost have been fun to watch him execute his self-control by balling his fists at his sides so he wouldn't reach for me, if the mating heat didn't get a rise out of me as well.

I'd stay far away from him as soon as the next opportunity came. As I tried to take my mind off him, I worried about my unknown new life in a city full of strangers.

What if everyone hated me?

I had only one friend, but Shade wouldn't be around all the time, and I shouldn't demand he babysit me. I was so nervous, all things considered, that I was no longer in the mood to observe the broad streets, the buildings, and the people strolling down the alleys.

If Shade and I were alone in the car, I might be more relaxed. I might have enjoyed the rest of the ride. I had so many questions regarding the new school and Shifter City.

"Uh, revered Alpha Heir," I said, turning to him but lowering my gaze, as I'd learned that looking into the eyes of the shifter was usually considered a challenge or defiance. I had no need to rile him up now. "You really don't need to accompany a humble newbie like me to the Shifters Academy. I bet Canary can guarantee my safety and even make me behave."

Shade didn't comment back, but I could tell he was trying not to laugh.

"I'm not escorting you," Sideburns said in a scathing tone. "As you said, you aren't important enough to be worth my effort."

Oh, burn.

"I am going to visit Princess Viviane, my intended," he said, reining in his temper. I had no idea why he was even angry. "Princess Viviane is a well-respected senior student in the Academy. She's supposed to graduate early next year."

"Cool," I said. "So you two will get married and have children soon? Sorry, I meant pups."

"That's none of your business," he grated.

Wow, where did this sudden hostility come from?

"No pups then?" I asked. "You aren't shooting blanks, are you, Your Highness?"

I could be mean-spirited when my supposed fated mate denied me and paraded his chosen in front of me like I was nothing to him.

Shade coughed then hurried on, "You'll have to forgive Pip for being so blunt, Jared. We already know that whatever is in her head will come out of her mouth, unfiltered. That's why you're sending her to the Academy to learn the rules."

"And shifters' manners and some fighting too,"

I added with a smirk. "According to Prince Going-gray, there's no free lunch, and I must be a contributing member of the shifter society. Haha, I look forward to it."

"I expect you to understand all these rules and follow them to the letter within a week," Sideburns said.

Even though his expression was stern, he still looked devastatingly handsome. I wondered if this fated attraction made me think he was good-looking or if he was truly easy on the eyes.

"I might need two and a half weeks to get myself sorted out, Alpha Heir." I wiggled my brows at him when he stared hard at me. "Or at least two weeks. Miracles don't happen overnight."

"You need to get serious, Pip," he grated. At least he was saying my name this time. It didn't sound sexy or like a caress rolling off his tongue though. "The training in the Academy is not a joke! Not everyone can graduate. It won't be fun staying at the bottom of the food chain. Perhaps Shade can tell you what it really means."

What an ass!

I batted my innocent eyes in an exaggerated way. "It's not a joke? Okay then."

"There'll be peer pressure right away," he stressed.

I widened my eyes. "Fuck me."

Shade laughed, but Sideburns glared at me.

"Awfully sorry, Highness," I said, patting my cheek lovingly. "See? I slapped my face for punishment." My voice turned stern, deep and mocking. "Remember, Pip, no swearing in front of your betters!"

I probably shouldn't joke, but anything was better than the awkward silence hanging between us. I also found that when I joked about things, I felt less impact from the mating heat. I decided that no matter how he treated me, I didn't need to react the same way.

Sideburns shook his head, as if he'd had enough of me. He didn't appreciate my spunk. Too bad I'd discovered that I had plenty of spunk when I wasn't being chased by hunters or being cut open on a table.

Whatever happened, I'd pull through this school thing and deal with the bullies by adapting faster than anyone else while not taking things too seriously.

"You need to get yourself in shape before the Moon Ceremony," Sideburns sneered with a vengeful smile at my confused look. He flashed his perfect white teeth. "It happens in a week."

"What does the Moon Ceremony have to do with me?" I asked.

"Every student in the Academy must shift into their animal forms and join the hunt," Sideburns said.

I blinked again. "Shifting and hunting?"

That didn't sound good. I'd been hunted as recently as two days ago, and I didn't want history to repeat itself.

He ploughed on, "And lots of battles where failure is unacceptable. A couple of accidental deaths are always expected during the hunt."

Was he fucking kidding? Did he want me to end up dead in the hunt? I'd be the most inexperienced shifter during the barbaric ceremony—if I could even shift. "Accidents" could easily happen to me.

But I wouldn't give him the satisfaction of seeing me unnerved.

"Cherry on top." I grinned. "You almost got me worried for a second there, Alpha Heir."

He narrowed his eyes, a bit pleased with himself. "So you do know how to worry."

"Yes, Your Highness!" I said. "I was anxious to know what color my wolf will be after I shift. Size doesn't concern me though." I winked at him. "Size isn't everything. You know what I mean? But being a wolf of color will mean the world. I want to be a rainbow wolf."

Shade had been quiet during the battle of wills between his brother and me, but now he couldn't help but roar with laughter. "That's what got you in a bind, Catnip? I hate to disappoint you, but there's no such thing as a rainbow wolf."

Sideburns, however, wasn't amused.

His eyes burned with silver fire, as if he couldn't decide if he wanted to punish me or whether he desired me more. Even though I wanted to kick him to the curb, a stream of heat also rose in my belly.

The Alpha Heir turned to sniff at me.

Nope. Nope. No way would I let him take in my scent again.

With nimbleness that surprised even myself, I leapt up, twisted my torso in the air, and landed on the passenger seat, all in one smooth move.

Shade arched an eyebrow. "How did you learn that kind of move, Pip?"

Sideburns bellowed behind us, making both Shade and me nearly jump out of our seats.

"Watch the fucking road instead of flirting, Shade!" he snapped. "Will you ever grow up and learn to be responsible? At least try to be a good influence instead of being influenced!"

"Yeah, Canary. Look ahead instead of at me." I punched Shade in the arm jokingly. "Sideburns— so sorry, with all due respect, I meant Alpha Heir— is right about responsible driving. And please, please don't let bad influences get to you."

"Who's the bad influence? You?" Shade chuckled. "You've got some strength in your punch, Pip girl."

I punched him again with a big grin. "Get out

of here. You can take a punch or two. You're a big boy, Prince."

Sideburns seethed so much I could feel his hot breath blowing the tiny hairs on the back of my neck. I doubted any of his subjects dared to taunt him this way. Well, he was getting some new experiences. It was all about the journey. Got to live a little, dude.

Luckily, we arrived at the Academy before Sideburns' illogical anger combusted me like the fabled dragon fire.

CHAPTER TEN

Shifters Academy was situated in a broad area of sagebrush and rocks, surrounded by a shock of colorful, rolling hills in the distance. It was a military compound with high walls. Behind the steel gate, two watch towers, one on either side of the campus, stretched into the sky.

I squinted at three heavily armed shifter guards on top of the closest tower.

"Is this an actual school or a prison?" I asked. "I can't tell the difference."

"Show some respect, Pip!" Sideburns said through his clenched teeth. He enjoyed finding every chance to scold me. "Our airtight security is for the protection of the students and the safety of the school. Also, the security team won't hesitate to take actions against any deserters."

Wow, that threat was definitely for my ears only.

Would the guards really shoot me if I tried to leave the Academy grounds? The school no longer sounded so peachy. The guards would pose an obstacle if I decided not to stay.

"To the undisciplined, a military school might sound like a prison." Sideburns wouldn't let it go. I had a feeling that he didn't know how to handle me, and he didn't like it one bit. He was the Alpha Heir. Even the toughest shifters submitted to him. I was a nobody. I didn't look tough, but I didn't have a submissive bone in my body.

"It's the finest Academy that has produced tens of thousands of elite warriors," he continued. "You're lucky I permitted you to be enrolled."

Yeah, yeah. I refrained from telling him that I'd never asked to be enrolled into anything and that I certainly didn't ask to be trained as a soldier to fight the shifters' future war. It wouldn't do me any good to stay on his bad side.

The sentinels on the high tower saluted, and I mimicked them and saluted back, only to realize they weren't saluting me but their princes.

The gate slid to one side. The guards inside the checkpoint booth saluted Sideburns as well.

Our jeep cruised through the open gate and stopped on the central road in the middle of a grand courtyard. Two escort jeeps and a black van parked outside the gate, waiting to escort their Alpha Heir away from the school.

Shade exited from the driver's side. I followed suit and got out.

Two guards stood beside the jeep on either side of the Alpha Heir, eager to serve.

I wheeled around, surveying the well-trimmed lawns around the courtyard and the maroon brick buildings beyond. The campus looked nice. I only hoped the students here were nice too.

My awed gaze fell on the statue of a magnificent wolf in the center of the square. It was over twenty feet tall and condescending.

"That's a sculpture of my ancestor," Shade said with a chuckle that was filled with pride. "His name was Fenrir, the Wolf God. The book of our family tree says that he rode over fire with twin flames burning forever in his eyes."

"No shit," I said with a grin.

Sideburns flashed me a hard look as he finished typing something into his tablet before stepping out of the jeep.

"First lesson, Pip," he snapped. "You'll learn to censor every word before it comes out of your mouth."

"Then I won't be able to speak for a month, good sir," I said, not dropping my smile. No kind of schooling would bind my tongue.

I turned to Shade. "Are we getting lunch? You can tell me more about this Fenrir wolf guy."

Suddenly, a crowd of students appeared, boys in gray and blue uniforms, girls in gray and red skirts and socks, flooding into the courtyard from all directions.

The boys looked at the Alpha Heir with reverence, but most of the girls either stole a glance at Shade or gawked at him. I heard some giggles as well.

"It's lunch break." Shade smirked, enjoying his popularity with the ladies.

I scowled at him. I hadn't been wrong about him being a man whore, and he flashed me a grin and winked at a giggling girl nearby.

A gorgeous tall blonde in a gray and red skirt uniform swept toward us like a force of nature, as if she owned half the campus. Maybe she did, since she carried the regal air of a princess. Then it dawned on me who she was.

Everything about Princess Viviane spelled royalty, power, and riches. Every feature on her face indicated her high breeding. Her makeup was also impeccable.

Her classic blue eyes fixed on Sideburns. It didn't take a genius to see that she obviously regarded him as her equal and the rest as trash.

"Jared," she purred and pouted. She used his first name to indicate their close relationship. "I thought you'd be back yesterday. I was waiting for you all night!"

She was staking her claim in public, but, in my humble opinion, she sounded a bit too desperate by telling the entire school she'd been waiting all night for him.

The princess didn't spare me a look but shoved me hard in the chest even though I wasn't exactly standing in her way. While I tried to steady myself, she ran into Sideburns' arms.

I understood that she didn't like me standing too close to her beau, but shouldn't she go after him instead, since he was the one who had walked to my side to scold me while secretly inhaling my scent?

"Ex—" I protested, my face flushing in anger. "Excuse me?"

The princess snapped her disdainful gaze toward me as if I wasn't a person. She'd shoved me intentionally to put me in my place. A lowly girl like me had no business standing close to a high and mighty Alpha Heir. I should have cowered ten feet away from him so as not to offend her.

"How dare you talk to me, dirty rat," the princess hissed.

"Hey, lady," I said good-naturedly and spread my arms. "I don't think I'm a rat shifter, unless you were speaking from personal experience and recognized your own kind."

The princess's eyes widened in surprise before rage took over. Yeah, I knew that outraged look. No one lower than her had dared to speak to her that way. I still had a smirk hanging on my lips, but I was ready for an attack and pictured doing a devil's kick to dent her pretty face.

Did I even know how to do a devil's kick?

The courtyard fell silent even though it was packed, and students dropped everything they were doing to watch with riveted interest.

"Who the heck are you?" Viviane demanded, red-faced. Even the roots of her blonde hair turned red. "You're dead!"

"Don't mind her, Viviane," Sideburns said, his hands gripping her waist. "She's nobody. That girl hasn't even shifted yet and knows nothing about our rules. Don't stoop to her level."

I chuckled lowly. Wow. What a match made in heaven! Yet his dismissal set bitterness brewing in my middle.

"Fine, since you asked," Viviane said and threw her arms around Sideburns' corded neck. "I missed you. You haven't called since you left my penthouse last time. We had a good time, didn't we? My throat still hurts from what you did, but I regret nothing and only want more."

She didn't mind anyone hearing as she narrated their kinky sexual escapade. And she thought I was trash.

Sideburns frowned at little, then said, "I missed you too, Princess."

She stood on her toes and leaned in to kiss him. He hesitated for a beat, his gray eyes darting to me before returning to her. And then he kissed her back hard.

I'd probably just have let it go if the princess hadn't shoved me and then called me a rat. She'd have struck me if Sideburns hadn't dismissed and humiliated me. Or maybe I just felt angry or even a bit jealous at being rejected. So I was up to some pranks and petty vengeance.

Suddenly, Viviane farted long and loud, like issuing a series of high notes. Sideburns pulled away from her, looking shocked. Then he farted too, shorter and sounding more like whining.

Now the courtyard was even quieter until someone could no longer hold back their laughter, then a couple more snickers burst out.

I chuckled too. This was fun. But I didn't stop there. It wasn't in my nature to hold back

"Anyone heard that?" I asked around with a smirk. "Someone has an accent. Is it French?"

I heard that the Great European Shifters Kingdom was based in Paris.

A roar of laughter rippled across the courtyard. Even Shade was laughing, and he'd been trying not to double over by the driver's side of the jeep.

"Silence!" Sideburns bellowed in fury. "Return to your stations!"

The crowd muffled their laughter and scattered.

Sideburns turned to glare at me, and his girl-friend's stare was full of venom and death.

"Toss that bitch out right now," she told him.

"That's exactly what she wants," he said. "We just dragged her here today. And we'll punish her by making a soldier out of her."

"But I don't want that rat girl in my Academy!" she said.

"The Academy isn't yours until you become my wife, Princess Viviane," he snapped with his alpha stare, and she flinched. "Just put up with her for a few more months, love." His voice softened. "This new girl is a stray wolf. She'll earn her keep here, and she won't cause trouble for you. I'll make sure of it."

Ouch. He thought he could speak for me. It wasn't exactly music to my ears to be talked down by my supposed mate as he tried to pacify another woman.

Did he really have to stomp on me to make his girlfriend feel better?

"Tell me this, because I don't get it." I chuckled. "How is it my fault that you lovebirds made funny ass sounds while expressing your great love? Royals and nobles fart too—"

The princess's eyes burned. "I'll kill the rat right now!"

Sideburns pulled her back.

Shade moved to stand beside me in a blur. Though his pose seemed casual, his shoulders tensed up. He would defend me, no matter who attacked me. I stepped three paces away from him. I wouldn't put him in that situation and drive a wedge between him and his brother. Besides, I could fight my own battles.

"Shut the fuck up for once, Pip!" Sideburns snarled, his handsome face twisting in anger. "Your big fucking mouth will get you killed one day!"

My jaw clenched, but it was probably smart to retreat now. The lovebirds were both heirs, and they could kill me by raising their pinkies. Besides, Sideburns wasn't worth fighting for.

"The road trip was too much for you, Pip," Shade said with a yawn. "Let's get you settled in." He stretched a hand toward me. "C'mon, Catnip."

"I'll take it from here, Prince Shade," a shifter girl wearing the same red and gray uniform as Viviane said in a bright voice.

The petite beauty had dark hair and a heart-shaped face. Her small nose was cute and tilted up. Her pink lips were ready to offer a friendly smile at any time. Though she was about five feet two inches, she had a great, curvy figure.

A piece of knowledge flew from my fractured memory bank and told me that she was of Asian royal heritage. She was one of the few who had remained in the courtyard when Sideburns shouted for everyone to leave. It had been brave of her to stay, or maybe she was just too curious to leave and would rather suffer his wrath than miss out on the rest of the drama.

Two other Asian girls flanked her. Both were half a head taller than her, one with dark auburn hair and the other with honey brown hair.

Shade blinked at the Asian chick, and then he smiled. "If it isn't too much trouble, Princess Danielle?"

Another princess. She was also of the elite class. No wonder she hadn't scurried away like the other students.

"No trouble at all, Prince Shade," Danielle said with a sunny smile. "Pip, the new shifter girl, will settle in with me and my other companions in my penthouse."

"No fucking way!" Viviane shouted. "The rat girl must go to the bunkhouse and stay with other lower shifters. That's where she belongs."

"Nope," Danielle said. "I'm officially offering Pip new status as a companion to the Princess of the Asian Shifters United Kingdom."

"She isn't even an Asian like you, Danielle. She isn't your pack," Viviane pointed out vehemently.

"She's—she's probably a mixed breed, some dirty blood."

"Do you really want to bring race into it, Viviane?" Danielle asked.

Sideburns frowned deeply at the girls' drama. "But you already have three companions, Princess Danielle."

Danielle bowed to him a little to show respect. "But you can see that I have only two companions left, Alpha Heir. Joelle returned to her family in Japan, and I've been meaning to fill her position for a while. Pip will be the perfect fit."

"What if Joelle returns?" Sideburns asked, still frowning like his ass was in pain.

"Then she'll have to stay in the bunk room," Danielle insisted with an easy smile.

"You just want to get back at me because you're so jealous," Viviane hissed. "But know this, Danielle: you don't want to cross me over that rat girl. Your tribe is small, and soon your title will be stripped from you, like what happened to your mother. No matter how you call yourself a princess, you're a second class."

Danielle stepped forward, her face turning red with fury, but I stepped in her way. Judging from the intel that I'd just gleaned, Danielle was in a weaker position. And that Viviane bitch had the Alpha Heir to back her up.

As a nobody, I had nothing to lose, but Danielle needed to tread more carefully. She had a tribe.

At the same time, I wasn't going to let her be humiliated like this when she had stood up for me. That took great courage and kindness on her side.

So I did what I did best.

Princess Viviane let out another loud fart that had a long tail and sounded like "blue...blue... rude..." before she finished her threats.

Those remaining in the courtyard except for Sideburns laughed.

"That rat girl is a witch!" Viviane cried out while she was still farting and pointing her shaking finger at me. Then she gasped and ran away with her hands covering her face.

If she hadn't, she might have shat herself. I wasn't kidding.

Danielle grinned and stepped toward me.

"Will you accept my offer to be my third companion, Pip?"

I smiled at her. "It's my honor, Your Highness. Should I curtsy?"

"No, Pip. We got rid of the custom two centuries ago. Call me Danielle."

She turned and curtsied at Sideburns just for the fun of it. "Alpha Heir, may we have your permission to take our leave?"

Danielle's other two companions also curtsied.

I mimicked them but went overboard by spreading my arms widely in a theatrical gesture.

"Bye-bye, Alpha Heir," I said sweetly at a thunderstruck Sideburns before turning to wink at Shade. "See you around, Canary."

With the princess's arm looped around mine, we left the stinky scene laughing. I think I could actually like it here.

CHAPTER ELEVEN

*P*rincess Danielle's suite included the entire seventh floor of a baby-blue brick building, and I got to have my own small room that overlooked a ring of distant orange hills.

If I ever had to escape, my best bet was to cross those hills and mountains, because everywhere else would be on the shifters' radar. But now, with a new sponsor stepping in to shield me, I could relax for a while.

I hummed a song in the shower, celebrating my good luck for bumping into Shade, then Danielle. I used a lot of soap and spent a long time in the hot water until I rubbed myself pink.

Danielle also had three servants, and they'd prepared everything for me, including a few sets of new pajamas. I was happy that I didn't need to do laundry, but I did wonder what my responsibilities might be as a companion.

Well, I'd do my best to earn my keep and repay her kindness.

Danielle and her two other companions, Summer and Paris, didn't attend the rest of their classes for the day. They were actually quite happy to use me as an excuse, as they claimed that all three of them needed to help the new wolf girl brought in by the two princes.

Before I pulled on a sundress that Danielle had given me, I wiped the mist from the full mirror in the bathroom and stared at myself. Now I knew how I looked.

I had creamy skin and a toned body. I was average height, but my every curve was in the right place. The only flaws I had were fading, criss-crossed scars on different parts of my body, from either being burned or cut. Soon I might not have scars, but I'd forever remember that my faceless and nameless enemies had cut me deep and burned me all over. One day, I'd find them and return the favor.

My gaze traveled to my face, from my golden eyes like liquid flames under long, thick lashes to my straight nose and high cheekbones.

I looked nineteen going on twenty, so pretty much Danielle's age.

My lips were full and pale, as if they needed to be kissed to bloom to life again.

I blushed at that wanton thought. Like that was going to happen, since the last thing my fated mate wanted was me. But then, who needed his kiss while he'd kissed another in front of me?

I tried to shake off the hurtful image of how Sideburns had kissed his chosen girl. I wouldn't be seeing a lot of him since I was inside the walls of the Academy now. Out of sight, out of mind.

I'd just stick to Danielle, Paris, and Summer and stay far away from that nasty European princess.

Thinking of my new friends, I shrugged on the sundress in a hurry and stepped out of the bathroom into the spacious living room.

All three girls lounged on the couches, eating popcorn and watching an old movie.

"There you are." Danielle gave me a once-over with a warm smile. "I was starting to get worried and was about to send Paris to see if you had drowned in your own bathtub, but I can see why you spent that much time in the shower. You clean up nicely."

"Pip's a knockout," claimed Summer, the girl with honey brown hair. Somehow, I got the feeling that she liked both chicks and dudes, which was cool. "No wonder Viviane shoved her away from Prince Jared. If she sees how our new girl actually looks, she's going to prohibit Pip from getting within a mile of the Alpha Heir."

Little did they know that I was actually Sideburns' rejected mate. Well, I wasn't going to broadcast the news and unnecessarily humiliate myself.

"Want some?" Paris, the girl with auburn hair and beautiful darker skin, offered me popcorn. I bet she was half-Asian and half-African.

I slid onto the sofa across from the girls and grabbed a few popcorn kernels and inserted them into my mouth, then I grinned at her in thanks.

"What's the deal with Princess Deep-throat?" I asked, inching toward Paris for more popcorn. "It's not like I stole her man."

"What did you just call her?" Paris let out a whistle.

I widened my eyes and put on an innocent look. "Didn't you hear that she gave Sideburns a blow job and that her throat still misses him?"

The girls stared at me while nodding.

"That was scandalous," Summer said.

"Who's Sideburns?" Danielle demanded.

My eyes sparkled as I realized how easily I mingled with Danielle and her companions, just as easily as I got along with Shade.

I vaguely recalled that my tormentors in that lab building had mentioned that I was a chameleon, and that I could absorb knowledge and become one within a new environment.

I didn't know what a chameleon was, but I guessed it meant I was highly adaptive.

"You girls need to go out more often." I sighed happily as I took over Paris's bag of popcorn. "We've established Viviane as Princess Deep-throat, or Blow Job. Sideburns is the Alpha Heir Jared."

Paris nearly fell off the sofa with giggles. "The Alpha Heir's sideburns are famous."

"I bet he spends hours a day trimming them before he flexes his biceps in the mirror," I said. "You can also call him Mutton Chops if you're in a bad mood."

Danielle wiped a tear from the corner of her eye.

"I like Shade, though, so he's just Shade instead of Canary," I explained. "You know, he's all golden locks, nice and soft."

The girls held their bellies and laughed more, but then Danielle stopped laughing and became solemn.

"Are you and Prince Shade an item?" she asked.

"*We* aren't an item," I assured her. "We are two items. We're friends without benefit and will remain that way. Anyway, there's one more. The big bad Jay. I call him Going-gray, and he hates it. He insists he isn't even forty yet, but he looks more than forty-three to me. He's lucky I didn't start calling him mean grandpa."

The girls roared with laughter again and forgot all about the rest of the snacks on the table, so I helped them out and consumed them like a locust.

"Prince Jay isn't even married," Summer said. She was keeping track of everyone's marriage status?

"Now you know why," I said.

Danielle tilted her head to the side and furrowed her brow. "Have you called the Alpha Heir Sideburns in front of him?"

"All the time." I nodded. "But I always apologize and promise him that I'd only call him Sideburns on a good day and Mutton Chops on a bad day in my head. But he still wouldn't have it. That's one of the reasons he sent me to the Academy—to reform."

I grinned widely at the girls, brushing off the reality that Sideburns had dumped me here so I wouldn't be his problem. "I'm going to learn manners from you."

Paris winked at me. "We're the politest shifters you'll ever meet in the Academy. But that is only when we don't bite."

Summer laughed. "You've come to the right place, Pip."

Warmth welled in my chest. I thought I'd been shot to Hell, only to come to Heaven and make friends.

I hoped this piece of heaven in my reality lasted.

"Hungry?" Danielle asked.

"Bless you for asking the most important question, Your Highness," I said.

"You look like you can eat," she said. "Summer, do the honors, please."

Summer grabbed an electronic tablet on the table and typed something into the screen rapidly. I scooted over to watch, so I could learn.

"You'll want good comfort food after making a very powerful enemy today," the princess said.

"The farting contest will be the talk of the Academy for a full semester," Paris announced, "since it's never happened before, and that it happened when they had their tongues down each other's throats."

"Stop it," Danielle chortled. "We don't talk shit here. We're ladies of manners who must be shifter role models for Pip."

"Will I get you all into trouble?" I asked, my face dropping. "I don't mind sleeping in the bunkhouse. Even a bunk bed is ten times better than where I used to sleep."

Danielle arched an elegant brow. "And miss out on all the fun you can bring? Not a chance."

"Our territory might be smaller than the Europe territory." Paris bared her teeth. "But our shifters' bites are harder and our claws sharper."

I widened my eyes and mock-cringed away from the girls. "I'm shaking in fear now."

"Tremble all you want, but you're staying with us," Danielle said. "I might be a smaller princess from a smaller shifter clan, but I'm still a princess. I can make up my mind and choose whomever I want to be friends with."

Summer smiled at me. "And you're the only one besides our princess who ever stood up to Blow Job."

We rolled on the sofa and laughed at Princess Viviane's new title.

CHAPTER TWELVE

*F*ollowing the map of the campus, I found the classroom. It would be my second class for today.

The school administrators had put me with the first years. Danielle, Paris, and Summer were second years, so we wouldn't attend the same classes most of the time. I was on my own.

After my first class and a couple unpleasant encounters, I had a basic grasp of the structure of this military school.

Viviane ruled this place along with Sideburns due to her family's influence and their relationship. The French princess's father was the King of the Great European Shifters Kingdom.

She'd graduate in six months and be out of my hair, so I thought she wouldn't cause too much trouble for me. But as the most powerful, popular shifter in the Academy, her pawns were everywhere; they were her eyes and ears.

Some of her fangirls who were in my class constantly gave me the evil eye. Other students kept their distance from me, as no one dared get on her bad side. So within the first day, Viviane had succeeded in making me an outcast.

I was all the more grateful that Danielle had the balls to take me under her wing. I'd heard that Danielle was constantly bullied, even though she was also a princess. Viviane didn't like to have any rivals, so with Danielle, she bullied her just enough to make Danielle's life miserable but not enough to get in trouble for harassing another fellow princess.

The reason I was late for the second class and thus got scolded by the teacher and earned snickers from my classmates was that I'd been stalked by Blow Job's lackeys.

Three big shifters had jumped me in the corridor. Only thanks to luck and my prank magic had I gotten away. The bullies got tangled with each other and fell over themselves.

"And they said shifters weren't fucking clumsy." I shook my head and made a snide comment, "Watch where you're going next time, you cute little monkeys."

The trio had called me nasty names and threatened to retaliate before I blew a kiss at them and rushed off.

The second class focused on analyzing the future war between the vampires and shifters. I knew nothing about current events, so I wasn't sure if I agreed with the professor's prediction or not, but I absorbed everything like a sponge.

And I filed the newsflashes in my head—

- All three supernatural cities—Vampire Castle, Mage Town, and Shifter City— were heavily guarded and magically warded.
- While the vampires and shifters were keyed up to start a new supernatural war, the mages promised to remain neutral and grant access to both parties if war ever broke out. Mage Town was situated between the vampires' and shifters' territory, and the mages would become even richer from selling magical weapons, potions, and offensive spells to vampires and shifters alike.
- The supernatural cities had separated from the rest of the human cities after the Federal Government collapsed. Most of the states ran their own affairs now, and they all competed to expand their

own armed forces to protect their
borders.

I SUSPECTED that the mages might be the force
encouraging the vampires and the shifters to fight.
I hated the mages since I strongly believed that
they were the ones who had held me captive,
tormented me, and then hunted me.

The class ended with an open discussion on the
horsemen. Some said War might still be on Earth,
but most students wanted to get all the forces to
work together to stop Death from coming to do
even more damage than War.

Whenever anyone mentioned the horseman
Death, my heart would skip a beat, then run erratically, and fractured nightmares or visions would
swirl in the back of my head, yet I couldn't catch
those horrible shapes. It was just a dark and chilly
feeling.

As soon as the teacher announced that the class
was over, I rushed out, jumping over obstacles and
landing on a few feet that stuck out into the aisle
to trip me. Instead of achieving their goal, two of
Blow Job's minions fell over their seats and landed
on their big asses on the floor.

I didn't linger and giggle, as I was looking
forward to meeting Danielle, Paris, and Summer

for lunch. I sprang to the girls as soon as I spotted them at the brink of the courtyard, waving my hands over my head at them in case they missed me, my backpack bouncing on my back.

Paris had gotten me the backpack filled with textbooks, notebooks, all the necessary stationery, and even a couple of snacks.

It was probably the first time I had owned anything.

They trio shook their heads and smiled at my eagerness, and I grinned back.

"Hey, what are we going to eat?" I asked. "Do we have to pay? All the meals in the military academy should be free, right, since they're training us to be vampire slayers for them?"

Danielle laughed and rolled her eyes.

"If you keep rolling your eyes, they'll get stuck one day, Princess," I advised. "And what if your wolf's face gets stuck like that?"

"That's never going to happen," she said, rolling her eyes again.

That reminded me. I needed to ask them about the Moon Ceremony. I must learn how to shift before then. The last thing I wanted was to embarrass myself in the middle of it and thus embarrass my new friends. If I proved to be uncool, they might dump me. Then what was I going to do?

I brushed the worries aside when I spotted Shade on the other side of the courtyard.

"Canary! Here!" I shouted, but there was no need to yell since he was already heading our way.

Danielle and the girls snapped their attention to him, stars in their pretty eyes.

"Did the prince scowl at me?" I asked them.

"Yeah, he kind of did," Summer offered happily. "What have you done?"

"As you all saw, I just waved at him," I said. "Maybe I should return his scowl. He doesn't deserve my big smile anymore."

Shade reached us and I scowled at him, even though he looked as hot as ever with a few strands of loose blond locks hanging over his bedroom eyes.

"What's wrong, Catnip?" he asked. "Why did you grimace? Do you have a toothache? The Academy has a good dental plan."

"It wasn't a grimace," I said, rearranging my facial expression. "You glowered at me, so I was returning the favor."

"Yeah? Well, I wasn't happy with you," he said, resuming his glare. "Now everyone knows I'm Canary!"

I looked at the girls, but they all turned away their faces, trying to appear innocent.

Busted! They were the ones who spread the rumor about his pet name.

I sighed. "It could be worse, Canary. Being popular with the ladies isn't all perks."

He slapped the back of my head, but it was more playful than punishment, so I didn't take it personally.

"How was class, Pip?" he asked. "Did you stir up more shit?"

"Me?" I said, frowning at him deeply before I gestured at the girls. "I don't stir shit, especially now that I have perfect role models who don't shamelessly fart."

The girls gasped, and Shade let out a strangled sound that was close to a chuckle.

"Be careful, Catnip." Shade lowered his voice. "Just don't go so far that you can't come back from it. You don't want your adversaries to connect the dots and then go on a witch hunt."

He was warning me. Sideburns might piece together the incident of his and his girlfriend's ridiculous farting and the accident of the tent falling on him. That would force the Alpha Heir to punish me, which was the last thing I wanted.

"Fine," I agreed, then turned to Danielle for introductions. "You know Princess Danielle already. The other two chicks are her fierce minions. The honey-haired one is Summer. She's a keeper. The delicious dark-skinned henchwoman is Paris, and she's a catch."

Shade nodded at Danielle and flashed the girls his perfect white teeth, displaying his bright smile. He just couldn't help but dazzle women.

"Then what are you, Catnip?" he joked.

I knew he was still attracted to me, but he'd never step between his brother and me. It didn't matter that Sideburns had chosen another.

"I reserved a table for us," Danielle chimed in, gazing at Shade. "Are you joining us, Cana—Prince Shade?"

Shade slanted me a hard look before turning to the princess with a softer, rueful expression. "Unfortunately, I can't, Princess. I'm part of the faculty now. It's frowned upon for a teacher to fraternize with students. I'll be your training coach in battle class this afternoon." He turned back to me. "I'll need to talk to you after the class, Pip."

"But you just said no fraternization," I reminded him.

He shook his head in frustration and stalked away.

"His loss," I grunted, "by refusing to fraternize with us, we have one less mouth to feed."

"You'll never need to worry about not having enough food, Pip," Danielle said. "We don't let any shifter go hungry."

The day was looking brighter. I never needed to worry about going hungry as long as I stayed with these girls.

I followed them into a fancy building of steel and glass on the north side of the courtyard. The second floor was an upscale restaurant. I was glad that I didn't need to worry about the dress code since everyone was wearing a school uniform.

The hostess led us toward a table next to a window. The four of us gathered around it, and I admired the pristine white tablecloth, fancy utensils, and the napkin folded like a swan.

"We come here often for their signature grass-fed hamburger," Danielle explained. "And the salad and herbs are picked fresh from their organic garden."

"Sounds awesome." Like that made any difference to me.

I grinned nevertheless and peeked out the window, the statue of the Wolf God staring back at me from the center of the courtyard.

"So you know Prince Shade well?" Paris fished.

I'd told her about Shade already, but the girls just liked to gossip about him.

"He's better than his brother in every way," I said.

"Try not to talk bad about the Alpha Heir," Danielle hushed me. "His girlfriend has already targeted you. Don't get on his shit list too."

I shrugged and sighed. "I'm already on his shit list."

Thinking and talking about Sideburns made me lose my appetite.

"Just be careful, Pip," Summer warned. She was the most cautious one among us. "You're new to our world. Shifter society operates under a strict hierarchy. Right now, you're under our princess's protection, so they can't attack you directly in the open unless you offend someone who outranks Princess Danielle."

"Fine, I'll cower," I said.

The girls' conversation soon circled back to Shade. He might be interesting, but I was more into learning about the clash between the vampires and shifters, especially a very specific vampire. But it seemed no one knew much about him, as if he was just a legend made from nightmares.

I also needed to gather more intel on the mages and find out about my hunters.

The waiter soon brought a big tray of drinks, and four plates with huge hamburgers and heaps of French fries on the side.

I stared at my food in glee. "It's big."

The hamburger was four inches high. I grabbed it with both hands, opened my mouth to take a bite, but only tore a small chunk at the corner with the sauce smearing across my cheek.

Danielle laughed, and the girls joined her.

"Let me show you how to eat an American hamburger properly," Danielle said and opened her mouth.

Oh my gods. I blinked. She neatly bit off a quarter of the hamburger. Paris and Summer followed suit. I was impressed, and then I was a bit intimidated.

I opened my mouth again, but it couldn't reach even two inches wide, and then I just shut it.

The girls giggled.

"Do you know why Americans have big mouths?" Danielle asked, trying to educate me.

"They were born with it?"

Danielle gestured at Summer to let her answer.

"They evolved after constantly eating big sandwiches and burgers," Summer said. "They were trained as children."

Danielle nodded her head in agreement. "My country folks warned me that Americans all had big mouths. I understood it only after I came here."

Danielle's father was the Shifter King of the Asian Shifters United Kingdom. There were many high-profile international shifters in the Shifters Academy, including Blow Job.

"If they can do it, I can do it too," I said.

I opened my jaw wide, eyes rolling back with the effort, and I held the burger between my teeth as if it were prey. I took a big bite and chewed in victory with a stupid grin splitting my face.

The burger did taste better with a huge bite. I swallowed quickly since it was rude to talk with food in my mouth.

"Wicked." I smirked. "We all have big mouths

now. We're officially big-mouthed North American werewolves."

Danielle rolled her eyes. "We are not werewolves, Pip. We're shifters."

"But we shift into a wolf, right?" I said, then realized that I might be the only one who hadn't shifted and didn't know how. "You know, about shifting, uh, I might have a few questions."

The girls leaned closer to pay attention to me while inserting handfuls of French fries into their big mouths. I smiled at them, and my heart filled with happiness.

Just a burger, some fries, and budding friendships could make me so giddy. My past life must be full of shit. And now, I didn't even want to find out my origin or if I had a family, things like that.

Maybe it was best if I didn't remember a damn thing. That one glimpse into the past of being a lab subject was already enough to turn my stomach. I didn't need to have my memory back to feel whole. I had a new clan now. Maybe I should move on with this good new life and forget about the hunters as well.

I opened my mouth wider, took a second large bite, and grinned at the girls. They all had their mouths full and smiled back.

Summer swallowed her food and drank her diet coke. I rushed to grab a large non-diet coke.

"You fit right in with us, Pip," Summer said.

"We're the Fantastic Four Werewolves," I said, then glanced at her barely touched French fries; mine were nearly polished off. "You want some help finishing that?"

Just as I was about to grab Summer's plate at her amiable nod, Viviane led a group of eight toward our table.

The girls' faces paled. Even Danielle sat straighter, her shoulders tense, her hand gripping her fork. I eased back in my chair, but I was ready for a good brawl.

"Look how all the Undesirables are getting together," Viviane said with a contemptuous smile, gesturing at us.

Her minions laughed on cue, their eyes skewing toward me. Two bigger girls in the group shot angry glares at me, still remembering how they had fallen over themselves when they tried to jump me. They looked like they wanted to get even.

Danielle stood from her chair and kicked it away from her. She put her hands on her hips and faced Viviane.

"What's your problem, Viviane?" Danielle asked. She was nervous, yet she stood up to the bigger princess, just as she'd stood up for me.

I motioned for Paris and Summer to stay put, but I shot to my feet to back up Danielle and mimicked her by planting my hands on my hips. I soon noticed I looked ridiculous being a copycat, so I dropped a hand, but the other hand remained on my hip.

I had a mocking grin on my face as I chewed my burger. It'd be fun to spit it in Blow Job's face if the situation called for it.

"My problem?" Viviane narrowed her eyes. "I've been lenient with you, yellow princess, so you snatched my prey in front of everyone. You'll learn a hard lesson by crossing me and shielding that rat girl."

"It's none of your business whom I befriend," Danielle said, shaking with anger. "I'm not afraid of you and your deranged army. Bring it on with all your dirty tricks. I've seen plenty of them these last two years."

"You've seen nothing yet," Viviane sneered. "But I assure you that you will soon."

"Hey chick, cool your small tits," I cut in. "You might think everyone is enthralled with you and waiting in line to see what you'll pull out of your overrated white ass next, but we're not interested. So move on, will ya?"

Viviane looked shocked that I had the balls to talk to her this way, and her followers all gasped at my audacity. Two heartbeats later, the French princess's eyes glowed with yellowish light. The bitch's wolf was about to break out and attack me.

Her minions growled as well, ready to shift and jump us.

Paris and Summer got to their feet, bracing for a fight.

I pushed myself in front of Danielle. When the battle started, I needed to be at the front. My hand twitched, ready to pull the hidden dagger out of my boot.

A short blonde dashed from behind Viviane toward our table and tossed a handful of dirt on our plates before I could stop her. My face dropped as I turned to look at my French fries, now ruined.

"You dumb fuckface," I hissed as I leaned toward the table. I grabbed a handful of the ruined fries and flung them toward the blonde. "You don't disrespect food when so many people in the world still suffer from hunger. Now eat dirt."

While she fended off my fries, her skirt dropped to her ankles, exposing her panties. She let out a panicked cry and bent to pull her skirt up, but Paris was quick enough to grab a phone from the table and snap a series of pictures of that blonde bending over in her underwear.

"Too bad global social media disappeared half a century ago," Paris said with a chuckle. "We could have gone viral on TikTok. But don't you worry, Blondie. The Academy's network still works, and you'll be famous."

"Shut up!" Viviane shrieked. Then she pointed a finger at me. "You dare attack *my* pack? Now that you started it, the Alpha Heir can't blame me for finishing it."

She snapped her fingers, and her goons closed in on us.

"Get the princess out of here," I told Paris. "I'll handle this bunch of hens."

"No," Danielle said. "We'll fight hens together."

Before we clashed with our foes, a male voice boomed, full of outrage and authority.

"What the hell is going on here?" Going-gray suddenly appeared between us.

What was he doing here?

His annoyed gaze found me first, as if I were the troublemaker.

"You again, Pip girl?" he snapped. "Can't you stay out of trouble for five minutes?"

"No, good sir, it's not me this time," I said. "It's so unfair that everyone always assumes it's me without investigating first."

Over Going-gray's dark, warning look, I realized which one I should direct the fire to. I thrust two fingers in the shape of a gun in Viviane's direction. "Blow Job led her mean crew over to harass us. First, she made a racial slur against good Princess Danielle, and then one of her lackeys threw dirt on our food. I'm sure there's some shifter rule about spoiling another's food. If not, make one as soon as possible."

I paused to suck in a breath. "And then that dumbfuck blonde's loose skirt dropped to her dirty ankles. Maybe she did that intentionally just to get attention—some shameless toads would do anything to have a second of fame. Know what I mean? Paris was quick to think on her feet, so she snapped some pictures. We'll put them on the Academy's network. Feel free to check it out later, sir. We want it to go viral, like old TikTok. Then Blow Job blamed us—"

"Shut the fuck up, you stupid rat girl!" Viviane screamed.

I noticed the entire restaurant had gone deathly quiet while I'd vomited my words all over. Well, at least Viviane's nickname had been exposed, and there was nothing we could do about it now.

Face burning red, Viviane charged me, but Going-gray blocked her. He was amazingly fast and strong, considering his age.

"While I'm here, no brawling will be allowed in this fine military school that I helped build," he snarled. "The one who lands the first blow will go to Solitary."

I blinked. Solitary? That didn't sound attractive.

Viviane trembled with rage. "Did you hear what she called me, Prince Jay? A lowlife insulting the Heir to the Great European Shifters Kingdom shall be put to death immediately!"

"In your barbaric backyard, maybe." Danielle puffed up her chest and snorted. "But this isn't your territory. This is the North American Shifters Kingdom ruled by His Majesty, King Grayson. You're just like me, a guest student in Shifters Academy. And Pip is under my protection. If Prince Jay deems we've broken any rules, I'll take full responsibility."

I applauded. At my gaze of encouragement, Paris and Summer clapped their hands too. But we all stopped as Going-gray glared at us.

"What did I warn you on the way here, Pip girl?" He focused his glare on me. "We gave you a new life, and you try to throw it away?"

That wasn't true at all. He and Sideburns had dragged me here, though I'd chosen to come with Shade, enticed by his friendship and promise in the end.

"But I didn't throw it away," I said. "I'm enjoying it. My friends and I were enjoying grass-fed hamburgers mixed with freshly picked herbs from the restaurant's organic garden and discussing why all Americans have big mouths, and then Blow Job—"

Going-gray put up a hand to stop me. "You cannot go around calling people names, especially those who are your betters! Viviane is a princess!"

154

"But I confessed to you on the road that I don't remember names well unless I know them, so I rely on visual aids to help me know who's who," I protested. "Like you're Prince Going-gray and the Alpha Heir is Sideburns. Surely, I mentioned all this, right?"

More gasps and a couple of coughs sounded from the back of the restaurant.

Going-gray stared daggers at me while he ran a big hand through his hair, as if he wanted to rearrange it to cover all the gray. He had more since I'd last seen him.

"Sir, can we be dismissed?" I asked with a cordial smile. "I don't want to be late for my next class. One of the teachers gave me a yellow card already."

"Wipe that stupid, smug smirk off your face," he barked.

I dropped my grin. "You got it."

"This isn't over," Viviane spat venomously. "I might have made a deal with the Alpha Heir to ignore this rat girl, but I'd like to know why Prince Jared even took pity on this urchin. Regardless, unfortunate accidents happen all the time here."

"Are you threatening my new companion?" Danielle demanded, her eyes on fire.

Viviane sneered. "You'll know when it's a threat."

She stormed off, and her minions flashed me a

death glare before running after their queen bee. I thought of making them fart all the way, but I'd be digging a deeper hole for myself.

"Congratulations, Pip girl," Going-gray retorted, his muscled arms folding across his bulky chest. "You managed to make a powerful enemy who will make your life hell on day two."

"Hell? Been there before." I grinned wider at him. "Dealing with BJ? Cherry on top."

CHAPTER THIRTEEN

*B*attle class turned out to be an open session with a mix of first, second, and third years.

Over two hundred coeds gathered in the training hall. Students paired up to spar or wrestle upon cushioned mats, while five instructors led the class. The main coach wore a ball cap and held a whistle in his mouth. I grinned when I spied Shade amid the instructors. He wasted no time opening the floor and explaining the rules.

The entire clan of female shifters hung on his every word, and the male shifters looked on enviously, like they wanted to be him. While Shade enthralled them, his words passed in one of my ears and came out the other, since I was busy looking around.

All this was so new and strange to me, yet I

meshed into the environment just fine. Maybe I was indeed a chameleon. I'd looked up the definition in a magical dictionary. Chameleon wasn't exactly a magical classification, but it defined a person who could absorb anything and become one with their settings.

Being a chameleon would increase my chance of survival in an unknown, hostile environment.

While Shade explained the rules of dueling, Viviane and her gang entered the training hall. Shade narrowed his eyes at the newcomers, and everyone turned toward the entrance.

"Sorry, Prince Shade," Viviane said with a confident, entitled smile. "We're a bit late. Apologies, instructors."

Shit. They were in this class too? I had such a bad feeling about this that my skin itched.

Danielle darted a worried glance at me before she pursed her lips with determination. I nodded. Whatever happened, we'd deal with it. Besides, there were so many instructors here, Blow Job would have to think twice about coming after us.

The instructors divided us into five groups, each with an instructor leading us. Unfortunately, I wasn't in Shade's group. I didn't expect him to give my any special treatment, but he was the only one who knew about my amnesia and might cut me some slack if I stepped out of line or trod on toes, which had become the story of my life.

Paris and Summer, however, ended up on Shade's team. The two girls jumped into a hug and high fived, but then they tried to look demure when they caught Danielle's and my unhappy looks. But I was less unhappy than Danielle, since I at least was still with her in the lead coach's group. We'd watch each other's six.

The sucky part? Viviane and three of her thugs, all built like brick walls, were in our group as well.

The training started as soon as the lead coach blew his whistle. I took inventory of everything, not missing a beat. That was how I learned. I absorbed the instructors' fighting moves, then compared their maneuvers and tactics, filing them instantly and coming up with the best combinations for myself.

Being a copycat was my strong suit.

My name was called, and I stepped onto the mat to face a shifter boy. He looked a year younger than me, and he wasn't much bigger. We parried, and I picked up some of his moves, improved them, and returned the favor. He was friendly, and I didn't act aggressively either.

After warming up a little, my nervousness vanished. I threw a thumbs-up at Danielle when she glanced my direction. She was parrying with a shifter of Latino heritage.

The shifter boy and I parted ways after one more bout. Then I came face-to-face with one of

Viviane's henchwomen. It was just my luck that she was double my size with bulky arms the size of my legs. She was more like a man than a woman. I'd call her Butch.

Butch stared down at me with a vile grin while Viviane, two mats over, swung a half-hearted punch at her practice partner—her partner basically let herself serve as a punching bag. Viviane watched us, evil delight glinting in her eyes.

So this was her way of keeping her nasty little hands clean—attack me indirectly by using her damn groupies. I doubt Sideburns would care. In fact, she probably set this up right down to making sure we were all in the same class.

"Peep, right, like Peeping Tom?" Butch asked mockingly. By the hungry look in her eye, I'd soon be a dish on her plate.

"Why not? I like Peeping Tom. He's got the balls to dig his nose in where it doesn't belong. And are you *Butch,* like a dude?" I asked with a smile.

A few chuckles rose around us. Not all students were on the mats, and not all of them were fans of Viviane and her goons.

Butch's face turned purple with anger. Not everyone could take a joke like me. "You won't have a smart mouth after I'm done with you."

"Is that so, Butch?" I asked and wiggled a finger at her. "Can't wait."

She swung her fist at me, and I ducked instinctively. She advanced on me and swung her arms again and again, taking advantage of her far reach and long limbs. For a big girl, her speed was impressive. I bet she practiced a lot in the boxing ring.

I kept dodging her heavy punches, left and right, dancing slightly back. Her fists flew by my ears several times. I let her display her moves, then I found an opening, twisting and darting behind her, and kicked her knee. She didn't go down, not as I'd expected. *Fuck*, Butch was strong. She elbowed backward toward my throat and slammed into the soft, vulnerable part.

It took me second to realize that she'd let me kick her so she could elbow me. Pain choked me, and I doubled over. I dropped to my knees and fell over, curling into a ball. My hand grabbed my throat, trying to soothe the hurt.

"Weakling!" Butch shouted. "Who's your daddy now?"

What did this have to do with my daddy? I didn't even know who he was.

It was against the rules to kick an opponent who was down, but it wasn't against the rules for her to place a foot hard against my body to claim victory. She twisted her heal into my gut, grinding into my skin while cheering.

Fuck Butch.

With both hands, I gripped her ankle and

twisted hard until her body began to fall. She couldn't stop the momentum and slammed into the mat face first. I leapt up and hauled her along the mat, surprised by my own strength. But then I was getting stronger every day without the hostile spells and drugs in my system.

I gave her a good kick in the back before I slammed her down again. My boot followed and pressed into her mouth, proving who the meaner bitch was.

"Now, would you like to tell me who your daddy is, Butch?" I chuckled.

Quite a few smaller students snickered. I bet they got bullied a lot too.

"That's enough!" the leading coach barked and made a time-out gesture.

I smiled and removed my foot reluctantly from Butch's face.

"This was fun," I told her. "Let's do it again, shall we?"

Butch jumped up and wiped her mouth with her sleeve before she spat.

"Coach Hanuman," Butch said. "The new girl cheated! She should be punished."

I blinked. "How was I cheating when I only mimicked your moves?"

"You shouldn't have copied me and then played dirty!" she yelled.

I smiled. "Well, sue me."

"Enough!" Hanuman blew his piercing whistle and pointed at the sidelines. "Both of you will sit on the bench until class is over. If either of you talks or causes trouble again, you will go to detention!"

He spoke fluently with that whistle in his mouth. That impressed me, so I was going to call him Coach Whistle.

Danielle made a beeline toward Coach Whistle, probably wanting to defend me against Butch, but I shook my head at her. Viviane shot me a malicious stare as if that could stab me silly.

Coach Whistle blew his signature whistle again to signal the next round.

Oh, fuck. Danielle was now paired against Viviane.

I trained my eyes on them, worry twisting my middle. Blow Job was a head taller than Danielle. From her build and pose, everyone could see that BJ was bigger and stronger and obviously had way more training than Danielle. The French princess was also one year ahead of the Asian princess.

They faced each other with death glares. BJ flashed a nasty grin at Danielle, and the nervousness in Danielle's eyes vanished the next second, replaced by determination and stubbornness. I admired her bravery even though she and probably everyone else knew this would be a hell of a match. It would take a miracle for Danielle to win.

Viviane had come to battle class with revenge in her heart. She probably figured that if she could make an example of Danielle in public, no one would stand in her way when she came after me.

Viviane brought her leg up to kick Danielle in the face. Danielle ducked to the side and rammed her fist into Viviane's calf.

Viviane took the blow while ramming her fist into Danielle's jaw, throwing her opponent's head back. Viviane's second strike found purchase on the side of Danielle face. Blood dripped from Danielle's mouth.

Every student, as well as the instructors, held a collective breath as they watched the duel. Nobody dared interfere with Viviane. Butch cheered beside me, and Viviane's other goons shouted excitedly like bloodhounds wanting to see more of the Asian princess's spilled blood.

I clenched my fists by my sides, my eyes on fire.

Shade stood on the far side of the hall. He started to head toward where Danielle and Viviane fought, but an instructor stopped him and said something about it being allowed in battle class. The fight would go on until one of them went down or yielded. As long as it didn't cause death, the instructors would allow it.

"Shifters are made of tough materials," another instructor commented.

Viviane kicked at Danielle's midsection, careful

not to use too much force that might make her fall. It was obvious what she was trying to do—keep Danielle upright so she could keep mercilessly bashing her. Another hit landed on Danielle's kidney, and the princess staggered. She didn't stand a chance. Viviane must have been trained to fight when she was a child. She delivered every move with precision and strength.

Before Danielle dropped to a knee, Viviane grabbed her hair and straightened her. Viviane's fist, tainted with Danielle's blood, rammed into her nose again. The sound of cracking bones echoed in the room.

The sadistic bitch was maiming Danielle for all to see and displaying Danielle's weakness.

Paris and Summer had moved to the front of the cushioned mat, trembling, tears in their eyes. I hadn't spent a lot of time with them, but I'd learned about their proud samurai shifter culture. They wouldn't plead to the instructors for their princess, and they'd never beg outsiders for help.

Viviane laughed and raised her bloody fist for another blow, her other hand pinning Danielle by her hair. But before she could land it, I dashed from the bench like an arrow and crashed into Viviane. Danielle dropped, as did Viviane from my blunt force.

I raised my fist and drove the knuckles into Viviane's face again and again before she could react. I was faster than her. I could be faster than anyone here.

She roared, trying to throw me off as I straddled her.

"How does it feel to be pinned down and trapped, cunt?" I spat on her face before jamming my fist into her eye socket. "Touch my princess again, and I'll blind you!"

For the first time, fear flashed in her eyes as I caught a glimpse of my savage look in them. She brought her fists up to punch me. She was very strong, but I was a hell of a lot stronger, and I was running on fucking adrenaline.

I felt her bones break under my brutal assault, just like what she had done to Danielle. I smiled vengefully. Blood dripped from my knuckles, and I was glad it wasn't mine.

From different directions, I heard stern orders to stop immediately. Shade shouted my name as well, but I didn't give a fuck. Princess Danielle had shielded me when I needed it, so anyone who hurt her must pay tenfold.

I grinned as I aimed a blow toward BJ's mouth, ready to knock out a tooth or two, forcing her to spend some bucks on dental work.

Two large, rough hands grabbed my fist before I could drive it home. I broke free and shoved them off. Those shifters were fast, and they grabbed me again. An arm wrapped around my

"That hurt, cunt!" I yelled, but my voice had lost some strength. "Your turn."

I had maybe two seconds before darkness overcame me, but I'd make those seconds count. "Let's make you a one-eared, Princess Blow Job!"

Even with my hands bound behind me and the potent sedatives flowing in my veins, I headbutted my forehead against BJ's before I twisted to the side, opened my jaw, and tore off the bottom half of her ear.

Viviane screamed.

I roared my victory while I spat half of her bloody ear into her face. I ignored the blood dripping from my teeth, mostly because my vision was beginning to fade.

"Prince Sideburns will like this new look." I chuckled like a psycho, the tone of my voice deepening. "But you don't taste good, actually, Deepthroat or not, Princess."

Speaking of which, Sideburns' roar shook the walls of the hall. My head swung lazily toward the entrance in time to see his massive, blurry figure charging toward me.

"What the fuck is going on?" he raged.

The Alpha Heir was a bit too late to the party. The lousy knight in shining armor failed to save his princess from losing part of her ear. But I couldn't voice the last insult as darkness pulled me under.

With the last of my consciousness, I heard Shade fight off those around me, then take me into his arms. The voices of Paris, Summer, and Danielle warned those away, and I imagined a protective ring around me.

CHAPTER FOURTEEN

a damp, bitter smell assaulted my nostrils.

I fluttered open my swollen eyes barely a crack. I could still feel the residual effects of the drugs coursing through my veins giving me a pounding headache. I bet they gave me a dose that could've killed a horse.

My gaze darted around the room: three concrete walls, another made from iron bars from floor to ceiling and a door locked from the outside.

I was in a jail cell. *In a cage.*

My heart thundered against my ribcage, and my blood turned to ice, even though my skin felt on fire. A memory surfaced of how I'd ended up here—punching the most powerful princess in a blind rage when she'd ruthlessly beat up Danielle.

I touched my neck to feel the needle mark. It had disappeared. In its wake, hunger pangs, a splitting headache, and ice-cold anxiety whirled inside me. What were my superior shifters going to do to me? They couldn't keep me here forever, right?

I'd had a glimpse into my past and concluded that I'd been a captive before too, though I didn't know for how long. If the shifters treated me the same—

Air caught in my lungs as fear clenched my insides. And this time, who would break me out?

Tears flowed down my swollen face. I couldn't be here. I couldn't be in a cage. I needed to think and find a way to crawl out of here. Would Shade be able to help me?

"Hello?" I called in a shaky voice. "Anyone around? I demand to talk to Prince Shade!"

No one answered. I pricked my ears but didn't hear any sounds. My senses reached further but still nothing. Every inch of this prison must be warded, and I seemed to be the sole prisoner.

I scrambled to my feet, steadied myself, and kicked at the iron bars. It didn't cause a ripple and only hurt my foot.

I slid down onto the cold floor again. It was best to preserve my energy. I cried for another minute to try to fend off my terrible loneliness and misery, but a wave of fatigue, probably still from the drugs, pulled me into the darkness. I welcomed it, anything to forget my current predicament.

A jumble of images, maybe memories, assaulted

my mind one after another, until they settled into one setting, in which icy darkness pierced me.

My eyes flashed open; the movement caused pain behind my eyes. I tried to understand where I was, only to find that the air was too thin to breathe. My sight gradually adjusted to the blanket of black surrounding me. I was lying on something hard, and six inches above me was a long sheet of plywood smelling of earth and mold. My heart skipped a beat. I was inside a coffin buried who knew how deep.

I screamed a sound so horrific I barely recognized my own voice.

An explosion came next, drowning out my screams and shaking my coffin. The wooden lid in front of me ripped from its hinges and flew upward, taking with it chunks of earth and debris.

My mouth closed and I gazed upward at a gorgeous male who stared down at me, his sapphire eyes full of rage, longing, sorrow, regret, and pain that this world couldn't carry.

I let out a whimper. "You came."

I'd seen that icy beautiful face before. The Vampire God reached his hand toward me, but just before I could grab his fingertips, a dark storm swept in and swallowed him and his desperate roars.

Before I could cry out for him, the scene blurred into the next one.

My heartbeat pounded in my frozen ears, drowning out the rapid sound of my bare feet hitting ice.

I was being hunted. The sound of men shouting and hounds howling chased me. I sprang over an expanse of endless ice with inhuman speed.

A group of armed vehicles raced after me, bullets zipping by me...

"Pip?" A voice reached me. "Pip? Wake up."

More voices called me urgently.

I blinked open my eyes, my legs thrashing, and I bolted up. My head hit the wall at my jerky movements.

"It's us, Pip," Danielle whispered.

I shook off the nightmares and fogginess in my head, peered at Danielle, Paris, and Summer, and grinned. My friends had come to visit me.

Danielle stood outside the iron bars, Paris and Summer flanking her. They all wore T-shirts and slim-cut jeans. Summer and Paris also wore light jackets.

Danielle had cleaned up and mostly healed, though she still had faint bruises over her cheeks and split lip. Looking at her, I realized that my own eyes were still a bit swollen with how much pressure I felt behind them. I must look like shit. I doubted they'd called healers to tend to me after throwing me in here.

Even so, my mood improved greatly at seeing my tribe.

I swaggered to my feet and moved closer to the bars. "No uniforms today, girls?"

Danielle rolled her eyes. "That's what you're worried about?"

Paris smiled. "No one wears uniforms on the weekend."

I groaned. "It's the weekend already?"

Summer peered around carefully before she yanked out two bottles of water and a few chocolate bars from inside her jacket. She shoved them to me quickly through the bars. "Hide these."

I glanced at my dirty, bloody uniform then at the cell. There was nowhere I could hide the smuggled bottles of water and bars.

"I'll just eat them now," I said as I gratefully accepted the supplies.

"Give Pip your jacket," Danielle ordered Summer.

Summer banged the heel of her palm against her forehead. "I'm so dense." She shrugged off her jacket and handed it to me.

I wrapped a bottle of water and the rest of the chocolate bars inside her jacket and laid it in the corner of the cell. Then I lifted a bottle of water, turned the lid, and took a long swig.

My parched throat instantly felt better. I bit off half of a chocolate bar, chewing quickly before I swallowed. "You girls are the best."

"Here." Paris removed a brown bag from inside her jacket as well. "Two large sandwiches for a big-mouthed North American female werewolf who beat the shit out of Blow Job."

All of us laughed, the mood lightening despite me being a jailbird.

I giddily accepted the brown bag. "Best breakfast ever! Thanks again, girls."

I placed it on top of Summer's jacket and bounced back to them. I'd consume the food later. Right now, I wanted to spend every second with my friends, regardless of my hunger.

"We can't stay long," Danielle said. "We bribed the guards for a brief visit. So, we'll just get to the point and give you the updates."

I nodded, my eyes becoming a bit misty. They'd taken a great risk coming to see me. I'd become a criminal by hitting the shifter princess. Danielle could have just walked away and kept her impeccable, clean record instead of being linked to me.

She eyed me, her throat moving as emotions twisted her expression. "You took the hit that was meant for me."

"You wouldn't have gotten that hit if not for me," I said, then rage shot to my middle. "The instructors and the guards should have stopped that cunt when she tried to maim you, but they did nothing."

I was also disappointed in Shade. He could've stopped the fight.

"It's shifter culture," Danielle explained. "We're

a brutal and violent species who stick to a strict hierarchy. It's never about being fair. It's always about power."

My eyes darkened. "It's always big dogs eating smaller dogs." I waved a hand to dismiss the thought. If I expected this world to give me some kind of justice, I was seriously mistaken. The only way to fight back was to become the biggest, baddest predator.

"How is BJ, anyway?" I asked, baring my teeth. "I might not get out of here, but if any of you bump into her, tell her I miss her."

"You'll get out of here!" Danielle said fiercely. "I've sent word to my father, but it will take him five days to get here after he gets the message. The horseman War destroyed global telecommunication and air transportation. The fastest way for supernaturals to travel is through a leyline, but leylines aren't reliable either. Dad has to go through three leylines to get to Nevada from Japan."

Paris added, "Our princess has been working on everyone in King Grayson's circle to persuade the king to delay the sentence."

"Sentence?" I drawled. "So they're going to execute me, the sooner the better, right?"

"If it weren't for Prince Shade that day, they'd have killed you on the spot," Summer said softly. "We have the prince to thank for that."

Danielle gave them a look before fixing her steady gaze back on me.

"I won't let it happen." She stepped closer, grasped my hand in hers through the bars, and whispered, "If they sentence you to death, we'll bust you out before that. I have a backup plan, Pip."

"No!" I shook my head vehemently. "The last thing I want is to get you girls in a bind. I don't fear death."

I'd been called Death's daughter, hadn't I? How ironic.

"You watch out for each other if I'm gone," I told them bravely before I expelled a heavy breath. "At least I'll die free and knowing I have friends."

Paris and Summer quietly cried.

"It won't come to that, Pip," Danielle assured me. "Prince Shade keeps close contact with us. He's hard at work to get Blow—BJ to drop the charges. He also pleaded with his brother to show you mercy."

Hearing about Sideburns left a sour taste in my mouth and sent a pang to my chest. It didn't surprise me that he would order the ax to fall upon me to appease his girlfriend.

Footfalls rushed toward my cell and paused at the other end of the corridor.

"The visit's over, Princess," a rough male voice called out. "You need to leave now! I don't want to get caught."

Danielle gave me a heartbreaking look. "You must hang in there, Pip. Just hang in there!"

I'd hang in here before I got hanged.

"Now, Princess, please!" the guard urged, and my friends rushed away.

I slumped to the ground, my smirk and bravado vanishing as I stared at the empty space where they had been moments before. The guard left around the corner too and never returned.

It was just me, silence and the darkness.

But I told myself not to be dismayed.

I scrambled toward the corner, my shaking hands opening the brown bag and removing the sandwich. This hungry werewolf was going to consume everything! Screw rationing it.

I licked my fingers after the last chocolate bar disappeared into my belly. I had nothing to do now. Troubled dreams and fragmented memories did not visit me again, but I couldn't sleep either.

I leaned against the wall, pulling my knees up against my chest, and my thoughts traced back to the Vampire God who had reappeared in my broken dream or memories before my friends' visit.

Who was the handsome devil exactly? It seemed galaxy fire burned in his sapphire eyes when he'd gazed upon me with intense longing and ravenous hunger. Did he hunger for my blood or want me as a woman?

I shook my head at my wishful thinking. He couldn't desire me. Even my fated mate didn't want me. Yet I was hoping to see the Vampire God again, just once, so I could ask him if he'd indeed come for me in that damned lab building.

My mind replayed the longing in his eyes as if by doing so I could find comfort in this cold, damp cell, as if I could deceive myself and hope that someone out there might truly want me.

Eventually, sleep came. For how long I didn't know, but when I woke, my muscles ached.

At the sound of footfalls coming toward my cell from down the corridor, I crouched low. Part of me came alive, like a shark smelling fresh blood, but the other part had shut down due to my fatigue and anxiety.

Someone had come to fetch me for my execution. There'd be no last meal. No trial. This could be a secret execution.

I didn't bother to move until I saw who stood in front of the bars, regarding me solemnly.

A smirk split my face, but I didn't rise to meet Shade, unlike how I'd bounced up when Danielle and the girls had showed up. I didn't want him to see my wobbly legs if I stood, so I sank to the floor instead, my legs crossed.

"Canary," I breathed in a cheerful tone, "did you come to sing for me? It has to be free since I'm short a few coins."

"Very funny," he said. "Glad to know you're still so entertaining."

My eyes trained on a brown bag in his hand. I couldn't help it, as a delicious smell wafted from its contents.

He shoved the package between the bars toward me. "Brought you burgers, chips, and drinks."

"Toss the bag over here, will you?" I asked, my smile still ghosting my lips.

He gave me a weary look, but at least it wasn't a pitiful one. That was why I always liked him.

He bent, placed the brown bag on the ground, and shoved it toward me.

I grabbed it before it reached my feet and peeked inside. I licked my dry lips. The good prince had brought me a bottle of apple cider as well. It was my favorite Martinelli's brand. I inspected the rest of the contents before I flashed him another grin.

"You even got me pickles? I'll eat them last though."

I was so thirsty that even my soul felt dry. I tore off the lid and drank half the bottle of juice.

"Easy, Catnip," Shade warned. "If you drink like that, you'll get sick."

Then he stopped himself. I already looked sick from starving and having nightmares. At least my

MEG XUEMEI X

eyes were no longer swollen. I could look at his handsome face in full view.

"Worry about yourself, Canary," I said, quirking a brow at him. "I'm doing swell."

At least he had called me Catnip, signaling his good mood, which meant he probably had better news.

Things were already looking up. First, the prince came instead of an executioner. Second, I got a meal. Then a dark thought crossed my mind. Maybe this was Shade's way of saying a final goodbye.

If so, I should demand a T-bone steak or even spicy sushi rolls.

And my fated mate hadn't shown his face or sent one single word. Maybe he was eagerly waiting to watch my head be chopped off.

Acid flooded my stomach, so much so that I almost stopped eating. But then, I told myself, what the fuck? I'd enjoy every good thing in my brief life until the last second.

I grabbed two chips and popped them into my mouth.

"Are these corn chips or potato chips?" I asked Shade.

"That's what you're worried about?"

"Princess Danielle said the same thing the other day," I said with a shrug. "I'm about to die, and you

182

want me to think big? If I didn't know you better, I'd call you an asshole."

He shook his head. "Sorry that I couldn't come earlier." His voice was raw and rough, as if he blamed himself for my situation.

I didn't blame him at all. It counted for something that he hadn't forgotten about me. I tossed a pickle into my mouth and moaned in pleasure.

His gaze landed on my lips.

"You're not going to die, Catnip, not while I stand here," he said fiercely. "If this was supposed to be your last meal, I'd have come a couple of days ago to bust you out and sneak you away from Shifter City."

My eyes widened, and I sniffed in gratitude. "You'd do that for me?"

"Of course. Meanwhile, I've been petitioning to have your death sentence removed." He ran a hand through his messy hair. Now that I stopped worrying about my weak, dirty state, I could tell he hadn't had much rest. Twin dark circles had appeared below his eyes. He still looked ruggedly handsome, though. Some guys were truly blessed.

"Viviane finally agreed to drop the charge, persuaded by Jared," he continued. "My father also agreed not to place a severe punishment on you, as both Jared and I pleaded with him."

I blinked. "Sideburns doesn't want me dead?"

Shade chuckled. "Only you'd dare to keep

calling him that." His face turned solemn. "It's not in him to let you die. His wolf would rebel." He paused for a second. "Jared might be a hard ass, as he has to constantly wade through political waters, but his wolf—all our wolves—think in a straight-forward, primal way. His wolf would never allow my brother or anyone to kill his fated mate. And you, Pip, are Jared's mate."

He dropped the bomb and waited for me to jump, but I made no move other than eating another pickle. His brother had warned him not to tell me, but, under the circumstances, Shade ignored his orders, which only said how good he was to me.

He narrowed his eyes, not thrilled at my apathy. "Well?"

"Yeah?" I asked before I swallowed the delicious pickle.

"Aren't you surprised?"

"Should I be?"

"Finding one's fated mate is the biggest thing in life! It's a once-in-a-lifetime, rare gift. Most shifters never find their mates."

"So? It hasn't been a huge deal for Sideburns. Actually, it's the opposite of a big deal."

Shade looked stunned. "You knew?"

I shrugged. "From the beginning. What do you think I am, Canary, blind?"

"And you didn't tell me?" he accused.

"Sorry I didn't try to depress myself even more," I snickered. But then my shoulders slumped, and I overcompensated by tossing a chip or two into my mouth.

Ever since I'd met Sideburns, everything about him depressed me.

I lifted my eyes to Shade. "What difference does it make if I know it or not? He never wanted me."

"He wants you," Shade said with a sigh. "That's why he prohibits every man from courting you or getting close to you."

I let out a low laugh without mirth. "He won't claim me as his mate, but he won't let anyone else have me either. He's such a treat."

"He's the Alpha Heir." Shade scratched his stubble. He hadn't shaved for a couple of days. "His marriage will be a political alliance. When Princess Viviane, the heir of the Great European Shifters Kingdom, is bound with my brother in matrimony, our family will become more than a powerhouse. With our combined forces, the North American shifters will stomp the vampire army. That's what's in my brother's head."

"I get it," I said. "BJ comes from a royal shifter bloodline, like your family. The joining of the two most powerful bloodlines can produce the next powerful bloodline. It's all about pure royal blood. I, on the other hand, am a lone wolf who doesn't remember her past. I'm a refugee, the lowest among the lower shifters. I have no power behind me. I have no ties. I'm also being hunted, and I don't even know why. It'll be an eye-opening event if the Alpha Heir ever picks me, fated mate or not. And yet," a grin reached my ears. "This nobody bit off the ear of the most powerful shifter princess."

"An earlobe," Shade corrected with a chortle. "Which the best healers in the city have patched up. And could you please stop giving ridiculous names to everyone? It's a horrible habit. And you're wrong about you being the scum of the earth."

I scowled at him. Who said I was the scum?

"You *are* special, Catnip," he said. "I can feel it whenever you're around. I felt it when I first spotted you. I see it, but Jared hasn't yet. Fate gave him a great gift, but he's tossing it away. One day, it'll bite him in the ass."

"Fate cursed us by pairing us with each other," I murmured.

The prince frowned at me. "You need to develop a sense of self-perseverance. You surprised everyone with your outburst of power and strength. They have no idea that you're actually more dominant than any shifter, including Jared. All the more reason you need to rein in your rage. Use it, but don't let it ride you or you may end up dead. I can teach you how to control your beast and your temper."

Now that I'd regained my strength with solid food in my belly, I rose to my feet and stalked closer to the bars to smirk at him. "But I can't pay you, Highness. You'll be disappointed that I don't have deep pockets."

"I'm not looking for money, but I hear the jingling of gold coins in the future." He chuckled. "I wonder if Jared regrets dragging you all the way here. I bet he didn't expect you to be such a headache."

I put up a finger. "First, he couldn't really drag me here. I came willingly because I trusted you, Canary. And second, the Alpha Heir can just exile me. Don't shifters have rules about banishment?"

I'd hate to leave Danielle, the girls, and Shade, but if it was my lot, I'd take it.

"He'll never let you go, Pip," Shade said quietly. "He might reject you for political gain, but his primal need is to keep you in his sight. He won't let any other man claim you."

"He doesn't own me," I said. "And he'll truly regret it if he thinks and acts as if I were his possession. He rejected me, and I reject him back."

Shade gave me a long look. "Did you feel the pull when my brother was close to you?"

I might not want to reveal everything to Shade, or to anyone, but I wanted to be as honest to my friends as best I could.

I nodded. "I can't deny the attraction, but it's just biological. It means nothing to me."

Shade sighed. "Jared is stupid for rejecting you so openly, but he also doesn't know what to do with you. One day, he'll realize that the sun doesn't always shine out of his butthole."

"So he dumped me in the Academy." I snorted. "But I like it here, because of Danielle and the girls. Plus, you're here. I know if I ever get out, BJ will try to make my life hell every waking moment. But some things are worth fighting for. And for me, friendship is worth more than gold."

Shade reached for me and squeezed my greasy fingers that held a chip and a pickle between them. "You'll get out of here soon, Catnip, I promise. And I always keep my promises."

CHAPTER FIFTEEN

hey decided to let me live and released me from my cramped cell a day later, just as Shade had promised.

Danielle, Paris, and Summer came to meet me. As we walked across the campus toward our building, many students gave us a wide berth. It seemed no one wanted to be near the crazy chick who had bitten off the most powerful princess's ear. But a couple of students waved at me. Guess I'd earned some respect by standing up to the biggest bully at the Academy

"That rabid rat should've been put down," someone said behind me. It must be one of BJ's goons.

"Ignore her," Paris said. "We prepared a feast for you."

"A feast?" I asked in glee. "Then let's hurry!"

The girls laughed, and we picked up our pace.

"And all-you-can-eat cakes," Danielle added to my great pleasure.

Once we reached the penthouse, I showered, changed into clean clothes, and rushed to join the girls in the living room. It was indeed a feast—all sorts of dishes, desserts, and drinks were crammed onto the table.

"Can the table hold all the weight?" I asked, a bit worried, though I immensely appreciated their efforts.

"Worry about your stomach holding the weight," Summer said with a smile.

I accepted the challenge and dove into the grand feast meant to celebrate my freedom.

"My father canceled his journey," Danielle swallowed a bite of cherry pie, "seeing how King Grayson had already signed the paper to release you. I'm surprised the king got involved in the Academy's affairs, even though this was a special case since you attacked BJ. There've been talks about merging all the shifters under one high king. King Grayson will need the support of BJ's father, the European Shifter King. But still, King Grayson didn't deliver you, a girl who doesn't have any ties, to the European king to please him."

Her message was clear. She suspected something and thought there might be something I hadn't told her. The princess was sharp.

But what could I tell her? That I was a girl without memories, country, or clan? And I was being hunted by powerful mages, vampires, and possibly other species? That I was also the rejected mate of the Alpha Heir?

Paris and Summer also peered at me, and I shrugged, my face closed off. A feeling of loneliness washed over me.

Danielle didn't press further but sighed. "Both princes pleaded on your behalf. I wasn't surprised that Prince Shade defended you, but it's kind of strange that the Alpha Heir also spoke for you. I heard that he also made a deal with Viviane and her father afterwards. Prince Jared will soon openly propose to BJ."

My heart skipped a beat. A stab of pain deep within my chest followed.

I shouldn't have cared, as Sideburns had made it clear that he would never choose me, but I still felt physical pain every time his rejection was brought to my attention.

It was as if I was being punished by the universe when it wasn't even my fault. The universe was a big, fucked-up place.

I schooled the emotions threatening to break my expression. "Whatever. They deserve each other."

"BJ has been pushing for their engagement for over a year," Danielle said. "She's finally getting what she's always wanted. The European Shifter King is keen for royal grandbabies."

"We need to tread carefully," Summer reminded us. "Especially you, Pip. Keep your guard up at all times."

I hated that we weren't in the same classes, since they were a year ahead of me. That left me alone most of the time during the day.

Paris nodded. "BJ won't let it go easily. She's the most vengeful bitch ever. If she doesn't come after you right away, it only means she's biding her time for something really nasty."

"I eat nasty like popcorn," I said, then shook my head. "Let's not talk about her anymore. I have bigger things to worry about like the Moon Ceremony."

No point fretting about what BJ might do. Might as well focus on what I could control and then try to enjoy my time with my friends. With how things had gone so far, I might not have many good moments.

"The Moon Ceremony is like a hunting party," Danielle said. "It's a big shifters' tradition that happens once a year. Every student shifts, then hunts in Humboldt Forest. Sometimes, the hosting royals, like Prince Jared and Prince Shade, will join us."

I looked up at them beneath my eyelashes. "So… uh, you all know how to shift?"

"Of course." Summer grinned. "Since we were children."

Son of a bitch. I rubbed my sweaty palms along my jeans. "I, um… I've never shifted before. I don't know how."

The girls' eyes widened.

"Where have you been all these years, Pip?" Paris said in a teasing and sympathetic tone.

Still, my chest tightened. "Here and there," I said.

"Pip was a lone wolf when Prince Shade found her," Danielle said. "I bet no one taught her how to shift, unlike us. But that's going to change."

While I'd been in jail, the princess must have learned a lot about me. I wondered if Shade was her source. Anyway, she was also a princess, so playing political games was part of her job.

"You're no longer a lone wolf, Pip," the princess continued. "We'll teach you, and you'll shift perfectly before the ceremony starts." Her expression darkened. "But you need to learn discipline and control your rage. You're loyal to a fault when it comes to your friends, but if you put yourself in danger again, we'll lose you for good." Her lips thinned with worry. "It can't happen again."

"Fine, I'll be careful," I promised, then reached for a slice of red velvet cake.

* * *

FOR THE NEXT couple of days, the girls spent every waking hour drilling me and teaching me to shift, but no wolf showed herself. We couldn't even get a simple whimper from the beast.

"Maybe I'm not a shifter?" I asked in dismay as three wolves growled at me to get me to follow suit.

Danielle had shifted into a beautiful white wolf, while Summer and Paris had fluffy fur in different shades of gray. All three had tried using their wolves to convince mine to pull her head out of my ass, but she ghosted all of us.

I simply didn't feel the animal inside of me, even though I couldn't deny I'd seen my hand turn into a wolf's claw when I'd fought one of my hunters weeks ago. Maybe that had been some kind of magic?

After uselessly growling some more at me, the girls shifted back into their human forms and got dressed.

"Our wolves sense that you're a shifter," Danielle said, her brows drawn together in confusion. "And the Alpha Heir brought you here because he sensed it too. He's one of the most powerful shifters and wouldn't have made a mistake."

Frustration and anxiety buzzed along my skin. "I hear what you're saying, but I'm telling you I feel nothing, which means they're going to kick me

194

out, and I'll have no choice but to accept my humiliating fate."

"Keep practicing," Danielle ordered. "Even if you can't shift now, you'll shift in the ceremony when thousands of shifters all change shapes. Your wolf will want to come out then. Trust me."

I did trust her, but I sure as hell didn't trust my pussified dormant wolf. It's too bad I couldn't because I would kick her ass for being stubborn and making me look stupid.

CHAPTER SIXTEEN

A fleet of buses traveled along the highway, escorted by armored vehicles, as we headed north.

I sat with my fellow first year students in a white and blue bus, separated from Danielle, Paris, and Summer. Some of Viviane's minions shared the bus with me and glared at the back of my head the whole time, but no one spoke to me. Somehow, my crazy reputation had preceded me, and no one wanted to lose an ear, I guess.

Speaking of which, I hadn't seen BJ since I had been released. I really wanted to see how her ear looked, like had it been re-attached properly? Could she wear earrings without one being lopsided? One didn't just forget things like that.

The bus rolled on for hours with a low rumbling sound until we reached the famous

Humboldt Forest. They parked in neat lines, then students filed out with excited, nervous voices. Our instructors herded us toward a large cobblestoned square and stopped in front of a three-story dome at the edge of the forest.

Central Nevada, which I'd passed through in Shade's jeep last time, was a vast landscape of sagebrush, hard dirt, and colorful rocky hills, but here, it was all lush greenery.

Armed shifter sentinels patrolled the perimeter. Anticipation and tension were high in the air.

My heart pounded erratically as I realized I'd indeed come to a hunting event. A sudden memory flashed—me running for my life from hunters in a dark forest. Cold sweat broke out in a line down my spine.

It was impossible to sneak away now.

The crowd had all gathered in front of the dome, gazing up at the royals on the terrace: Shade, Viviane, Danielle, and a few new faces I'd never seen before. But I bet they were shifter royalty as well. Standing behind them were high-ranking officers.

The small royal crowd parted, and Sideburns stepped in front of them. My heart stuttered. I couldn't control my body's reaction at the sight of him. Heat pooled low in my abdomen until I literally felt like panting.

As if there was an unseen mystic line

connecting us, the Alpha Heir's gaze found me right away amid thousands of shifters. They paused briefly before he tore his gray eyes away.

The lines on his handsome face hardened. Fucker must think that was my fault too. I sighed, letting go of the petty bitterness. He'd helped me, saved me even. If he hadn't, the king would have had me hanged.

Sideburns' deep voice boomed over the square as he announced the opening of the Moon Ceremony and its significance. He was good at making a grand speech. Fucker had been groomed to be the heir since he was born.

While everyone listened intently to his inspirational speech, his words passed through my ears like a cool, autumn wind.

The more he talked, making a big deal out of this spectacular event, the more my stomach twisted into knots. What if I failed to shift while everyone else did at the Alpha Heir's command? So far, I knew I was the only one in the entire school who hadn't shifted into my animal form.

I shouldn't have come with Shade. Now I was going to be the number one embarrassment in public. Before I could come up with an exit plan, a wild wind swept over the square, answered by howls.

Then, all around me, everyone tore away their clothes and began to transform.

One second, they were all human, the next, wolves, bears, panthers, and tigers surrounded me, but wolves held the majority.

Fuck, fuck, fuck!

Shift! I commanded. *Please, wolf, if you're here. Please just get the fuck out, even if you have to claw your way to the surface. Turn my skin to fur and my face to a muzzle. Just do it!*

I didn't hear a howl inside me to answer my call; not even a whimper. How could I pull something from nothing?

I tried again, using Danielle and the girls' method to peek deep within me, my eyes squinting so hard they ached. I groaned when nothing happened.

Still me, the same ol' Pip, vicious and curious, but none of those qualities could help me shift.

As if they could smell my frustration, every eye, animal and human alike, stared at me, waiting for the last member of the hunting party to shift, so they could run into the forest to hunt.

I darted my panicked gaze around wildly, trying to locate Summer's and Paris's wolves, only to be met with a lot of glares and growls. Only the high-ranking shifters hadn't shifted yet, since they'd let everyone else get a head start. And now I was wasting everyone's time.

Standing on the terrace, Danielle gestured frantically for me to roll with the punches and just shift.

"Uh?" I shrugged helplessly as chaos crowded my mind like hundreds of buzzing bees.

Shade snapped his fingers and mouthed, "C'mon, Catnip! You got this!"

I got nothing! I clenched my teeth to fend off waves of anxiety slamming into my chest and wiped beads of sweat growing larger on my forehead.

I desperately called to my beast. At this point, I'd settle for shifting into a mouse if I could, but only mocking silence returned my frantic pleas.

Maybe this shifting thing just wasn't for me. Everyone had mistaken me for a shifter. The joke was on them.

BJ, her cold gaze focused upon me, sneered loudly from the terrace. She leaned closer to Sideburns, whispered something to him, then let out a peal of vicious, derisive laughter. He stared down at me with a flash of disdain and disappointment.

The angry, contemptuous look from my supposed fated mate pierced my skin like hundreds of needles.

Rage burned through my middle, hotter and sharper than the imaginary blade Sideburns had jammed into my gut. A scorching sensation surged through me, smelling of burning embers and pine.

Magic.

It ripped through me in what felt like a raging storm, all thunder and lightning, battering my insides. My heartbeat quickened, jolted by a kick of adrenaline. Wild wind ruffled across my stretched skin, and then fur appeared and raced across my body while my bones stretched and snapped painfully into their new form. It happened so quickly, I didn't even have time to cry out from the brief, painful reconstruction. And then the agony was over.

One second, I was Pip the girl, then the next, I dropped to the ground on all fours as a wolf staring down at a pile of torn clothing, but I didn't care. Crisp air filled my bigger lungs, and I howled in delight.

I pushed up with my hackles, my belly departing from the cobblestoned ground. I dipped my head and gazed down at the ivory fur on my chest, then at my paws. A rainbow streak decorated each of my front paws.

I twisted my head to look over my shoulder, and from the corner of my eye, I caught another broad rainbow splashed generously across my back.

Wolves were usually black, white, brown, gray, or golden, but I was an ivory wolf with rainbows.

Gasps and murmurs rose from the terrace, and the other wolves around me howled.

"Freak!" BJ shouted.

"Not a freak, but one of a kind," Shade said, "a descendant of a pure, strong shifter bloodline." He'd said a rainbow wolf was impossible. I bet he was more than impressed now.

Sideburns couldn't take his eyes off me. BJ nudged him to focus his attention back onto her. My wolf was too overwhelmed to care about their little games when thousands of shifter animals howled and roared all around me.

My wolf raised her head and howled again, then ran after the other shifters and followed them into the forest.

I was one of them now. I'd shifted.

I'm a wolf, I said three times to myself, yet I still didn't feel that much different. I still had the same thoughts, same urges, and probably smelled the same too.

A ray of light kissed my muzzle. I let out a huff and leapt over the undergrowth in an arc, my paws landing on soft layers of leaves.

Non-shifter animals scurried away, dashing through bushes in utter panic. A flock of birds flapped their wings, screaming warnings, and flew above the canopy to get away.

Shifters' hunting calls, primary and bloodlust, echoed in the forest. I halted as I remembered how I'd been hunted. The terror I'd felt was still fresh in my head.

I decided right then what my wolf would do. She would not hunt smaller, weaker animals. She'd only seek the predators.

I diverted from the main hunting party and trotted toward the part of the forest the other shifters seemed to be avoiding. I thought of finding Danielle, Paris, and Summer, but in the vast forest, it was hard to track them down amid thousands of other shifters. And I had no idea how to track as a wolf. If their minds were on the hunt, I didn't want to spoil their fun.

I trotted in the opposite direction from the other shifters; their howls of bloodlust echoed in the distance now. I paused in a clearing, deciding it was a good idea to practice being a proper wolf.

First, I arched my back, then I realized that was what a cat would do. I abandoned the bad habit in favor of stretching my hind legs.

I snapped my head left and right to check for danger, then I flicked my ears to listen to all the sounds in the forest and learn to distinguish their layers and subtleties. After I was done, I put my nose to the ground and sniffed, mimicking what a wolf would do to track game or enemies.

An image of a vast expanse of water formed in my wolf head. I shot forward between the foliage, slashing my tail, my paws thumping against the earth.

Slow down, I told myself. *Get used to being a wolf.*

In no time, the forest gave way to a vast, clear lake. I came to a stop at the edge of the water and peeked into the surface. My wolf's reflection stared back at me. Where my human eyes were full of mischief and curiosity, my wolf's eyes glinted with cold, sharp intelligence and predatory intent.

I liked Pip the wolf. My tongue lolled out in a wolfish grin.

A sudden wind bristled through my fur, bringing with it the scent of something foreign to the area. A branch snapped and animals scurried away, followed by the whistling wind. My ears swiveled to listen.

Someone or something was coming my way. Several of them actually. *Wolves.* Their paws hit the forest floor in an urgent rhythm.

I had company.

Should I greet them with a swishing tail and a big wolf grin? I turned away from the lake and padded toward the brink of the forest just as a dozen wolves arrived.

I put on my best smile, at least my version of a friendly wolf smirk, but the other wolves answered with snarls.

I squinted at the leading silver wolf, a flash of realization hitting me.

It was BJ and her pack. And their intentions smacked me in the muzzle.

They'd tracked me and found me here, and they had come to do what BJ had planned to do the moment I'd set foot in Shifters Prime Academy —kill me.

And I'd just created the perfect opportunity for her to get rid of me as a lone wolf in a secluded part of the forest.

A low, malicious snarl rumbled in the back of BJ's throat.

I tucked tail and bolted down the lakeside without waiting for her killing order. The enemy pack didn't howl as they raced after me, but I howled like a maniac, calling for help.

I hoped some shifters who weren't loyal to BJ would hear and come to my aid, but my howls only brought five more hostile wolves from the edge of the forest where I was heading.

They rushed toward me, cutting off my escape route.

They'd planned this somehow, which meant they'd followed me, and me and my wolf had been too busy prancing through the forest to notice. They wanted me dead, and I was making the job easy.

After counting their numbers, I ceased howling. If Danielle, Paris, and Summer came, they'd be walking into a trap. There was no way the four of us could match two dozen wolves. No wonder BJ ruled the Academy.

But if Shade could get here...he wouldn't get here in time. When I'd rushed into the forest, he'd been on the terrace, talking to some royal lady and fully dressed.

I was alone, and this inevitable battle would end soon.

I was a new wolf who had just learned to put one foot in front of the other while chasing her tail for fun. The dozens of wolves closing in on me had been doing this for years and were all highly trained, vicious fighters.

I bared my teeth, intent on maiming as many enemies as I could, but then I caught sight of BJ. I should take her out first. If I failed to tear out her throat, I'd try to gouge her eye out. I had already made her a one-eared wolf. It would be fun to make her a one-eyed wolf as well.

Fear gave way to courage, and a war song pumped in my wolf's veins. I threw my head back and howled into the sky one last time, then I turned my tail and charged in the direction of the silver wolf, but that cowardly bitch had seven wolves lined up in front of her to protect her, and they bolted to me as one.

A brown wolf lunged at me from the side, intending to slam me down with her weight. She was damn fast and had calculated the exact moment to crash into me. I would have been sent flying into the lake—which was a good way to kill a wolf since most wolves couldn't swim—if I hadn't lowered my belly against the hard dirt and skipped forward to avoid that blow.

It wasn't a move a normal wolf could pull off, but I had. The brown wolf flew over me and dove into the lake headfirst with a splash. I'd have cheered if I could afford the time to do so.

Without missing a beat, I lifted my head and kept on the collision course against BJ and her pack.

My tactic was to change direction at the last second and squeeze through the space between two wolves to reach BJ, and then I'd give all I had to swipe my claws against her throat.

Half a dozen wolves surged forward, ready to torpedo me. If I had one mishap, I'd be done for. It was too late to turn around and flee. Besides, there was no way out when they had me trapped like this.

Now! my wolf snarled.

At the last second, I leapt into the air, up and over the running wolves, and slammed into BJ. We tumbled down together, but she twisted her throat away from me to avoid my blow.

Her wolf was well-trained. She turned swiftly from defense to offense and slashed at my neck with her claws. I ducked, but she still managed to tear a gash into my shoulder.

I ignored the pain and tried for her throat again.

Our wolves clawed at each other, snarling and engaging in a life-and-death battle. My claws opened a thin line on the side of her neck, and she retaliated by slashing my muzzle.

Blood poured out of me.

I willed my claws to turn into blades like when I had slashed open the hound, but that didn't happen. I opened my jaw, dove for my enemy, delight glinting in my eyes as I saw raw fear in hers.

But a wolf from behind took me off guard and clamped down on my hind leg to hold me in place. I yipped in pain as its teeth buried deep into my flesh, but my cry was cut short when two other wolves slammed into me, sending me flying.

Air exploded from my lungs as I crashed into the hard ground. Despite the pain, I forced myself onto all fours.

Two dozen wolves surrounded me, three rings deep to prevent my escape. They snarled with bloodlust, ready to pounce and finish me off. But by the hungry look in their eyes, they wouldn't kill me quickly. They'd tear me apart first.

Fear pooled in my belly, and fury pulsed in my veins.

This bunch held no honor. They only knew how to fight dirty.

I spotted BJ standing outside the circle like the coward she was. I doubted I'd get another shot at her, but I'd given her many wounds to remember me by.

I turned slowly in a circle, snarling and seeking out the weakest link to break through. My paw kicked up a twig. This gave me an idea.

Taking them off guard, I rolled in the dirt, getting sand, dirt, and twigs onto my fur and tail, then I raced in a tight circle at high speed. The debris flew from me and hit the surrounding wolves.

While they were surprised and enraged, trying to blink the dirt and sand from their eyes, I bumped away two wolves and leaped in an arc toward BJ again.

This time, she was more than prepared and jumped to the side to avoid me. Two wolves, who appeared to be her bodyguards, charged me at the same time.

A large gray wolf threw me off course, and we collided and wrestled against each other. Her fangs clamped down on my jaw and held on.

She was larger than me and clearly much more experienced in battle.

The other wolves lunged at me. One tore open my side while another bit into my shoulder. I howled in pain, trying to shake them off frantically and claw my way out.

But I knew I wouldn't get out of this. My luck had finally run out.

When I thought I could have a new life in Shifter City, I'd actually headed toward my death.

A surge of anger rushed through me and with a howl, I flexed and shook all the wolves from me. My claws slashed out and raked one across the throat. Blood sprayed from the wound and arched through the air. The wolf's limp body collapsed on top of me.

As I attempted to wriggle out from under the dead wolf, BJ leapt to my side and swiped her sharp claws at my exposed throat. She no longer bothered to taunt me. She obviously wanted to get the job done quickly and move on.

But before her claws met their mark, she went airborne. The wolves snapping hungrily around me were also heaved backward by a great force.

A roar thundered so mightily the forest shook. Foliage fell, and dirt flew into the air.

A black wolf stood tall beside me, snarling, his gray eyes searing with rage and power. My wolf recognized him immediately. Sideburns' wolf snarled and roared again before scanning the threats, ready to deliver a death sentence.

Every wolf dropped to the ground and showed their bellies in submission, including BJ.

The Alpha Heir's wolf had tracked me here too.

Of all the people and all the wolves, it was the mate who had rejected me who had saved my ass.

I let out a whimper of pain and rose to my paws, ready to use this opportunity to limp away, but the black wolf lunged, faster than lightning, and blocked me. I blinked at him, and he nudged his jaw gently against my shoulder to push me down.

He wanted me to rest while he handled things. I'd be a fool to disobey him under the circumstances. He was, after all, the only one standing between me and my attackers.

I sat on my haunches and waited, my head dizzy from the loss of blood. The wolf's rough tongue rolled out to lick my wounded muzzle.

All the other wolves let out whimpers and lowered their heads to the ground as they realized the truth. I was undeniably the Alpha Heir's fated mate. The man could hide the truth and deny me, but his wolf could never fight his primal instincts and needs, which were to feed, defend, and claim his true mate.

BJ's wolf released an outraged howl. Bitch hadn't seen this coming. The black wolf responded with a warning snarl that rippled with power. The silver wolf lowered her head and whimpered.

She trained her eyes on me, hatred and murderous jealousy brimming in their dark orbs.

This wasn't over between us. I knew with absolute certainty that the French princess would not allow me to live. She'd take any opportunity to kill me.

My rainbow wolf raised her front paw and managed to show her the middle claw.

CHAPTER SEVENTEEN

*J*ared's wolf continued to stand between Viviane and her pack, defending me. That was something I hadn't expected. The resentment I harbored for the man reduced to a faint pulse. He had finally earned his name.

Viviane's silver wolf made a whimpering, pleading sound, wanting to approach Jared's black wolf. The princess in her human form had staked her claim on Jared in the courtyard, but the relationship between their wolves presented differently.

The black wolf growled to warn her away. She skidded back and whined at the rejection.

The man and the wolf were at odds and wanted different things.

The brown wolf that had first attacked me

growled to back up her princess. From the blood-lust in her eyes, I knew she wasn't willing to give up the kill just yet, not even in the presence of the Alpha Heir.

She stalked to the side toward me, planning to get past the black wolf. The black wolf snapped his massive head toward her. The brown wolf lurched, and the black wolf hauled himself toward her, meeting the brown wolf in the middle and smacking her to the ground.

She yelped in fear, an ounce of sense returning to her. She rolled onto her back in surrender. The black wolf only snarled in rage, then opened his powerful jaw and tore out her throat with his massive teeth.

With blood dripping from his fangs, he looked up at the other wolves as if to remind them that anyone who defied him would be killed merci-lessly. It was that simple.

BJ and her pack whimpered pathetically, begging for mercy. The black wolf snarled louder. He wanted her and her pack gone.

BJ let out a low howl, then shot into the forest. Her minions followed, giving the black wolf a wide berth and running after their princess with their tails tucked between their legs.

Within seconds, the enemy wolves were gone. The sound of their paws padding against twigs and leaves faded.

The forest rustled despite the lack of a breeze. New presences appeared in the forefront of my awareness, but I didn't feel threatened.

I pricked my ears, listening. The Alpha Heir's elite team was coming.

Jared's wolf had reached me in the nick of time. If he'd come seconds later, Viviane's wolf would have killed me. Jared's wolf was more ruthless and impulsive than the calculating man inside him. If it were completely up to the man, I doubt I'd still be alive. But then, as the Alpha Heir, Jared didn't act on his primal instincts. He was a major political player and let that guide his thoughts.

The guards, all in their beast forms, spread out in the forest to guard their boss and secure the perimeter.

I yipped a quiet thank you to the black wolf and indicated that I should probably get going, but the black wolf blocked me again before I could limp away. He herded me to a spot by the lakeside and pushed me into a crouching position, then he started to check my wounds and licked at any he found, starting with my injured shoulder.

His licking immediately soothed my pain. He could heal me because either he was the Alpha Heir, or we were fated mates. His power and energy sank into me, and in front of my eyes, my wounds began to close.

A feeling of contentment settled inside my

belly, making me want to purr. For a second, I wondered if Jared the man would also do this for me and treat me so tenderly. But I was sure of one thing: I liked his wolf ten times better.

The black wolf licked me for probably half an hour, until he was sure he'd healed every wound.

My wolf grinned at him. The black wolf tilted his head. Then he trotted to the lake, dipping his muzzle into the water to wash himself clean before he returned to me.

The black wolf regarded me, liking what he saw. Tenderness, possessiveness, and protectiveness twinkled in the depths of his beautiful gray eyes. I swallowed and let out a wishful whimper. I'd hoped the man could have looked at me like that when he'd first learned I was his fated mate.

I gazed back at him, seeing my golden eyes like liquid flames in the reflection of his own. The black wolf rolled out his pink tongue and licked my healed muzzle in affection. I swayed my hips playfully, then I licked his muzzle, returning the favor and thanking him again.

The guards stayed at the edge of the forest to give us privacy. At this point, Viviane, her minions, and Jared's close circle must all know that I was his true mate.

As I licked him again, a low rumble vibrated from the black wolf's chest. He pressed his muzzle between my shoulder and my head to inhale my scent.

A sudden heat rose in me, pooling in my belly. I recognized it as the mating heat, even though the sensation was very different than when I was in my human form.

The black wolf nipped my fur, raw male need pouring off him. His tongue licked the back of my ear, sending a stronger wave of heat shooting into me.

I yipped and whimpered as primal, urgent need to surrender to my mate seized me and the mating call sang in my bloodstream. Jared gazed back at me through his wolf's eyes, conflicting emotions darkening them to cold winter gray. The man also desired me, yet he didn't think I was enough. He never thought I was good enough for him.

The beast might want me with his every fiber, but the man had rejected me. Even now, Jared didn't exactly express that he would choose me.

Fated mate or not, I was no one's bitch.

I'd be a fool to cave in now, even though the unbearable heat and need urged me to surrender myself to the Alpha Heir. But I was fortunate that even in my wolf form, I still thought like Pip. Cold logic told me that I had no standing in the shifters' community. If I allowed myself to be the Alpha Heir's plaything and side dish, I'd never get my dignity back.

And I'd lose more than my pride.

Cold clarity pierced through the mating heat, and an icy wind cooled my body, stopping me from making the mistake of rolling over and giving myself to the Alpha Heir, an asshole in my book.

The black wolf pushed his heated muzzle into my neck, ready to pin me to the ground in the throes of passion. I used my strength and shoved him away hard.

He let out a low growl, not understanding why I'd suddenly grown cold. I stared into his questioning eyes to let him see and feel what I really felt.

His chest rumbled, and my wolf growled back before I turned and dashed away.

CHAPTER EIGHTEEN

a full mirror covered the entire wall in the private training room. It was exactly what I needed.

I'd shifted into my rainbow wolf three times, and I still couldn't get enough of how amazing and mind-bending the process appeared. But then, I couldn't catch it all, since one second I was in my human form, then next, I was a wolf.

"Quit it, Catnip." Shade couldn't take it anymore. "I've never seen any shifter vainer and more self-absorbed than you."

"That's not true. I just want to get used to this shifting gig while making sense of it," I said before shifting back into my wolf.

I twirled and turned my head to study my rear in the mirror. I had a nice ass. I flicked my tail, pleased to see a rainbow streak along its length.

"You can't exactly make sense of it," Danielle said. "Shifting is magical."

When I wheeled back to the front, my wolf's reflection stared back at me, her eyes like golden flames, similar to how I looked in my human form, but more intense and brimming with icy intelligence.

From the mirror, I saw Shade shake his head in irritation. "I've never seen a wolf act like this before. It's not normal."

I skidded to the left in a dancing move, then leapt to the right in an arc. Paris and Summer laughed at my silly wolf. I grinned back, then arched my back. My sleek wolf leapt across the room and brushed past Shade to irk him some more.

"Stop fooling around," he barked. "That's enough shifting for you today."

The prince also forbade me from shifting more than four times a day since it'd consume too much energy and even cause harm. But I didn't feel tired. I felt exhilarated to experience this newfound freedom.

Worried he might come after me and grab my tail to show me that he meant business, I slowed my movements.

"Shift back, Pip." Shade grunted his command. "If you don't, I'll make you do a hundred extra pushups, then lift weights before we go into our fighting lessons."

I hated doing pushups and weight training. I wanted to go straight to fighting, but Shade insisted on us following his strict methods, especially after what had happened to me at the lake.

When Danielle, Paris, Summer, and he had learned that BJ and her pack had nearly killed me during the ceremony, they'd raged. Shade was especially upset, so he'd come up with a plan to make me one of the best shifter fighters. His private coaching schedule included hand-to-hand combat as well as sword fighting. He wanted me to increase my chances of survival, and I totally agreed with him. He'd also mapped out nightly outdoor sessions to train my wolf to track, escape, and fight with claws and vicious bites.

He'd also attributed my overcoming BJ and biting off her ear in the first battle class as a fluke due to the element of surprise on my side and my raw strength and savage attitude.

Danielle, Paris, and Summer, who insisted on sitting in on my private lessons with Shade, nodded at his every word.

When I'd told them about Jared and me being fated mates and that he'd rejected me as a man but his wolf rebuffed BJ in favor of me, they'd been shocked but promised not to tell anyone. I was pretty sure Jared had done the same with his men as he wouldn't want anyone to know about us either.

"So that was why King Grayson signed the release paper instead of executing you," Danielle had pondered aloud. "The king must have known, and the royal family's tight circle must all know about it by now. And with BJ seeing it firsthand during the ceremony, you've become her biggest threat. She won't rest until you're out of the picture for good."

"Thanks for putting me in a better mood." I'd shrugged and then offered to keep my distance from the girls to keep them safe, considering that I'd been marked for death. "I don't mind sleeping in the bunkhouse with the rest of the students. I'm not above them or anyone. I just hope people in the bunkhouse shower. I have a sensitive nose these days."

"Don't insult us, Catnip," Paris had said, using Shade's term of endearment for me.

"You won't be separated from us, ever," Danielle had assured. "End of discussion."

As soon as I shifted back into my human form, Shade mercilessly put me to work on my pushups. He also decided to include the girls in our lessons. While he enjoyed trading fists with Danielle, he made Paris and Summer cross wooden swords in the ring.

For some reason, he always gave me the most tedious tasks.

I did twenty pushups, bored to tears, so I started replaying last night's erotic dream. It had felt so real that I wasn't sure it was a vision or a lucid dream.

I was with the gorgeous vampire again. His face was something I'd never forget.

I could still feel the slight burn of that bite in the pulsing veins on my neck. The pleasure that had rippled through me after had felt damn good, I didn't think such sensations were possible.

"You taste like darkness and sunlight at the same time," he'd told me, his eyes mesmerizing, his voice velvet and sensual beyond this world. "I'll never let you go. I'll come for you, Bride."

He'd thrust into me, his massive cock granite hard. It'd filled me and stretched me to the limit. I'd screamed, half in horror, half in pleasure, as if I was torn between Hell and Heaven.

And his cock—

"Why did you stop doing pushups, Pip?" Shade demanded, jerking me back to the present.

"Uh? I did? Why?" I asked and found myself prone on the mat, my core still throbbing with heat.

Shade sniffed, and his cornflower-blue eyes suddenly glowed with heat. The girls snapped their heads toward me.

Crap! Shifters could smell arousal. To a male shifter, I must smell like a bitch in heat right now.

My face burned hot, and I blamed the Vampire God for appearing in my vivid erotic dream. In the back of my mind, I kept believing that he'd come for me one day, as if my lost memory told me that we had unfinished business.

While a tinge of fear washed over me at his coming, the dark part of my soul longed to see him.

I was fated to be the mate of the Alpha Heir, but my fated mate had rejected me. Now I couldn't stop thinking about another man, who not only craved my blood like nectar, but also my body.

Fate must have big plans to screw with me, over and over.

CHAPTER NINETEEN

I survived another week in the Academy without being maimed or killed, which I considered a win, though I continued to be harassed. BJ's minions hadn't given up trying to bump into me in the corridors or trip me in the classroom. I also often found dead rats or live scorpions inside my locker, and once I found a doll that looked like me being cut with knives and pinned with dozens of needles. The gang even resorted to voodoo stuff and painted "cursed" with pig's blood on the wall of my locker.

To spare myself the grievance and avoid whatever nasty surprise lurked in wait, I no longer opened or used my locker. Everything went into my heavy backpack, and I carried it everywhere.

Despite my burdens, I never forgot who I was —Pip, the prankster, who never sat on the sidelines and never let anyone push me around. I liked good jokes, so I responded eagerly to BJ's mental warfare.

It helped that I discovered an uncanny ability for using prank magic. Somehow, I could always track and single out my attackers to cause unfortunate "accidents" to those evildoers. The water would run cold or run out when they were in the middle of their showers, or maybe their boyfriends couldn't get an erection just before they got down and dirty together. This was the only time I felt like the universe was on my side and actually listening to my calls, because birds always knew right where to pick their next shitting spot—mostly on the heads of BJ's cronies.

Now, most of them, including BJ, either wore a broad hat or carried an umbrella with them at all times.

My magic couldn't do real damage, that I'd learned, but it could annoy the hell out of my adversaries, which made me giddy. All I had to do was picture a deed, and my magic would make it happen.

Maybe I should practice making my mind-over-matter magic bigger and more lethal, so I could tackle any foe.

BJ and her goons became increasingly frustrated since my retaliations were always worse than their harassments. They were sure that I had something to do with the pranks, but none of them could prove anything. All they could accuse me of was saying that nothing strange or bad ever happened to them until I came to the Academy.

After a while, they ceased to harass me but resorted to glaring instead, but I always smiled back. Yet I wasn't fooled into thinking they'd stopped plotting against me. When their revenge came, and I knew it would, it would be big and deadly.

Despite my feud with BJ, I liked my life at the Academy. I had shelter, food, and friends. I even felt relatively safer. BJ's shenanigans were peachy compared to the horror I'd experienced at the hands of the mage hunters, and I'd only caught a glimpse of my treatment.

I DRAGGED a large piece of pepperoni pizza onto my plate.

"We're one, though our beasts have their own minds, personalities, and tempers," Danielle said, trying her best to explain our inner wolf while we ate in the dining room of her suite. "When we're in our human form, our human wills, thoughts, and traits dominate. But in our animal form, we follow our beast's instincts, and her primal needs can often override our social inhibitions. Most of the time, however, it's harmony between our two halves, but sometimes there can be conflicts."

Well, with me, it was all harmony. The beast was me, and I was her. I didn't feel any split personalities or interests.

"I think that's why the Alpha Heir's wolf acted differently toward you." Danielle placed a slice of vegan pizza on her plate and cut a piece with a fork and a knife. "However—"

Someone knocked hard at the door.

I glared at it. "Whoever it is, we are not sharing this pizza, especially with someone who uses their knuckles to bang on our door."

"We have plenty, Pip," Summer said. She rose, gave my shoulder a light squeeze, and walked toward the entry way.

The door opened revealing an agitated Going-gray.

"Prince Jay." Summer bowed slightly. "Can we help you?"

Going-gray peeked inside, and Summer politely stepped aside to let him have a good look. We had nothing to hide.

Going-gray's critical gaze landed on me. "I have a message for Pip girl."

"Surprise, surprise." I grinned at him to further irk him. "I must be important. But you should have just said 'knock, knock.' And we would ask, 'who's there?' then you'd answer, 'Prince Going-gray'. Much better than pounding on our door."

The girls gasped, then muffled their laughter. Danielle shook her head at me to tell me not to aggravate the cousin to the Alpha Heir while she tried not to laugh as well.

Going-gray stepped inside and closed the door behind him.

"That mouth of yours will get you killed one day," he said as he parked himself in the center of the room and crossed his bulky arms. "This information that I'm about to tell you is sensitive."

"How sensitive?" I asked curiously while delivering a chunk of pizza to my mouth. Danielle used a fork and a knife, but I liked to use my fingers.

"Clean yourself up and make yourself presentable, Pip girl," he ordered. "The Alpha Heir will pick you up at seven."

"What for?" I cried out. "I didn't do anything wrong. I've been treading very carefully, like a good, little mouse, since I got out of jail."

Over Going-gray's hard, unconvinced look, I blurted, "Someone waking up this morning and discovering an eyebrow vanishing had nothing to do with me."

Yep, I made one of the bullies lose her left brow in retaliation for her spitting on the ground when I passed. I didn't like people spitting. "She shouldn't even whine about it since she still has the other one."

"Don't give any details," Paris hissed to shush me. "They'll take it as a confession."

Going-gray narrowed his eyes. "Did you have something to do with that?"

"Prince Jay," Danielle chimed in with a polished smile. "Everyone loses an eyebrow now and then. You don't need to worry about that."

Going-gray looked even less convinced.

"You should know that it's been brought to the Alpha Heir's attention all the recent unrest at the Academy," Going-gray drawled in his grating voice. "Burnt food, showers not working correctly, pipes breaking, random bird attacks... and oddly all of it is focused on Princess Viviane and her friends. And recently, they've started having girl troubles."

I squinted at him while putting on an innocent yet nosy look. "What kind of girl trouble?" I swept a hand at my friends in the room. "We're all girls. Maybe we can help?"

"You've done enough, Pip girl!" Going-gray said. "Especially since they're accusing you of all these strange happenings."

"They can't be serious," Danielle protested. "Please don't listen to their vicious lies, Prince Jay. You know whatever is running wild on campus has nothing to do with Pip. She's with us all the time, except when she attends her classes."

Going-gray snorted. "Princess Viviane never had acne before; now she does. She has to drink potions made by mages to get her skin issues under control. Her friends have started growing unwanted thick body hair, even though they shave their legs every day. Mustaches have also appeared above their lips, and they are losing hair from their heads. And worse, two of Princess Viviane's male bodyguards grew boobs." He crossed his arms tighter over his chest as if he could fend off the curse of getting boobs.

I widened my eyes, and the girls followed suit to play innocent as well.

"Oh my gods," I cried. "That's terrible!"

"My heart goes out to them," added Danielle.

Going-gray shook his head. "Something smells rotten, Pip girl, and I know it has something to do with you. Somehow, you always make shit appear."

I opened my mouth to argue but he raised a hand. "Don't distract me. I came to tell you that the Alpha Heir has extended a dinner invitation to you, and you aren't going to brag to anyone outside of this room."

The girls and I shared a stunned look.

A dozen thoughts whirled in my head, and I felt a pang in my heart. This invitation had come too late.

"I appreciate the invite," I said, "but I'm afraid I'll have to decline."

The girls gasped.

Going-gray's eyes nearly bulged from their sockets. "How dare you insult the Alpha Heir and turn down the great honor—"

"Well, throw me in jail again," I said with food in my mouth this time. He didn't deserve my shifter table manners anymore.

Veins pumped on Jay's neck. "No sane woman would reject the Alpha Heir."

I smirked at him. "There's always a first. Why don't you give the great honor to Princess Blow Job, aka BJ? I'm confident she'll jump on the opportunity, and then the Alpha Heir will get the treat of a deep throat and—"

"You forget your place!" Going-gray's face reddened with anger. "Last time, you were tossed in jail because you bit off Princess Viviane's ear. What kind of savage animal are you?!"

"Wolf," I offered. "I'm a North American female werewolf."

"If it weren't for the Alpha Heir, you'd be dead instead of standing in front of me huffing disrespectful words. If you want the Alpha Heir to continue to protect you, you'll learn how to compromise!"

He looked like he wanted to jam his fist into my jaw. I bet that would hurt like a bitch. He swore colorfully and turned on his heels, about to storm off.

Danielle rose from her seat. "Prince Jay, I'm so sorry for the unexpected turn of events. Could you wait a second and give me a moment with Pip? She's my responsibility, and I'll make sure she listens to reason to avoid an untimely demise."

Danielle dragged my sleeve until I followed her into her bedroom. She closed the door. The princess's lovely bedroom had a beautiful rug in the center, a set of ivory vanities against the wall next to glass bookcases, and a grand piano in the corner near the full window.

I slumped into a vibrantly hued Proust armchair. I loved to sit in that chair whenever I was in her room.

"I think Jared sent Going-gray to threaten me in case I refused to go to dinner," I said. "But I'm not going to take his crap."

"You'll dine with the Alpha Heir tonight," Danielle insisted. "I'm not asking you to sleep with him or anything, but you need his protection. Mine isn't enough anymore, though it kills me to admit that. Plus, this could be a turning point between you two. Be the bigger person and give him a second chance, especially since he saved you on the Moon Ceremony. Maybe tonight he'll promise to dump BJ. After all, he is your fated mate."

"He won't ditch BJ," I said. "You didn't hear what he planned for me before I came here. Who would be so coldhearted toward his true mate? I can't trust him even though he saved me twice. He'll always want power more than he'll ever want me."

"I'm not asking you to trust him," Danielle said. "Just go to the dinner tonight and see what he has to say and report back. That's all. Take one for the team, please?"

Danielle was thinking of my best interests. I was lucky to bump into her and the girls on my first day here. She was part of my pack now so I needed to quit acting like a lone wolf.

I jogged from the room and flashed the older prince a grin. He wasn't touched, but it was obvious that he was relieved that Danielle had talked me down.

"The Alpha Heir will pick you up at seven," he repeated. "Dress properly and don't embarrass him, Pip girl."

"Aren't you the picture of joy, Highness?" I said. "I hope you come by more often."

He ignored me but nodded at Danielle respect-fully and exited as fast as he could. I guessed that either he couldn't stand me or he didn't want to go home with a pair of boobs.

CHAPTER TWENTY

*J*ared showed up at the princess's suite at seven sharp.

At least he didn't send Going-gray to fetch me. That showed me some respect, but I hadn't expected it, considering how he regarded me. But as Danielle had said, something might have changed after his wolf had chosen me.

He wore a Yale-blue shirt that subtly showed his hard muscles beneath it. His tailored slacks displayed his powerful thighs, and his shoes were shiny and spotless.

He'd combed back his dirty-blond hair, and he'd shaved his sideburns. He was probably smart for doing that if he didn't want his new nickname to spread like wildfire.

The Alpha Heir's gray eyes flashed with heat as they roved over my body. My stupid heart flut-

MEG XUEMEI X

tered, especially when I noticed how handsome he looked when he wasn't giving me a stern stare.

"You look nice, Pip," he said.

"So do you, but where are your sideburns?" I asked.

Danielle coughed to remind me to act properly. Right, she'd drilled me on the dating rules for hours until I couldn't take it anymore.

"I shaved them to try and prevent the spread of your ridiculous nickname for me." Annoyance and impatience had edged back into his voice. He wasn't used to letting anyone talk to him like this without punishing them.

"Good for you, Alpha Heir," I said. "As for this dress you appreciated a moment ago, Princess Danielle swore there'd be no pizza for a week if I didn't put it on. The girls also painted my face. If going to dinner means jumping through these hoops, I'd rather skip dinner next time. You know what I mean? And despite their insistence, I refused to wear stilettos."

Jared looked down at my flat sandals, and I wiggled my toes to drive my point home.

"No way will I wear those pointed high-heel shoes that could make me twist an ankle, not even for Your Highness. No offense."

The girls groaned collectively in the back-ground. I'd tossed all their coaching out the window within the first five minutes.

"Shall we go, Lady Pip?" Jared asked, his voice still tense.

"Uh?" I blinked, since this was the first time being called a lady, and not by just anyone, but by the second most powerful shifter in North America.

The Alpha Heir offered me his elbow, and I pinched his muscles to test their strength before I laid my hand on his arm. Huh, shifter society and its endless rules.

Danielle, Paris, and Summer all bowed at Jared before he whisked me away outside. He guided me toward a black armored car, escorted by another black armored car, and both cars rolled out of the gate of the Academy.

A member of Jared's Ace team drove while we sat in the back. I mirrored Jared's upright posture, even mimicking him by placing a hand on each of my thighs.

I didn't bother speaking, and I was fine if he didn't talk to me either. When it came to my unwilling fated mate, I no longer held any expectations. If I had, I'd be setting myself up for disappointment.

But I almost failed to control my tongue and asked him what his French princess would think of him taking me out to dinner. But then they weren't officially engaged, plus he hadn't said this was an actual dinner date.

So I left it at that and twirled my finger around the tips of my lilac-blue hair as I peeked out of the window.

The car drove fast through the landscape of sagebrush and rolling hills.

Jared cleared his throat and finally spoke. "How's school, Pip?"

"Not bad."

He got reports all the time, so he must know what was going on at the Academy. I wondered if he also knew that his girlfriend still planned to off me. I not only needed to watch my six, I needed to watch my friends' even more. I'd never told Danielle, but I'd been keeping an eye open even when I slept. It had started to take a toll on me.

He turned to me with a sigh, and when his eyes met mine, they glinted within the darkness of the vehicle. "I know I've been busy, but I want to talk to you about certain things and clear the air."

"I appreciate it, high sir, but I'm a shifter of low status. You don't really need to treat me to dinner, and you certainly don't need to clear any air with me, since there isn't anything that needs to be cleared. If you regret this dinner invitation already, you can revoke it right now and take me home. Or drop me off right here, and I'll fetch a ride home. In this dress, I'm sure it won't take long."

He tensed but words kept falling from my mouth. "And don't worry. I'm not a freeloader, unlike some people. I'll do my best to learn while I'm at the Academy and be a contributing member of society, as Prince Going-gray warned that I must earn my keep. I also understand that when the war breaks out—it might happen sooner than I can blink twice—I'll be shipped to fight on the frontlines. No problem. And before my enemies stab me to death, I'll do my best to take down as many vamps as possible. Hopefully, my sacrifice will make a difference and make the world a better, safer place."

He shook his head, a smile threatening to break his serious expression. "You won't be put on the frontlines, no matter what, but I appreciate you trying to sidetrack me, a gift I'm sure you're well aware of. Let's stay on topic, please, so we can discuss matters of importance."

"What's more important than gaining more power and winning the future war, high sir?" I asked, hiding my sarcastic tone. "I'm not sure I'm up to the task of discussing anything else, but then again, I am but a low wolf girl."

"You can call me Jared when we're alone," he said. "And can we stop with the theatrics? You're way more intelligent than you look. I've learned my lesson when it comes to underestimating you."

I grinned at him. "Are you saying I look dumb? You do know how to flatter a girl, Your Highness."

"You don't look dumb, Pip." He sighed. "You know you're gorgeous."

"Then you're more dangerous than I thought," I said.

He'd never said nice things to me before. And when a man flattered a woman, he usually wanted something from her.

He'd never said nice things to me before. And when a man flattered a woman, he usually wanted something from her.

He laughed. It was a rich, pleasing sound, and it was the first time I'd ever heard it. This side of him surprised me and made my core clench with sudden need. I could try my best to ignore this spark between us, but it wasn't in my power to control my body's reaction to him. There was a reason Fate deemed us compatible biologically.

"You should laugh more often," I nearly purred, then warned myself not to flirt.

"I will try."

The air between us suddenly became thick and awkward.

"Where are we going?" I asked.

"It's sort of a surprise. I have a place outside of town that I have been longing to visit for some time. The view is fabulous, and we'll have good food and the privacy we need."

So he wasn't taking me to a fancy restaurant where everyone in Shifter City knew his face and would gossip about the Alpha Heir taking on a new girl. He would keep our meeting tightly under wraps to keep his girlfriend from catching wind of it.

That also explained why we were driving along a less-traveled road.

I remained unfazed. I wouldn't react until I knew what he was up to, which was probably to no good.

"I know you don't know much about me, but I'm not one who likes to be surprised," I said.

"Could have fooled me." He winked at me.

Now that surprised me. The Alpha Heir didn't seem to be a winker or the flirting type, which were Shade's specialties.

I stopped cold, and a sense of peril rolled over me. All the tiny hairs on my neck stood on end.

Jared drew his eyebrows together in concern. "Pip, are you all right?"

I peered out the window. We were cruising along a low bridge above a creek with woods on both sides. This would be the perfect place to ambush and attack us if anyone had the mind to. On this old bridge, there were no other cars except Jared's and his guards' that trailed behind us.

I caught a flurry of movement outside the car.

"Something isn't right," I said in a tight voice.

"This is shifter territory. No one would dare—"

An explosion sounded. The guards' car behind

us flew into the air. It flipped a couple of times before smashing into the railing of the bridge and tumbling down into the creek below in a ball of flames.

Plumes of smoke puffed into the air, smelling of gasoline and pine. I sensed the shifters inside expelling their last light of life. All four of them were dead.

That explosion had to have been infused with black magic. Bulletproof vehicles didn't stand a chance against such a heavy onslaught of magic.

The air also reeked of dark power.

"Go!" I screamed just as two streams of magical fire shot toward our car. The first stream passed through the window, slammed into the driver, and melted his face.

The second jet of magical fire landed under the car. The flames engulfed the tires, the stench of burning rubber filling my nostrils.

My heart hammered so violently I was afraid it might break through my ribcage. I thrust my hands forward to brace for impact as the car skidded toward the railing before spinning out of control.

"Stay down!" Jared shouted at me, his hand pressing me down and covering my head as if he feared another ball of fire might melt my face too.

The car slammed into the guardrail. I barely managed to catch my breath before I heard a man's bass-like voice call, "We have no quarrel with you, Alpha Heir! Hand us the girl, and you can walk away."

I breathed laboriously and looked at Jared, icy fear pumping in my veins. They'd let him live if he promised to surrender me. If the Alpha Heir was killed, the king and every shifter would turn over every stone to hunt down the killers.

Jared didn't want me anyway. It shouldn't be a hard decision for him.

"You think I'll let you live after you killed my men?" Jared snarled, his voice escaping through the broken windshield. His gaze darted all around as if searching for a way out. I did the same.

"That's unfortunate, Alpha Heir," the male voice called back. Several more men and woman appeared and circled the car. "But let me remind you, we have no quarrel with you. And to show our good faith, our employers will compensate you for the collateral damage. Just give us the girl, and we'll be on our way. You'll never see us again."

I trembled, fear coating my skin.

If they took me, my fate would be worse than the one in the lab building, I was certain of it.

"Get out of the car and make a run for it into the woods," Jared ordered in a hushed voice. "I'll slow them down for you."

He lashed out, his leg kicking open the back door on my side near the guardrail, while he still shielded me with his body should we be shot at again. I rolled out of the door and crouched next to it. Nine assassins, all wearing masks and dressed in black, closed in on us.

Two mages stood several paces away, fireballs twirling on their palms, ready to toss at any second. I felt like some of them were members of the same hunter group that had chased me off the cliff.

They'd found me somehow.

They'd probably been waiting for me to cry or beg first.

Before they could react to my movements, I retrieved two daggers from the hidden belt around my thigh and tossed them at my nearest foes. One drove into the forehead of a short, bald mage near me, and the other punctured the throat of a female mage just as she tossed a ball of fire at me.

Shade's training had paid off, and I was thankful that I'd strapped those daggers to my thigh before I'd left the princess's suite.

Jared leapt next to me and shifted midair into his warrior form. The eight-foot-tall monster lunged at two mages, who had just recovered from the shock of watching their peers drop at my throwing knives. None of them had expected Jared to be that fast and powerful, but they'd never seen the Alpha Heir in action.

Jared bellowed as his claws tore out a mage's

throat, then thrust into the other mage's chest without missing a beat. The beast's roar of rage probably loosened a few mages' bladders as well. That was one of the shifters' psychological tactics —to pump fear into their enemies and make them freeze.

Before the mages dead bodies could hit the ground, Jared wheeled, whipped out a gun, and fired a series of bullets into the others.

Effective!

My gleeful mood turned sour as I watched the bullets bounce from invisible shields in front of the mages. It must be spells that protected them from modern weaponry, but anything old school, like my daggers, were still working.

I lunged at a pig-eyed mage, intending to reduce their numbers further and even the odds. A jet of black spells shot toward me, and I felt a wave of scorching heat, but before the spells slammed into my chest, Jared threw himself in front of me, faster than an arrow.

The spells exploded on his back, some slashing open his skin and the rest lighting him on fire. Burning flesh and fur permeated the air. My chest tightened in sickly, overwhelming fear and then seared with rage, yet I couldn't help him put out the fire. If I did, we'd both be dead or captured.

Jared didn't let the horrible burn slow him

down. He leapt over twenty feet and landed hard onto a mage and twisted his head off.

I charged another. I spun, kicked, and swept his feet from under him. He dropped to the ground on his side. I followed him down and pumped my fist into his eye socket. At the contact, he fired what looked like purple lightning directly into me.

It didn't fry me like it may others, but the pain was real and crazy intense. I ignored it. In my blind rage, my hand transformed into bladed claws, just like it had before.

The mage's small eyes widened in fear, yet his hatred was more potent.

"You shall never be set free, *Death's daughter, a plague set on Earth*," he said in an ancient witch tongue with a demonic origin, yet I understood it perfectly. "My master should have aimed to kill you rather than capture you."

"Who's your master?" I hissed as I tore off his mask.

I didn't recognize his sharp face or auburn hair.

"You will never know, as our tongues have been magically bound, but he'll find you and drain you—"

I had no use for him.

I raised my bladed claws and sliced off his head. As I jumped off him to look for my next target, I saw there were only two more mages left, the man who had initially spoken to us and a dark-haired woman.

The man exuded a sinister vibe. His eagle mask covering his long face didn't help either. The women next to him looked to be in her thirties. Judging from her magical signature, she was more of a witch than a mage.

Somehow I knew these things, even though I still couldn't remember my past.

The woman clutched the man's arm in panic. "We must leave now! Ore—"

Both Jared and I lunged at them. The eagle-masked man shoved the woman toward us, then smacked a vial potion to the ground. A band of dark smoke engulfed him before Jared could grab him.

The woman's eyes widened as Jared's claws took her head off before she could finish throwing any more spells at us. Her half-formed spells dissipated in the air, leaving a faint purple mist in their wake.

Chests heaving, we scanned the area to look for more threats. When I didn't sense any, I looked back at Jared. A few wisps of flames still danced across his back. How was he still standing, let alone fighting?

I tore a jacket from a mage's corpse and throw it on Jared's back to snuff out the remaining flames. His upper torso had been badly burned, and a gash on his back gushed blood.

He seized my hands to stop me from helping him, rage and relief searing his gray eyes. He inspected me quickly to check my injuries. Mage blood stained my dress, and I had a few cuts and bruises along my face and arms.

"We need to go before the mercenaries bring in reinforcements," he said, his voice laced with fury and grief. "We'll have to leave my men behind and come back for their bodies later."

I nodded. "How do you know they were mercenaries?"

"They were hired guns," he said. "Let's go."

I sprang toward the bridge after him. "You'll need treatment soon."

"I'll live," he said. "Can you run as a wolf?"

"Yeah, but I don't know this area."

"I'll lead," he said with a faint smile. "I won't summon my soldiers before I know who betrayed us. My cabin isn't far. Stay close to me, okay?"

I nodded, worried about the possible traitors in his ranks. If he called for help now, there was no telling who would show up. If the bad guys came before his loyal men arrived, we'd be in a hell of a lot of trouble.

"I won't stray," I assured him.

His Adam's apple bobbed up and down, then he shifted into his massive black wolf.

I did the same. As my wolf's eyes gazed down at my paws, I was glad that the twin rainbows still remained.

The black wolf leapt across the railing like a massive arrow and landed in the creek not far from the wrecked car. He snapped his head toward it and howled in grief for his fallen men.

Sorrow crashed into me too. I didn't know the shifter guards well, but they were my kind. Selfishly, however, I was relieved that Shade hadn't been in that car, something that could've easily have happened as he'd accompanied Jared on many dangerous missions before. I wouldn't be able to deal if something had happened to him.

I leapt over the railing and landed in the creek as well, although not as gracefully as the black wolf. He gave me a nod before he rolled in the creek for a few seconds to cool himself off and lessen the burn. Then he trotted toward the forest, blood soaking his fur from his shoulder to his chest, streaking down his body.

I raced behind him to watch his back, my ears straining to listen for any unusual sounds. My wolf eyes focused and sharpened to the darkness. My paws padded rapidly on the leaves, my heart pounding, as I was still running on adrenaline. The danger wasn't over yet.

The black wolf picked up his pace. Trees and undergrowth blurred past as we ran. A couple of

smaller animals scurried away, sensing big predators among them. I prepared to fend off other
predators should they show up thinking they
could take down a pair of wounded wolves.

I snarled now and then sending warnings into
the dark forest.

The scents of crisp autumn air and apple and
cinnamon were welcoming to my nostrils, but the
thick smell of blood set me on edge.

We needed to find a shelter soon, and I needed
to tend to the black wolf or he might bleed out.

I whined anxiously, and the black wolf
growled, urging me to keep going. We'd probably
been running for at least thirty minutes at high
speed—a powerful wolf could run faster than a
racing car, but we didn't have the stamina to main-
tain that kind of speed—when I smelled the lake.

I spotted a cabin ahead. The black wolf no
longer sprinted but dragged himself forward and
huffed in labored breaths. My wolf padded beside
him before I sprang ahead toward the cabin.

The black wolf growled, leapt, and caught my
hind leg to drag me back. I read his intention. He
didn't want me to risk myself, and my wolf rolled
her eyes. He could barely stand at this point. But
arguing or fighting him would just waste energy.

The black wolf sniffed deeply. I'd done that
already. We were alone.

He approached the cabin, his big muzzle

pushing open the wooden door. I padded in after his massive body and used my hind leg to kick the door shut behind us.

Ahead of me, the black wolf collapsed to the floor.

CHAPTER TWENTY-ONE

*J*ared's wolf had held on by sheer will until we were safely inside the cabin.

I quickly took in the interior of the cabin, which was more comfortable than pretty. Simply decorated, the cabin had full facilities and decent furniture. It was also clean and well-maintained.

I trotted across the living room toward the bathroom. I needed to shift back to my human shape, find a medic kit, and patch up Jared. But then a memory surfaced.

A medic kit might not help much while Jared was a wolf, and it might cause more harm than good to get him to wake up and shift back into his human form, something he might not have energy for anyway.

That left only one option. I would lick his

wounds like he'd licked mine. It could work again. I hoped.

I dashed back to the black wolf, whose breathing had turned shallow and ragged. He'd also fallen unconscious. Blood soaked his back and chest as he lay on his side. Two-thirds of his torso had been burned. Fur was missing and parts of his skin were blackened. A less powerful shifter wouldn't have survived, let alone made it all the way to this cabin.

The Alpha Heir was a hard man with a strong beast.

I crouched beside him and began to lick the wounds on his chest. As soon as my tongue brushed him, the cuts began to heal. I could've cried in relief. In that moment, I was glad we were fated mates so I could save him. The magic between us was undeniable.

I moved toward his back and stroked my tongue across his wounds faster until every gash on his back had closed and he no longer bled. Then I started treating his burns.

The black wolf was beautiful and powerful. He wanted me more than the man. I didn't know what to do with the man, and the man didn't seem to know what to do with me either.

I sighed, not wanting to think upon it further. I'd had enough trouble for one day, but I looked on the bright side. We had survived and destroyed a few enemies in the process.

I pushed myself to my feet despite the hunger and fatigue weighing down my limbs and brain. I needed to clean myself up.

Using my muzzle, I opened the wooden door and went to sniff the perimeter to make sure we were still alone in the area. Satisfied that I didn't smell or sense any threat, I galloped toward the lake.

The water was cold and clear. I jumped into it, submerged myself in the shallow water, and stood back on my paws to shake my fur. I repeated the process while also rinsing my mouth a few times. The entire time, my eyes never left the door of the cabin, and my ears pricked to listen to the sounds around me. Leaving a wounded Jared behind made me anxious.

After I cleaned myself, I returned to the cabin and shifted back into my human form, and locked the door.

I gave my naked form a quick look, then darted a glance at the black wolf. His breathing was no longer ragged, but he was still out. It'd take a while for him to wake up, as he needed time to heal and recharge. He'd lost a lot of blood.

I padded into the bedroom with quiet steps, searched the drawers, and found a clean blue shirt. I shrugged it on, the hem reached to my knees.

Too exhausted to do anything else, I returned to the living room and sprawled on the sofa while watching the black wolf on the floor. The adrenaline had worn off, leaving dark thoughts churning in my head. A riot of emotions, mostly fear and worry and uncertainty, swam in my mind and tightened my chest.

The shifters had been proud that no one could breach their fortified city, yet the mages had gotten through and openly attacked the Alpha Heir and his guards. One mage had gotten away, vanishing into a dark fog.

I had no doubt that the hunters would regroup and come after me again. If they could break into the city, surely they could find their way into the well-guarded Academy, a place already full of my enemies.

Those nasty fuckers might even grab me in my sleep and hurt my friends, if given the chance.

I swallowed hard, my heart racing with icy fear as I pictured how the hunters could hurt Danielle, Paris, and Summer. If I stayed with them, I would only bring them danger. I thought I had more time to learn to defend myself better, but I was running out of time. I had to leave the Academy soon.

The black wolf growled but still didn't wake up. His breathing had finally settled into a steady rhythm. It wouldn't be long before he wakened.

Knowing he was okay comforted me more than

anything. It was my primal instinct to protect him as well. When the next wave of fatigue pulled me under, my heavy eyelids closed.

* * *

THE AROMA of cooked meat tantalized my nostrils and forced my eyes to open. It took a moment for my vision to focus as Jared, in his human form and dressed in a casual gray T-shirt and blue jeans, entered the living room with two plates in his hands.

He'd cleaned himself up nicely and looked ruggedly handsome. His dirty-blond hair was still wet from a shower. A strand fell across his forehead, and he jerked his head to the side to shake it away. He smiled at me as I slowly sat up, rubbing my eyes and trying to blink away the last of my sleepiness.

I had to admit that when Jared smiled, it was as bright as a ray of sunshine. His sternness disappeared completely, and was replaced by stunning male beauty.

"I made hotdogs for us," he said. "Come."

I jumped from the sofa and sauntered toward the table. Jared's gaze traced along my bare legs, potent heat simmering in his gray eyes.

My face burned and need rushed through me.

He pulled the chair out for me, and I thanked

him while I perched on the seat, staring at a plate of three hotdogs topped with pickled peppers.

"Looks delicious," I said. I could eat anything at the moment.

"I'm sorry you didn't get the fancy dinner I had planned for you," he said ruefully as he sat on the other side of the wooden table. "There isn't much food here except for hotdogs and pancakes, but I'll make it up to you."

"You don't need to do that." I smiled back at him. "Food is food, and I'm not picky."

I grabbed a hotdog and took a bite to prove my point.

"Not bad. It's fresh and juicy." I wiped sauce from the corners of my mouth with my finger, then sucked my finger past my lips.

Jared tracked the motion with his heavy gaze, desire coating his expression.

I arched an eyebrow while my hearted fluttered. He dragged his gaze away from my lips and let out a pent-up breath. The physical attraction between us hung thick in the air, and there was nothing either of us could do about it.

It was purely a biological reaction between mates, and Fate deemed our bodies very compatible.

I tore my thoughts away from the dirty image of my naked body entwining with Jared's long, hard, and muscled one and eyed his untouched plate of food.

"Aren't you going to eat that?"

"You can have it," he offered.

I gave it some thought then shook my head. "I'd be a terrible person to take food from you. You're wounded and need meat more than I do."

"It's my job to provide and protect you," he said, then stopped, as if worried I'd take it the wrong way. He'd only said what was in his thoughts.

"Don't worry about it," I said, trying to diffuse the sudden tension. "As the Alpha Heir, you have big responsibilities."

He nodded and bit into a hotdog. In less than a minute, he'd finished all of them, while I still had half a hotdog left.

"I almost lost you, Pip," he breathed, fear permeating his gaze for the first time. My heart skipped a beat when I realized he truly had been afraid for me.

"I'm still here." I smiled. "We're still here, and most of those fuckers died."

"Thank you for guarding me while I blacked out," he said.

I wondered if he knew that I'd also healed him. He might have attributed his recovery to his power and ability of regenerating quickly.

"No problem," I said. "You'd have done the same. And you didn't give me to the mercenaries."

"I would never!" His fierceness turned to grief, and he swallowed hard. "I lost four elite guards tonight. I'll have to go back for them soon and bring reinforcements."

I reached for his hand to offer him some comfort but stopped myself. Instead, I said, "I'll help."

"Pip," he said, giving me a measured look. "Vampires have been hunting you, and now mages want you too. Why? What do they really want?"

A sudden burst of anger shot through me. "Yeah, I stole something from them!"

He arched an eyebrow. "Pip?"

"I told you already that I don't know why those nutcases came after me," I snapped. "They were hunting for a girl of my age and my height, probably, and haven't worked out yet that they're chasing the wrong girl! I'm just a plain, ordinary girl who seems to always be in the wrong place at the wrong time."

"You're anything but ordinary and far from plain."

"So you *know* what they want from me?" I sneered, no longer wanting the last half of the hotdog. "Enlighten me, sir, please. Or you can just deliver me to them and get it over with."

"You misunderstood me, Pip," he said, remaining cool, unlike before when I'd riled him up and he'd been all mean and harsh. "I'm only curious about their motives, but no matter what they are, I'll never give you up." His voice turned fierce. "I'll never give you to anyone. I'll eradicate them all before they can lay a finger on you. I swear this to you here and now. As long as I breathe, you will always be safe."

I blinked. A wave of warmth rippled across my chest. Jared and I might have gotten off on the wrong foot, but we were trying to get along now. And I wasn't some emotionless rock. Any shred of kindness touched me. I didn't think that I had received much kindness in the past. I might have spent all my life in that lab building being experimented on.

I shuddered as a violent chill rocked me.

"Are you cold, Pip?" Jared asked in concern.

"Why?"

He rose and extended his large hand toward me. For some reason, I accepted it. Maybe I needed a bit of comfort too. He led me to the sofa, sat down, and pulled me onto his lap.

I was surprised, but I didn't try to get away. I wanted to be right here, safe within his warm arms.

"I won't lose you," he whispered in my ear, and a pleasant sensation tingled on my skin. "You belong to me."

My heart fluttered like a moth's wings. Was he

finally going to admit that I was his fated mate? Was he choosing me over BJ?

"What about Blow—Viviane?" I blurted out.

His body tensed beneath me. "She's nothing but a political arrangement, a means to an end. But you're different. You're the real thing. That's what I was planning to tell you over dinner. My wolf sees you, and now I see you too. You're mine and no one else's."

The possessiveness and heat in his deep voice made my heart stutter, and his warmth radiated through me. I snuggled closer to him, drawn to his scent of powerful male and pine. I inhaled it and wanted more. I wondered if he smelled this good to others, but I was his fated mate, so we would always smell good to each other.

He buried his face into my hair to get my scent into his lungs too.

"I won't allow anyone to take you from me, Pip," he vowed. "I haven't been able to get you out of my mind since the day I first laid eyes upon you. I tried to fight the pull between us, but now I know I can't win this battle, and I'm tired of resisting you. I don't want to deny myself anymore." A rumble of hungry desire vibrated deep within his chest. "I want you more than anything. Pip, darling, know this: even when I tried to escape you, you haunted my dreams every night."

This was the first time Jared had admitted he

wanted me. He was a hard man, and it must have taken a great deal for him to make this confession. I doubted anyone would want me as much as my fated mate, but then the image of the Vampire God flashed across my mind like a storm, making me hot and cold at once.

I'd never dreamed about Jared. I'd dreamed about the Vampire God and hoped to dream about him again. But it could be a defense mechanism after Jared had rejected me. I'd wished another man wanted me, so I wouldn't be swept into the "unwanted woman" category. And in those dreams, while the hot vampire desired me, he craved my blood more.

I couldn't help but shiver, remembering his fangs piercing my throbbing veins.

But I was meant to be with Jared rather than with that vampire monster, especially now that he had admitted I was his fated mate and that I belonged to him. Maybe this fated mate thing wouldn't be easy at the beginning, but eventually it should work out.

It had made a big difference that he hadn't given me to the hunters. He'd also taken fire and spells meant for me and killed my enemies. He'd risked his life all for me. I swallowed in gratitude. My past hurtful feeling of being rejected vanished.

"You're my mate, Pip," Jared whispered, his warm breath igniting a line of fire across my skin.

"Do you know what that means? I never expected it to happen, but then you came, and you turned my world upside down."

"That's not true," I said. "I didn't turn your world upside down. I only played a couple of pranks, which couldn't be avoided."

He gazed at me, lust clouding his gray eyes, turning them a shade of silver. Lust swirled to life within me as well, and suddenly I didn't mind being the moth. I craved the burn only my fated mate could give and yearned to feel his searing touch.

"Jared," I murmured.

His mouth came down on mine, searing me.

My breath caught, every coherent thought abandoning me.

His kiss commanded my lips, demanding I open up to him. I easily obeyed, and his tongue thrust inside me to claim my mouth. My heart thundered. My blood surged to areas of my body that needed his attention.

Part of me wanted to push him away or slow the process, but the dominant part of me roared with raw need. We'd both fought this attraction for some time, but for different reasons. Yet it had all come back to this, and we could no longer ignore our lust toward each other. We were fated mates, biologically perfect for each other.

Who could fight that?

But maybe we were still going too fast, considering what had just happened.

I wanted to tell him to slow down, but my body was weak within his embrace. I tried to form an articulate thought, and then a wave of mating heat crashed into me.

Mating fever coursed through my bloodstream, rendering me boneless. All I could think about was having his cock inside me.

Liquid flames licked my slick pussy; aching need pounded through me. I then realized that I wasn't wearing underwear. My bare bottom was perched right on Jared's hard erection.

His kiss deepened, bruising me, which was just what I needed. His tongue mated with mine, sweeping and thrusting. Pleasure gripped me. I twirled my tongue to play with his, accepting and surrendering to his seduction, because nothing felt better.

The mating call increased its volume, drowning out everything else like a rumble of thunder.

I wanted to fuck him and be fucked by him—that was the only thought dominating my mind. I wouldn't care if I burned up right now, or the world burned with me.

I was a bitch in heat, literarily. I could no longer fight this urgent carnal need, and I didn't want to. I wiggled my ass against his erection while I tore open his shirt, my hands tracing down his taut muscled chest to his hard, flat six-pack.

He groaned against my lips, his lust a storm wrapping me inside. I couldn't escape it even if I wanted to.

He inserted his rough hand into my shirt, moving up and caressing my skin until it cupped my heavy breast. I let out a gasp, and he ran his hand over my breast, groping and fondling it. His fingers kneaded and twisted my nipple.

He was so skillful that for a fleeting second, I wondered how many women he'd bedded before me.

Had he played with Viviane like he was playing with me? I shook off the unpleasant image. There was no need to go cold all of a sudden. Jared was choosing me now. He was going to mate with me and leave her in his past.

His hands explored me further, and my back arched at the sensation. My fingers sank into his thick mane to pull him closer to me.

His lips left me as he pulled my shirt over my head. His lustful gaze dropped to my breasts. I was curvy in all the right places.

"You're so lovely, Pip," he murmured.

I smiled at him as I ogled his gorgeous body, lust racing through me. The Alpha Heir was all hard muscles. Every line marked him as a powerful warrior.

He kissed me again before pulling away, harsh lust darkening his eyes.

"Do you want me to fuck you?" he asked huskily.

I doubted that I could say no to him at this point, and I bet that he couldn't stop even if I said no. We were both goners.

"Fuck me," I breathed out as my inexperienced fingers fumbled with the fly of his jeans. He eagerly assisted me, then he lifted as he pulled his jeans down to his ankles before he kicked them away.

His thick, beautiful cock, slightly curved, sprang free. My heart pounded and my blood raced at the sight of it. Yet I was a little concerned. Could I accommodate such a large cock?

My unbridled lust made the decision for me. I'd give it a try no matter what.

Jared chuckled lightly. "Not what you expected?"

"I didn't expect anything," I said, my breathing shallow and short. "I never imagined your cock would want me."

He whispered into my ear, "I pictured your tight little pussy every night while I pleasured myself. Now that I finally have you here, I need to fuck you hard over and over again."

He heaved me up, his mouth closing around my

nipple as the tip of his hard shaft pressed against my entrance.

"Jared," I whispered. "I'm not sure—"

"You'll be fine," he crooned "You're already wet for me. We're mates. Your body was made for me. I won't survive this day if I don't get to fuck this tight pussy."

He spread my legs and thrust into me.

I gasped at the sharp pain, and he stilled.

"Do you want me to pull out?" he asked in a restrained voice. "Are you a virgin, Pip?"

"I don't know," I gasped, my chest rising and falling. "Give me a moment."

A wave of mating heat rushed into me like a storm, and the pain was gone as fast as it came. I was so wet that Jared made a low groan in the back of his throat. He couldn't hold back. He thrust up hard into me.

I moaned in pleasure. All I needed was his big, hard cock filling me. I sank my fingernails into his shoulder and started to ride his length up and down.

Jared hissed, lust and pleasure twisting his face, and his wolf peeked out, gazing at me with wild passion.

"I've never wanted another woman like this," he gasped as he grabbed my hips and heaved me up and down.

I slammed my ass down to his base over and over.

The pleasure was getting even more intense, and pressure kept building, pushing higher and higher. I quickened my rhythm at the burning urge. Jared thrust harder and faster.

We panted, our breaths mingled. He groaned and I moaned, both in the complete grip of our mating frenzy.

The sound of flesh slapping against flesh was shamefully erotic. Jared and I fucked each other like two wild animals.

The sofa groaned and quaked beneath us. For a second, I feared it might break, but then I no longer cared.

A beastly rumble vibrated from Jared's chest. The beast was thrilled at this mating, and I could feel his searing lust. Jared slanted his mouth over mine while his hand moved to rub my swollen clit quickly and roughly.

I cried out at the incredible sensation and pleasure.

We fucked at blinding speed, increasing friction to the maximum.

"This is the best bang I've ever had, woman. You're truly made for me," Jared panted and thrust into my molten depths. In and out. In and out. He pounded into me with abandon. "I can't get enough of this tight pussy. After this, I need to fuck you from behind. And you'll come for me again and again."

I'd heard that the shifters' favorite position was doggy style, and I couldn't wait to try it.

"Fuck me however you want," I moaned breathlessly. "I'm yours today. Talk less and fuck more."

"You asked for it," he growled. "I hope you can take it."

"Oh, I can take it," I said. "Worry about yourself."

The mating fever roared through me as Jared thrust into my core with his alpha shifter's brutal force. It was more than I could take, and I exploded around his cock.

Jared grabbed me to him tighter, thrust into me wildly, and shuddered with his own release.

My haze of lust gradually receded while my partner stayed hard inside me.

We gazed at each other, lust still brimming in his bright gray eyes, when a symphony of howls rose in the distance and echoed across the forest.

A band of shifters had come for us.

CHAPTER TWENTY-TWO

We broke away from each other, and Jared's shaft remained hard. He let out a curse, unhappy that shifters had come so soon. He'd planned to fuck me from behind.

I slid from his lap and scrambled to pick up my clothing off the floor. Jared pulled up his jeans while I shrugged on the oversized shirt.

"Shade and Jay will be here soon," Jared said over my worried look. "They tracked us to the cabin sooner than I expected. I want more time alone with you."

I nodded for no reason. I wasn't sure what to make of what happened. Everything had become a blur while we'd been caught in the moment, controlled by the mating fever. Or maybe I should take responsibility instead of being a wimp and blame everything on the circumstances.

The fact was that Jared and I had mated, but I had no idea where we'd go from here. So I perched on a chair, sitting up straighter than usual, and waited while Jared went to the bathroom.

Within a minute, shifters reached the cabin. Shade pushed open the door and stepped inside, Going-gray right on his heels. Both looked tense and worried.

The others didn't come in, but I heard them outside guarding the cabin and patrolling the perimeter.

Shade's gaze landed on me, taking in the scene. Worry disappeared from his brilliant blue eyes and was replaced with something else. Anger? Sadness? I couldn't tell as his face was an unreadable mask. Shifters had good noses, so he probably could smell his brother's scent all over me.

I grinned at him, happy to see him despite my face burning.

Going-gray stopped in his tracks, his eyes widening, then he tore his stare from me. He'd also registered that the Alpha Heir and I had had sex.

Shade moved toward me, crouching in front of me to make sure I was unscathed.

"We learned about the attack an hour later," he said. "You okay, Pip?"

I nodded. "I'm fine."

I'd healed fast, and only a few discolored

patches remained, especially on my legs and back. They didn't go away easily.

Just then, Jared came out of the bathroom and growled at Shade threateningly.

Shade sighed in exasperation, threw up his hands in a gesture of surrender, and stepped away from me. "Cool off, man. I'm not going to do anything. I wouldn't even if you hadn't marked her. It's not in me to step over boundaries and encroach on your territory. But Catnip is my clan, and I can't help caring for her. I'm not and never will be a threat to you in any way, brother."

A wave of warmth and sadness washed over me, but I knew better than to grasp Shade's hands in mine to show my appreciation for his friendship while Jared was all territorial. I wouldn't drive a wedge between the brothers.

Jared ceased growling and rubbed the dark stubble on his jaw. He nodded at Shade in understanding before training his demanding gaze on Going-gray.

"Report, cousin," he ordered, his face cold and hard and full of rage. The Jared I'd spent alone time with for a couple of hours had vanished, replaced by the tough Alpha Heir. "I assume you've already surveyed the scene at the bridge? All four of my guards are dead."

Going-gray snapped to attention with his

hands clasped behind his back. He was good at kissing ass. Always was and always would be.

"We inspected where you were attacked," he said. "Vampires weren't involved this time. It was all mages. We counted eight bodies, and one escaped. If we meet the mage who slipped away, we'll know it's him. We haven't been able to identify any of the assassins' bodies yet. But rest assure, we'll get to the bottom of this. Our investigation team is working around the clock."

Jared paced the room. "This was a planned ambush."

"Someone in our ranks must've betrayed us and leaked the intel about your secret route to the mercenaries." Shade paused for a second to rein in his fury and sorrow. Shifters were a tight-knit clan. Some of the warriors who perished might've been his close friends. My heart went out to him and all the warriors and their families. The four guards had been collateral damage. I was the one the mages really wanted. "We brought the guards' bodies back. They'll have proper burials, and their families will be taken care of."

"I can't believe mage's dared to attack our Alpha Heir in our territory!" Going-gray snarled. "We need to push the matter hard, Alpha Heir, and get High Mage Daeva to answer for this crime. Rogue mages attacking in our land is outrageous and utterly unacceptable."

I wondered who this Daeva was and if she was the one who had sent those two groups of mages to hunt me.

"We'll investigate this assault on our own first," Jared said, a cold, calculating light flashing in his gray eyes. "Daeva isn't the only power in Mage Town. Something has changed within the mage's circle. After we obtain solid evidence, we'll head to their headquarters and demand justice. You have my word. This attack won't go unanswered or unpunished."

"Do you know why they attacked, Alpha Heir?" asked Going-gray.

Jared glanced at me. "They wanted Pip and demanded I hand her over."

"Again?" Going-gray narrowed his eyes at me. "What is it about you, Pip girl?"

"The fuck if I know," I growled, trying hard not to lose it. "I'm being targeted for no reason. And I'm sick and tired of you drilling me with the same questions over and over!"

Part of me was suddenly relieved that we'd killed those mages instead of capturing them alive. I had no idea what kind of dark secrets they'd reveal about me.

I'd smelled the mages' fear of me. What if I was a monster that shouldn't have been unleashed, like that pig-eyed mage had said before I removed his head? Now that I thought back, I'd killed without any hesitation or remorse, even though the hunters were my enemies.

Violence seemed as natural as breathing to me.

I didn't know what I was, but if Jared and Shade learned it before me, I bet they wouldn't treat me the same again. They might even lock me up, and I couldn't allow anyone to put me in a cage again.

Ugly truth or not, I had to be the one who uncovered it first, then bury it if it was bad. When I was ready, I'd go hunt those fuckers and all my tormentors.

I wouldn't be kind to any of them.

"Be respectful, Pip girl!" Going-gray barked. "I hate to keep warning you."

"She's tired," Jared said, sending me another glance, desire hiding in the depths of his eyes. "It's been a trying day for her."

"Maybe the mages want a rainbow wolf." I didn't hide the sarcasm from my voice. "Who doesn't like rainbows?"

"I don't," Going-gray said. "I like rain. We need more rain for sure."

Jared's gaze still lingered on me. "Your wolf is beautiful, Pip."

My heart fluttered, and a small dash of happiness warmed my chest. It was the first time he'd ever praised me in front of others. It seems mating had changed his attitude.

"Let's get back to my manor," he continued. "We need to brief the king. And Pip needs to have a healer take a look at her."

"I'm fine," I assured him. "I'd appreciate it if you could have Shade take me back to the Academy. I don't want Princess Danielle to worry about me."

"I'll take no chances with your safety," Jared said. "Especially now that we know you're being hunted. You'll stay in the manor tonight. It's the safest place. Shade will inform Princess Danielle. And when you return to the Academy, I'll assign you two guards."

Shade and Going-gray traded a glance. The Alpha Heir had never sent guards to protect Viviane.

Jared had gone from ignoring and neglecting me to overprotecting me. I didn't want any guards hindering my movements, and I didn't want anyone to dictate my path. Yet I didn't want to fight the Alpha Heir either when our relationship had just started.

Should I expect a relationship with him after this? I shook my head at my idiocy. I shouldn't expect too much just because we'd had a good fuck on a sofa, caught up in the heat of the moment.

But then, it couldn't just be casual sex either. We were, after all, fated mates.

"Shade, Jay," Jared said before we headed

toward the cabin door. "Remember, what happened here stays here."

A rush of cold air banished any remaining heat within me.

I guess it was just a good fuck after all.

CHAPTER TWENTY-THREE

A dozen military vehicles waited on the road outside the woods. Heavily armed shifters were everywhere.

I was placed in the backseat of an armored black van in the middle of the formation. Jared took residence in the car ahead of me, and Shade got in the jeep behind me. I guessed the logic of the arrangement was that if one of us got hit, at least the others would survive. It was a not-placing-all-the-eggs-in-one-basket kind of thing.

Somehow, Jared insisted on Going-gray staying with me in the same vehicle. He was still jealous of my friendship with his brother. And after he'd mated with me, he wanted to keep Shade and me apart all the more, even though Shade had vowed to be a rule-follower and a team player.

After an hour of driving at high speeds, our

fleet of cars turned into a tree-lined street. Then, after a few more turns, our fleet entered through a security checkpoint and past a tall, iron gate that opened wide for us.

A splendid mansion rose in the distance, and my jaw fell open in awe.

"That's King Grayson's Palace," Going-gray explained as he glanced at me. "Alpha Heir's mansion is on the east side, less than half a mile away. It's easier to manage security with both the king and his heir in the same location. I'll take you to the Alpha Heir's manor where you'll rest for the night. Prince Jared and Shade will go see the king directly."

I was surprised that he'd told me all this. Maybe Going-gray finally felt sorry for me, or maybe he thought Jared and I were going to be an item, so he needed to get on my good side as well.

But he'd definitely softened his attitude toward me.

At the crossroads, the car with Jared continued on toward the mansion. Our car made a left turn, cruising along a curved path of a lush garden before it parked in front of a blue, three-story mansion.

All the way here, shifter sentinels, either in their human or animal forms, guarded every crucial point. Some of them blended into the shadows, but I could see them just fine. Going-gray wasn't wrong. The security was airtight here.

The car door opened for Going-gray and me, and then I was whisked into Jared's mansion before I could look around further.

I didn't walk tall with my chin held high like Going-gray. I hunched my shoulders as a sudden wave of uncertainty washed over me. I didn't want anyone's attention either.

The stylish foyer led to a magnificent hall with a marbled floor, crystal chandelier, expensive rugs, and a designer entertainment set.

Subconsciously, I couldn't help but peer down at myself. When Jared had found me, all I owned was a tattered sleeping gown. I didn't even own a pair of shoes. And now I was wearing a borrowed baggy shirt. No wonder Jared, the second most powerful man in Shifter City, thought Fate was treating him unfairly by saddling him with me.

Quietly, I followed Going-gray up the spiral staircase, traipsed down a pristine corridor on the second floor, and stepped into a grand suite. The two guards who had been trailing after us paused at the door and stood on either side, their legs braced in a solid pose.

"This is the Alpha Heir's living quarters," said Going-gray. "He spends most of his nights here."

"Good to know, sir," I murmured dumbly,

unaccustomed to him suddenly treating me like a lady.

Or he was treating me like Jared's supposed mate. No matter how much he disapproved of me, Going-gray was an old-school shifter. He knew that Jared and I had had sex. To an old-fashioned wolf, it was considered mating, like I was already unofficially married to Jared.

I snorted inwardly. We were far from that. Yet my pulse raced and my mind was a tangle of emotions as I reeled from the significance of mating with Jared.

"I can stay in a guest room, sir," I offered. "I bet the Alpha Heir has some spare rooms."

"You'll stay here," Going-gray said firmly. "You don't need to call me sir anymore, Pip girl. I'll have a maid bring food and a change of clothes."

"Thank you, good sir," I said.

He shook his head and walked out.

I looked around the lavish open-plan sitting room. Life here would be more than I had bargained for if Jared officially accepted me as his mate.

I would have status. I'd level up.

And this place would become my home.

Home. I tried to search for the feeling of having a home, but my memory remained a blank sheet.

With a sigh, I collapsed onto a white leather sofa and hugged a cushion to make myself warm and comfortable. Yet I still felt nothing. Even with the prospect that this could be my home, I didn't feel like I belonged here.

I shook my head. I was overthinking things. But I couldn't expel the empty feeling. In this magnificent suite, I felt more alone than ever.

I rose to my feet, jogged to the window, and gazed at the blooming garden below in the artificial light. Tall roses framed the whorls of the paths. There were so many of them that they looked like a field of stars. I wondered if those roses had thorns.

My thoughts drifted freely as I reviewed tonight's events.

I'd survived another hunt and even gotten laid. I'd experienced intense pleasure. So why was I in such a foul mood?

The door opened behind me. Two pretty maids, one younger and one older, entered and bowed slightly to me. The older one held a stack of clothes in her hands, and she placed them on top of an ivory chest. The younger maid lowered a large tray of drinks and three covered dishes on the center table.

I thanked them with a smile. They kept their gazes on the ground instead of looking at me, but they nodded, retreated, and closed the door lightly behind them.

At the Academy, everyone stared or glared at

me because I was a low wolf girl. But here, as the woman who was brought to the Alpha Heir's suite, no one, not even the elite guards, dared to make eye contact with me, as if I was suddenly above them.

It must've been a miracle that Jared or Going-gray hadn't struck me down when I'd glared at them right in the eyes and even threw insults in their faces the first day we met.

I retreated to the bathroom to take a long shower, then changed into a silky shirt and dress pants, and came back to the living room to devour the delicious steak, bread, and salad. They even brought me mango ice cream.

If I stayed with Jared, I'd live a pampered life. I'd be respected, but not because of who I was, but because of who I was to the Alpha Heir.

And I would be safe hiding within a fortified mansion with guards surrounding me.

CHAPTER TWENTY-FOUR

A shower of sunbeams pouring through the window hit my face and woke me up. I bolted from the sofa where I'd fallen asleep last night.

I blinked away my sleepiness and looked around. I could tell no one had entered the suite after the maids had brought me clothes and food, which meant Jared hadn't spent the night here.

Anxiety brewed in me. I needed to get back to the Academy, a familiar world to me.

Just as I returned to the living room after refreshing myself in the bathroom, a knock sounded on the door.

"Are you decent, Pip girl?" Going-gray called from outside the door.

"What do you mean by 'decent,' Prince Going-gray?" I shouted back. "I'm a decent person."

The door flew open. Going-gray, in his uniform, strode in, the younger maid on his heels.

He gestured at her, and the maid put the breakfast tray and coffee on the table, bowed, and retreated.

"Prince Jared and Prince Shade won't be around today," Going-gray said. "They were called to deal with some thorny issues outside the city. What do you want to do? Do you want me to show you around, Pip?"

I shook my head at him as I lifted the coffee mug and took a swig. The coffee in the Alpha Heir's household was amazing.

I lowered the cup. "Would you be kind enough to send someone to drive me back to the Academy? I don't want to miss any classes."

"It's Saturday," he said.

"I have private lessons."

"I see. You're a busy girl."

"I try, you know," I said. "Plus, you warned me to earn my keep before you guys tossed me into the Academy. So I have to train harder than anyone else, and when you send me to the frontlines to battle vamps and make Shifter City safe and make the world a better place—"

"Not this shit again," Going-gray cut in. "We'll never send you to the frontline."

Only because I had sex with the Alpha Heir.

"I'm not hungry," I said. "I want to go back to

the Academy. I don't want my friends to worry about me."

He gave me a long look, as if trying to read me. "There's nothing for you to do here anyway, and I'll only grow more gray hair if I have to spend the whole day with you." He motioned his head toward the door. "Come on. I'll drive you back to the school, and two guards will be assigned to you from now on."

"But it's the Academy. It's warded to keep the bad guys out. I don't want anyone to follow me around."

"Too bad," he said. "You'll have to take the issue up with Alpha Heir when he visits you again."

My heart fluttered like a butterfly's wings as hope stirred within me. Jared would visit me again? So we were going to have a relationship, officially. I wanted to ask when Jared would come to see me, but I bit my tongue so I wouldn't appear desperate.

"Just remember, Pip girl." Going-gray paused as if wanting to choose his words carefully. "At the Academy, not everyone likes you, especially those more powerful than you. Just watch your step."

He was warning me about Viviane, which meant no matter what happened between Jared and me, she wouldn't fade into the background. She'd probably fight me over him.

So I told him about one of BJ's friends who blamed me for her constipation.

"I don't want to know those details," he barked. "You need to have a filter. Don't let whatever passes through your head come out of your mouth. Keep your head down and keep your big mouth shut in school, and you'll have less trouble. Got it?"

I saluted him with a grin.

He glared at me. "You need to take things seriously, Pip girl. Things are different now."

As soon as I stepped into the princess's suite, Paris and Summer bombarded me with dozens of questions.

Danielle quirked an eyebrow at me, assessing my new state. The gorgeous dress she'd given me had been ruined in the battle, and now I was wearing a shirt and pants.

"Get Pip some cakes and coffee first, and then she'll talk," Danielle ordered.

"Thank you, Your Highness." I bowed in gratitude.

Pairs snorted and dragged me to the pristine kitchen and had me sit on the island. Danielle and Summer followed. Summer lifted the coffee pot and poured the black liquid into four mugs and pushed a pink mug in front of me.

Danielle usually drank black coffee, but the rest of us loved a lot of cream. I was the only one who was also addicted to sugar, though.

And after what I'd gone through? I poured five packets of brown sugar into my steamy coffee. When I went for one more, Summer snatched the packet out of my hand.

"You'll get fat if you consume sugar like that," she said.

"Who cares?" I rolled my eyes. "All sizes are beautiful. Plus, shifters burn calories like locusts going through grass."

"Let Pip have whatever she wants," Danielle said.

I drank my sugary, creamy coffee blissfully before I also devoured a plate of pancakes.

"So what happened?" Danielle asked. "We heard there was an attack."

"I happened," I said.

I smiled at my friends, my eyes a bit misty. This almost felt like home, so much more than Jared's mansion. I might not know my family, but my new pack felt like one.

"I have a confession," I continued. "And when I'm finished, you can decide if you still want me to stay here with you or not."

I planted my palms on the marbled island as I looked them in the eyes one by one, then I told them everything I knew about myself and everything that had happened to me… except the sliver of memory concerning the Vampire God. That one I'd keep to myself.

My narrative started with an unedited version of being hunted and ended with what had transpired in Jared's remote cabin and spending a night alone on his living room sofa.

The girls were shocked into silence for several seconds before they exploded again with fierce comments and more questions.

"I can't even imagine how terrifying that must've been," Summer said, "to be in such a dark place. But you've risen to the light, Pip."

"You risked a great deal by telling us." Paris grasped my hand. "We won't betray your trust."

"What Pip said stays in this suite," Danielle ordered. "She's pack." She looked at me with a nod. "Thank you for placing your trust in us. We'll do everything we can to protect you. We are your home now."

I'd protect them back with everything I had. I might not have much, but no one could take away my loyalty to my true pack.

I grinned at them, tears shining in my eyes. "We're the Fantastic Four Werewolves."

Danielle rolled her eyes. "Shifters. A werewolf has to be bitten and then turned."

"Maybe we should find a real werewolf and compare notes?"

"You don't want to compare notes with werewolves," Summer said. "They have nasty tempers."

CHAPTER TWENTY-FIVE

*T*he Nevada sun was about to set. I sprang across the west side of the campus toward the library, hugging a stack of heavy books to my chest. I didn't put anything in my locker because BJ's goons were getting creative as to what they were putting in it. They could have the space. I let them have fun wasting their energy by being uselessly petty.

These books were overdue, so I needed to return them and try to persuade the librarian not to fine me. I'd even prepared a few, amazing excuses.

Suddenly, the sky darkened, and shadows moved across the campus like unseen wings. All of my senses prickled as an instinctive alarm rang through me. The small hairs on my neck stood on end. A presence, dark and predatory yet extremely powerful, had made itself known.

My blood hummed with a thrill instead of fear, something predatory in me rose to meet the challenge.

My gaze swept the sky, then the ground, until I found my target. Time froze. I stood frozen, my muscles locked tightly, and my breath caught.

The Vampire God stood ten yards away from me, shadow and mist coiling around him. Menace and power rippled off him like the beginning of a dark storm.

The sight of him in the flesh was like a punch to the gut, and his icy, powerful beauty took my breath away. I couldn't tear my eyes away from him. Nothing mattered except him.

And his name, *Marlowe,* rolled over my tongue from a sudden long-lost memory.

His rich brown hair flowed to his sculpted chin. His straight, high-ridged nose marked his godly heritage. That perfect face must have been forged from a pure, dark god.

My gaze dipped to his sensual lips that had given me oral pleasure in my dream. I wondered what it would feel like if he savored the tender flesh between my thighs for real. I blinked, forcing myself to snap out of the inappropriate trance.

I'd been mated to another male. I'd had sex with the Alpha Heir, my supposed fated mate. Why would I crave this stranger who stood a few yards away and who might not even be real?

I blinked again. The vampire was still there. He was real, alright. His sapphire eyes locked onto mine, as if nothing else mattered to him anymore now that he had me in his sight.

I was the laser-focus of the baddest predator walking the Earth. It might not be a good thing, but it was also addictive to have his sole attention.

One instant, he was this darkest, most vicious and formidable vampire, then the next, his aura changed, as if he'd just stepped out of the darkness and brought starlight with him all for me. His cold marbled face turned so carnal that all I wanted was to touch him, even just once in my lifetime. It was as if the dark part of my soul craved him.

Hunger, longing, and pain burned in his eyes. I parted my lips and expelled a pent-up breath. Others might be terrified of the Vampire God stepping out of the myth, but I didn't worry about his thirst that subtly twisted his features as he inhaled the air with my natural perfume in it.

He craved my blood. It called him like a siren song. And still, I wanted to flirt with danger, for he held the answers I needed.

My blood buzzing with need, I stepped toward him, unable to resist his pull, unable to deny the same siren song in my veins.

Marlowe had come for me, just as I'd wished in

my every fiber. But he shouldn't be here. I needed to warn him. Even if he had a dark god's power, this was a perilous place for him, alone in the midst of one of the most fortified enemy shifter territories.

"Pip!" Danielle shouted behind me.

I wheeled around and spotted the princess sprinting toward me, her bosom bumping up and down. She was usually composed and coolheaded.

Had she spotted the vampire as well?

I shifted my position to pose myself directly between them. I wouldn't let him hurt her, and I'd have to explain to her that—

A sudden absence of the dark power and presence tugged at my heart. When I snapped my head in the direction of the Vampire God, he was no longer there.

The dark shadows had lifted from the sky and the surroundings. The last rays of twilight on campus faded altogether.

A feeling of profound loss swirled within me. Why did I feel this way toward this vampire who had just stepped out of the myth? He was basically a stranger, and in my dream, he'd craved my blood more than life.

Yet a stubborn thought latched onto my mind, telling me that my soul knew this being at the deepest level. My memory just couldn't catch up.

Danielle skipped to a halt in front of me. Her brown eyes were on fire with righteous anger.

"Princess, are you okay?" I wheeled toward my friend.

For a second, Danielle couldn't speak, as if she was having a hard time breathing. I stepped closer to her. She then gasped as if her lungs had just resumed their normal function.

"I felt a sudden wrongness here," she said, rubbing her forearm. "Like this incredible, dark danger…"

"I won't let anything happen to you," I said. "I'll always stand between you and danger."

"I know, Pip, but this isn't about me," she said softly. "I need to talk to you." Her lips thinned to a hard line. "Let's find a quiet place where no one can hear us."

"Okay," I said. "Just wait here for a second and I'll be right back."

I scrambled to the spot where the Vampire God had materialized then disappeared.

I half-shut my eyes and inhaled deeply. His lingering scent was still here—sage, powerful male, and rain on a dark spring night.

"Pip, what are you doing?" Danielle asked behind me.

She'd followed me. She might have sensed danger and menace from the Vampire God, but she hadn't perceived his brief presence right here. His dark power had shrouded him.

Regret and sorrow at his vanishing wrenched my gut. And the question remained. Why had I reacted so strongly to him?

What if he never came back?

Danielle glanced at the stacks of books weighing me down. We were near the library. She took a couple of heavy hardcover books from my hands.

"Let's find a private room in the library," she said in a low voice. "It's about Prince Jared. I just found out that he officially became engaged to Viviane last night."

* * *

I DROPPED the stack of books on the table, and a couple of them tumbled to the floor. Neither Danielle nor I minded them. The princess closed the door to the study, and I turned to look out the window. Night's darkness was pushing the last of the sun's light away in a haze of blues and blacks.

Chaotic buzzing filled my head. Blood drained from my face as Danielle told me everything she knew.

Jared had proposed to BJ last night, a day and a half after he'd had sex with me. He hadn't called or visited me after he'd fucked me, all because he was planning on marrying my nemesis.

I, his supposed fated mate, meant so little to him.

A wave of dizziness assaulted me, and I swayed. Danielle rushed to me and helped me sit down on a chair.

"BJ threw a party at midnight to announce the pre-engagement," Danielle continued. "I don't think the Alpha Heir himself has made the announcement, but the news I brought isn't false. I saw the engagement ring on her ring finger a couple of hours ago. It's huge and sparkling. I knew how this would hurt you, Pip, but I had to tell you."

"That's what friends are for," I said, tears spilling onto my cheeks. "To keep me from making a fool of myself."

I grabbed the edge of the round table with both hands to prevent myself from falling apart, my knuckles whiter than paper. My legs felt weak.

I'd already made a fool out of myself by surrendering to him, by offering him my maidenhood. I couldn't recall what kind of abuse I'd suffered, but when Jared and I mated, I'd been mostly sure that I had been a virgin.

And I bet as experienced as he was, he'd known it too. Yet he'd still cast me aside like this, even though he'd claimed that I was his mate in the heat of passion and that I was the best fuck he'd ever had.

My stomach clenched in pain. The contents in its pit threatened to come up. By sheer will, I kept them down and only allowed the bile to rise to the back of my throat.

My mind had a hard time processing all the miserable changes. It almost felt like my fated mate had slapped me in public when not long ago, he'd wrapped me tightly within his arms. He'd kissed me deeply and thrust into my core with fierce protectiveness and possessiveness.

He'd whispered sweet things to me, and I'd thought he'd finally chosen me. I'd given him a second chance, ready to start a new relationship.

But that wasn't how the Alpha Heir's mind worked when it concerned me. And he could blame it all on the mating fever or a moment of male weakness.

He'd treated me like a used shirt, and now I couldn't get over his betrayal.

Danielle stood by my side and wrapped both arms around my shoulders to support me. I leaned my head against her chest and started sobbing.

"I was a fool to trust him, Danielle," I said.

"Weren't we all?" she said. "We encouraged you to go on a date with him. We talked you into giving him a second chance. But believe me, you aren't alone. Every woman makes a bad judgment at least once in her life. We learn from our mistakes. And in your case, you didn't have much choice when the mating call drove you to the brink of insanity if you didn't mate with him." She swallowed hard. "Finding one's fated mate is the rarest thing, and it blew my mind that he threw it away like that. It's unforgivable. If you want to confront him, I'll go with you right now. We won't let him do this to you!"

I lifted my head from her chest and peered up at her through a mist of tears. "Then what? Fate might have tried to saddle him with me because of our biological compatibility, but we still have free will. He's made his choice."

"A fated mate isn't just biological, Pip," Danielle whispered. "It's magical. It's the greatest gift from the universe and beyond."

"It doesn't guarantee that you'll get a good guy," I said bitterly. "However, it wasn't a total disaster. I might have given him my body, but I never gave him my heart. And after he hurt me like this? I don't want him back. I might feel miserable right now, but I'll be fine. I'll move on. I won't let Jerkface and BJ crush my spirit. I'm not some weakling, Danielle. I don't rely on men to make me fucking happy."

I wiped away my tears with my sleeves until the last trace of my sadness disappeared.

"I'm done crying for him, but, if you don't mind, I'd like to be alone now, Princess."

"Of course." Danielle sniffed. "But know this: you have a pack, and we're here for you."

Redness rimmed her eyes. I was so absorbed in my own misery that I hadn't noticed that my friend had cried with me and cried harder.

"Hey, it's okay." I punched her forearm playfully even though I felt broken inside. "I'll be okay. I still have you girls."

"You'll always have us," she said.

The princess kissed the crown of my head and gathered the books from the table and the floor. She'd return them for me.

Danielle exited the study and closed the door behind her.

Hollowness expanded in my chest, then out of that wounded hole, a lustrous cord swirled out.

The mating bond.

I let out a strangled, mirthless whimper.

The bond was raw and new, but it was only half-formed. It seemed that the universe also knew that Jared hadn't committed to me.

Nor did I want to bond to him after learning that he'd tossed me away.

Why did it show up now? Why did it even form? A white-hot rage shot into me, and I mentally yanked it, trying to fling it out like trash.

Pain tore through me, so severe that I dropped from the chair and doubled over on the floor.

The half-formed, irremovable bond was a thorn in my soul.

I vowed to find a way to burn the half-bond. I wouldn't even allow its ash to remain in me.

Rage was a blizzard in me, but I forced myself to stay still and calm instead of charging out on a war path to the Alpha Heir. He wasn't worth it.

I sat in the dark room for a long time until a librarian issued a warning about the library closing through the intercom. I dragged my numb, fatigued body that still brimmed with rage out of the building and into the chilly night.

The wind sent a wave of hostile energy rushing over me. Two or three blocks away from the library, an ambush had been arranged for me. My senses were getting more astute. Ironically, it could be a perk from the regrettable half-formed mating bond with the Alpha Heir.

Instead of fleeing in the opposite direction, I stalked toward the trap.

One block. Two and a half blocks. A dozen figures slid out from the shade of the trees and bushes as I strolled down the path. BJ and her pack surrounded me, cutting off every exit point. But I didn't plan on retreating.

"What's up, dumb cunts?" I asked casually.

Power brimmed in me, and my hands turned to

claws. I could be a nuisance, but I didn't know the extent of my prank magic. It seemed that being mated with Jared had unleashed some hidden powers in me.

"Foul-mouthed slut," BJ hissed. "I promised the Alpha Heir, my fiancé, that I wouldn't cut you to ribbons. But heed this warning. You and he are done. Yes, he fucked you like a whore. He told me all about it. It meant nothing to him. You're nothing to him. He just needed to screw you once to get it out of his system."

I felt sick all over again, yet I controlled my trembling.

"Jared and I have something real," BJ continued, flashing her hand in front of my face to display a large, gorgeous diamond ring on her ring finger. "We have an understanding. He won't break his promise to me, and I'll be his future queen." She sneered. "He never promised you anything, did he, other than bending you over and fucking you like a cheap prostitute. Think again if you believe that you're his fated mate, that you're special enough to be a queen one day. Not in a million years will he ever choose you, rat. He's mine, always was and always will be. He just got an itch that one time, and you scratched it for him. You're pathetic."

I smirked. "He told me I was the best fuck he'd ever had, and I didn't even need to offer him a deep throat. However, have him by all means. Jerkface is no more than a pair of used socks to me. Feel free to tell him that. Oh, and keep the good blow jobs."

"How dare you?" BJ's face turned purple with rage, her eyes glowing yellow.

If she or anyone attacked me, I'd take them down. I didn't care. I would not let anyone dominate me, not even Jerkface.

I swaggered ahead, not bothering to ask a bulky shifter who blocked me to step aside. I lashed out, faster than lightning, and kicked her in the knee.

She fell, and I stepped over her.

The gang tried to lunge at me as one, but BJ called them back.

My heartbeat didn't rise above its normal rate. It didn't even pump in fear, probably because I couldn't feel my heart anymore. I didn't break a sweat either. I felt deadly calm and cold. It surprised me, considering I still had a storm brewing within me.

"Take what's mine again, and I'll end you!" BJ shouted behind me. "And before that, I'll put you through Hell. Try me, and you won't have a moment's rest, even though I promised my man not to put you down like the trash rat you are."

"Kiss. Kiss," I said.

I waved a hand. The wind swept a current of dirt and dead leaves toward BJ and the gang. A swarm of insects attacked them too.

"You're dead, bitch!" BJ shouted, and her gang began cursing me profusely.

"You first, cunts," I shouted back with a peal of laughter. "And love you back too."

Some random students who had been watching from the sidelines appeared disappointed. They'd expected a big fight. Everyone loved to watch bad things happen to others.

"Fuck off," I told the douches.

A wave of dire feeling slammed into my chest. I lifted my gaze just in time to see two plumes of smoke rise into the reddening sky amid a surge of flame several blocks away. That was the building where Danielle, the girls, and I dwelled.

A second later, an alarm blared through the air.

Cold panic pierced me, and I broke into a dead run toward my dormitory building.

CHAPTER TWENTY-SIX

Shifter sentinels milled around the burning building, the majority of them trying to put out the fire, a few of them patrolling the area and talking into walkie-talkies, while a couple of them guarded the entrance and maintained order.

I darted toward the building, but a pair of guards stepped into my path and blocked me.

"No one is allowed to go in," a shorter guard said harshly. "Are you blind? The building is on fire!"

"I live here," I hissed.

"Back off," the other guard barked. "We're still investigating the arson. Don't make me arrest you."

"You back the fucking off!" I screamed. "Princess Danielle and her companions are still inside! I know it!"

"We'll take care of it," the shorter guard said, his jaw tight.

I wasn't going to put my friends' lives in some guards' hands.

I shoved him in the chest, and he stumbled, surprised at my strength. He recovered the next second, snarled, and swung an arm at me. I ducked and booted him in his rib, sending him to the ground. I burst toward the entrance.

Four more shifters advanced on me, brandishing their electronic batons, ready to subdue me.

I leapt in the air and did a roundhouse kick without an anchor to support me. It was an impossible move, judging from the surprised looks on the shifters' faces, but my powers were being reactivated one by one.

Then, wasting no time, I jumped through the opening I'd just created and approached the entrance. Yet more guards were coming toward me. Some of them pulled out guns.

It'd take much longer to get through the guards, and my friends might not have that much time.

"Danielle! Summer! Paris!" I roared. "I'm coming!"

In an instant, I shifted into my rainbow wolf.

One leap, and I reached the second floor of the building, my claws hanging onto the edge of the windowsill. I peeked down to estimate my new situation should any of the guards try to shoot me, but no one raised a gun as they all stared up at me, shock on their faces, as if they had never seen a wolf climb and leap like I had.

They probably thought it was a waste of a bullet to shoot down a rebel wolf, since the fire and smoke might just do the job for them. Heat scorched my skin, but at least I had one less thing to worry about without the shifters trying to gun me down.

Fire or whatever wouldn't stop me from getting to my friends.

I turned my head up in determination as I calculated my next move. One more leap, and I'd reach the third story and crash through the window to get to my friends. Then I heard Danielle shouting my name below in a wailing voice.

I looked down again. Danielle and Paris, both in tattered and bloody clothes, carted Summer out in their arms. A couple of guards were trying to take Summer from them, but Danielle and Paris shoved them away, snarling fiercely.

One look at Summer, and I knew her spirit had left her body a while ago. I'd sensed a death, but I hadn't thought it was my friend while I'd been distracted by the Vampire God, then by my own rage and misery at hearing about Jared's betrayal.

With a wailing howl, I dropped to the ground

in a crouch and shifted into my human form. I coughed the smoke from my lungs, then dashed toward my friends. Danielle and Paris stumbled down the stairs with Summer in their arms, a long gash in Summer's neck. Her throat had been cut, and she'd been left to bleed dry before Danielle and Paris found her.

A sharp pain pierced my heart. Grief sank into my bones.

The sentinels barked orders and escorted us away from the blackened building. I bowed my head, unable to look at the grief in my surviving friends' eyes. My whole body turned cold as ice.

I knew what I must do next.

My enemies had started mental warfare against me by killing my friend. They had tried to flush me out of the Academy. Another dark thought iced my mind. The hunters had called me Death's daughter. Could it mean that I was truly cursed and would bring death to those I cared about?

I'd brought this on Summer. I hadn't had any friends; at least I didn't carry the memory of it. I'd had no pack. Now I finally had something and someone in my life, yet I only brought them danger and death.

I had to leave them. I was terrified to go solo and saddened to have to drift alone again, but if I didn't, I would have no friends left when my enemies slit all of their throats in their sleep or toasted them alive.

My path would be hard, but I'd take it. I'd learn to lurk in the shadows like a ghost, track my hunters, and kill them all.

Only then would I return to my pack.

GOING-GRAY ARRIVED WITH A TEAM. The interrogation went on and on. It was a waste of time. The killers had vanished, and the fire had covered their tracks. All the sentinels got was a whiff of two rogue shifters.

It'd been established that we had a traitor or traitors among us who were working with hostile mages. The investigation on the attacks on Jerkface and me hadn't had any breakthroughs, but both attacks seemed to target me.

Only this time, it'd gotten my friend.

Danielle and Paris had finally let Jay's men take Summer's body to prepare it for burial. The men then brought us to a safe house in a gray concrete building on campus, with six shifters guarding us.

Going-gray stayed with us and kept asking questions.

Both Danielle and Paris had told him the same story three times. Just as I'd speculated, Danielle had lingered in the library for almost an hour after she left me in the study, in case I needed her.

Paris had just come out of the shower when Danielle entered the suite. Danielle had asked about Summer's whereabouts, and Paris had said she hadn't seen Summer the whole day. Danielle had then knocked on the door to Summer's room. When she didn't hear an answer but smelled blood, the princess pushed the door open and found Summer, lying in a pool of blood, her throat slit open.

Then fire had suddenly erupted in the suite, as if some kind of spell had been activated. The entire suite had started burning and smoke had been everywhere.

We knew the rest of the narrative—Danielle and Paris had carried out Summer's corpse, and I'd arrived too late.

Jay also made me recount my confrontation with BJ and her gang twice. A terrible thought flitted through my mind. Had Viviane had a hand in this? Was she the traitor who had worked with the mages to take me out, and when that failed, they'd resorted to killing my friend to hurt me?

My throat moved up and down as a storm coursed through me. I'd find out who was responsible, and they'd all pay dearly.

I brought two glasses of water, one for Danielle

and one for Paris. They silently accepted the drinks.

"Where's Prince Shade?" I asked Going-gray. "Shouldn't he come with you?"

I hadn't seen Shade since I'd left Jared's cabin in the woods. I think he was deliberately avoiding me.

Going-gray darted a glance at my friends, as if debating whether he should reveal the intel in front of them. Two of his men who had escorted me from Jared's manor to the Academy a couple of days ago were also in the room, positioned by the door.

"Prince Shade accompanied the Alpha Heir on a classified diplomatic mission," Going-gray revealed. "They're out of the city and won't be back for another day. I've sent a messenger to inform the Alpha Heir about the attack on Princess Danielle's companion on campus."

If and when the shifters went to war with the vampires, the shifters would have to pass the mage territory in Oregon.

"Did they go to Oregon?" I asked. "Everyone's been talking about renewing negotiations with the new director of the mages, but I don't care. I just want to find out who killed my pack member and make them beg for death. Maybe the new director of the mages is behind sending the rogue shifters or if someone else in the Academy is the traitor. The rogues couldn't have gotten in easily without inside help."

"Don't speculate without hard proof." Going-gray gave me a measured look. "It won't do you any good, Pip girl." He sighed. "I'm not sure why I'm even telling you this. The Alpha Heir went to Mage Town to demand they hand over the rogue mages who attacked him and his royal guards. We won't rest until we have them. Prince Shade is good at negotiation, so the Alpha Heir brought him along. While we demand the new director police their own as effectively as we police our own, we need to have a good diplomatic relationship between us. And now this attack happened in the center of the Academy, one of our most secure structures. It's unacceptable. War's coming, Pip girl. One way or another."

He hadn't needed to tell me this. But even after his cousin had chosen another woman, Going-gray still treated me much better than before. Maybe he felt sorry for me.

"Everyone's safety in the Academy is our top priority," he said before he rose.

"Prince Brock," I called.

He looked at me with surprise, since I hadn't called him Going-gray.

"I've been the target, as you know," I said,

choosing my words carefully. "Even though the mercenaries have got the wrong girl, they are hanging on to the idea that I'm *the* girl. And now my friend has died because of me." I swallowed hard. "The longer I stay here, the more danger I'll bring to my friends. So, sir, I ask for permission to leave the Academy, for the safety of my friends and the other students here."

Danielle and Paris had been huddled together the whole night. For the first time, I didn't join their band. I didn't offer them comfort either. Words were cheap in this situation. I kept my distance, as I couldn't bear to look into their eyes and know I was to blame. The guilt was eating me alive.

They stirred, however, at my words.

"You're not leaving us, Pip!" Danielle said, her brown eyes widening. "I forbid it. We must stick together. What happened isn't your fault! You hear me?"

I fought back my tears, but I remained silent.

Going-gray gave me a long look, then sighed again and rubbed his hands.

"Despite all that has happened, Pip girl, the Academy is still the safest place for you," he said. "You have no idea how much more dangerous it is outside the walls. We'll double the security around you girls."

"I doubt it'll be enough," I said quietly. "I can't put my friends in danger any longer."

I'd solidified my decision. I'd take the target off my friends' backs and lure the enemies away with me.

Going-gray gestured for the guards to exit. They nodded, walked out, and closed the door behind them.

"I'm saying this only once off the record, Pip girl, considering you're Shade's friend," he said in a hushed voice. "The Alpha Heir may have different plans than you. He's trained to put his duties and responsibilities above his personal needs or even his personal happiness. But no matter what plan he has, he can't just let you go after…you know." He scrubbed a hand down his face. "Leaving the Academy or Shifter City isn't an option for you. All the guards have been briefed that you aren't allowed to leave the Academy grounds under any circumstances."

My heart skipped a beat, and blood pounded in my ears. Jerkface had anticipated that I might want to leave Shifter City after his engagement to my nemesis became official.

Rage flowed through me, but I reined it in. There was no need for me to tell Going-gray that I wasn't leaving for Jerkface's sake. Heartbreak and humiliation rated low in my book. I was made of sterner stuff. But when my friends' lives were in jeopardy, I'd do anything to prevent harm from coming their way.

"I'm so flattered that Jerkface would pay me all this attention," I said flatly.

Going-gray gave me a sharp look and made his way toward the door. "It's been a tough day for you girls. Try to get some sleep. I'll check in on you in the morning."

He walked out, shut the door, and barked orders at the guards outside. I heard his footsteps receding.

Danielle and Paris had dozed off on the sofa, exhaustion and grief haunting their faces. I pulled a blanket over them as I took them into my memories.

Then I found a pen and drafted a letter on a piece of paper:

Princess Danielle and Paris,

I must leave the pack. Please forgive me. But I promise this isn't goodbye. I'll return after I eliminate all threats against us and avenge Summer's death.

With all my love,

Pip.

Pondering for a second, I added:

P.S. I know a guy I haven't told you about who can help me. I'll find him. Please don't worry about me, as I won't be all alone in the wilderness. I'll be hunting those who hunted me.

I made a point not to mention Marlowe, the mythical Vampire God.

As soon as I left the Academy grounds, both Marlowe and the hunters would track me down. I only hoped that the vampire found me before the mages.

CHAPTER TWENTY-SEVEN

*I*t took me some time to work out the windowpane in the bathroom of the guest room on the second floor. The window was warded, but most spells didn't work on me, especially now that my magical strength had increased. Also, the ward was basically designed to prevent intruders from getting in not getting out.

I popped out the window after dismantling the ward and poked my head outside. No sentinels had been placed on this side of the wall. The main force had gathered at the entrance of the building. I slid out through the open window headfirst and glided down the wall like a lizard.

Once again, I surprised myself by being able to pull it off when most people would fall, their head knocking against the ground. My hands landed first beside a row of shrubs. I heard someone approaching and instantly crouched low beside the flowery bushes.

A guard strolled around the corner and disappeared to the other side.

I adjusted my backpack that contained food and other supplies for a couple of days and snuck along the low bushes, trying my best to merge into the shadows as I headed toward the north side of the campus.

There were two guard towers, one on the east and one on the west. I'd scale the north side of the wall, then run for the hills. My plan was to head northeast and get into Idaho, the human-controlled state. From Idaho, I could reach Washington State, the vampire realm, without crossing the mage territory in Oregon.

It wasn't like I trusted vampires, but Marlowe could assist me better from Washington State, even though the vampire realm was currently controlled by Lucian, his rival.

The last thing I wanted was to be caught in the conflict between him and the shifters, so I was leading him away from shifter lands.

I scurried along the edge of the campus, ducking when I saw any guards. It took me more than half an hour to reach the northeast wall, all the while staying off the guard's radar watching from the two towers.

No one was around this part of the property.

I'd done my due diligence and scouted the entire campus. This part was its only blind spot. And now nighttime provided perfect cover.

I took a deep breath, giving Shifters Academy, once my haven, one last glance. This was it. I was leaving everything behind. I'd be on the run. I'd be hunting while being hunted.

I touched the wall with my fingertips, an electric buzz rolling over my skin. These spells, though potent, weren't killing ones. They were meant to knock out intruders.

I wondered if I had dealt with enough spells in my past that I recognized them, like a muscle memory.

I had to admit that I might have a harder time working through the spells draped all over the wall if my strength hadn't increased since I had mated with Jared. Did he get stronger as well? I hoped not. Color me petty, but I didn't want him to reap the benefits from our partially-formed mating bond other than that passing pleasure.

I shook him from my mind and refocused on the current task, testing the strength of the spells again until I was confident they wouldn't knock me out cold.

My hands turning to claws, I leapt, my body half-shifting to best climb the wall. I was more of a chameleon than a wolf, so I could adapt and make myself more like a lizard at the moment.

I climbed up at high speed, ignoring the pain and slight burning sensation caused by the spells. It would be over soon.

I reached the top and climbed over to the other side, carefully avoiding the sharp iron spikes while I flattened myself to avoid being detected by the guards in the towers. I slid down the other side of the wall with a big grin on my face.

I fucking made it!

I was probably the first student who had broken the record of climbing over the wall of the Academy unscathed. I wished my friends could see this and pat me on the shoulder for my achievement. Shade had been right. I was a bit vain.

Thinking of my friends, my eyes became misty, but I fought back the tears and gazed at the distant hills under the dark sky.

There was freedom, but at what cost? Danger and loneliness would be my companions, and I'd have to hunt for my own food.

Before I jumped to the ground, my senses suddenly bristled and sharpened, picking up something. Presences that had been out of my range before popped up on my radar.

Just then, intense lights from dozens of flashlights and headlights shot toward me, pinpointing me on the wall like a fly.

I squeezed my eyes shut as several flashlights shone directly into my eyes. Those pricks!

"Pip girl!" Going-gray barked smugly. "Come down now, nice and slow!"

"Easier said than done!" I shouted back.

I couldn't do it nice and slow, as I could no longer hold on to the wall. My claws vanished. I plunged toward the ground, and the shifters spread out and besieged me, cutting off my escape route.

I was caught in the headlights like a fucking bunny.

"Turn your fucking lights off, men!" I snarled. "Are you going to shoot me now?"

"No, no, no," Going-gray said, still pleased with himself for outsmarting me. "You're too important to shoot at. We'll preserve you at all costs and protect you even from yourself. The Alpha Heir told us this might happen, so I took precautions, and it paid off. No more running off like a thief in the night."

I glared at him, but it was damn difficult to use my eyes to kill him, since I had to raise two arms to shield my eyes from the intense lights. Going-gray stood tall ahead of a small shifter army like a pompous ringleader. He grinned ear-to-ear. This was the first time he had gotten the upper hand, and he was savoring every moment.

"You've been waiting for me to run just to catch me!" I accused.

"You got that right, Pip girl," he said. "I was curious to see how far you would get."

"Then why don't you set me free and let your men chase me?" I challenged him. "Make it an interesting game. Let's see how far I can go without you ambushing me like this again."

Several shifters grunted their approval. Shifters loved to chase and hunt, and this bunch was made up of elite warriors who couldn't pass up a challenge.

"C'mon, Chief Going-gray," I said, trying to provoke him. "Don't tell me a bunch of big, bad shifters are afraid of a little girl like me." I jerked a thumb at my nose to make a point, and half of the shifters growled at the insult. "Or are you all too old to outrun me?"

"Nice try, Pip girl," Going-gray sneered. "You might look like a wolf, but you're a fox in disguise. If you think you can trick a veteran commander like me, you're mistaken. I caught you, fair and square. Come back with us. Now."

"This isn't fair play," I said angrily. "You set a trap and then you outnumbered me."

"I agree on both counts, and I ain't ashamed to show you that the world never plays fair," Going-gray said. "It's always the ones who have bigger guns doing the talking. I have the biggest gun here, so I call the shots." He flashed another grin at me like an evil grandpa. "If you try to run, we'll tase you and then pump sedatives into you. You won't feel good even after you come back around. Or there's the easy way—you come with us with a can-do attitude and good manners. You pick, Pip girl."

He really enjoyed seeing me frustrated. It was like he finally got his small revenge. His niceness toward me in the safe house had all been a fucking show.

"You can't do this," I said. "You know I'll bring danger to my friends! I can't lose any more of them!"

"I've taken that into consideration," he said. "I appreciate that you have the capacity to think of others besides yourself, so I'm not going to take you back to the Academy and jeopardize Princess Danielle's safety. You'll be put in a fortified military compound in the center of Shifter City under house arrest until further notice."

I blinked. At least he had more sense than I'd thought.

"What further notice?" I demanded. "How much further?"

"That depends on your behavior," he said. "We'll have to wait for the Alpha Heir to decide. Your fate is in his hands. However," he rubbed his stubble that was going gray as well, "I can assure you that he won't harm you, no matter how insufferable you can be. Consider that a blessing."

"Has anyone else ever told you that you excel at kissing his ass?" I asked.

Going-gray growled. "Don't be a sore loser. Just admit that even with that brain and power of yours, you lost. However, no one has ever come this far and climbed that wall without passing out, so you can feel a bit better about yourself. I'd love to chitchat more, but I don't have all night." He removed something from his pocket and handed it to a guard. "Now hold still so we can place this magical cuff around your ankle. Next time you try to cross the perimeter without permission, you'll get a nasty shock and our security team will be alerted."

"Aren't you a real treat?" I snickered. "But if you want me to wear that fucking shackle, you'd better put it on me. I don't know your men, and I will scream if any of them touches me."

Going-gray let out a long-suffering sigh. "Fine. Let's get this over with. I want to go home and catch a couple of hours of sleep before dawn!"

He took back the ankle cuff from the guard and stalked toward me, two of his men peeling off the group to follow him, as if I were a dangerous criminal that needed to be manhandled. Going-gray raised a hand to stop them, knowing it wouldn't look good, and I bet that he was more concerned that I'd ridicule him.

He stopped a foot and a half from me and

squatted to secure the cuff around my left ankle. I took the opening and swung my fist toward his face to vent my anger. I'd enticed him to come to me, and he had taken the bait.

Before my fist slammed into his face, his hand shot out and grabbed mine, faster than lightning. It was a shock how fast he was, considering the fucker was ancient. He was pushing on forty!

Something pricked my leg, followed by a rush of hot liquid.

"What the fuck?"

I glanced down. He'd just injected me with sedatives.

My head began to swim.

I could resist a high-voltage electric shock and most spells, but for some reason, drugs were the bane of my existence. My body just didn't react to them well. My fragmented memories told me that my former captors had also kept me sedated with drugs.

I really needed to figure out a way to counter the drugs after...after...

I dropped to one knee—I refused to drop to both knees to try and preserve my dignity—my glare on Going-gray grew weaker as the world began to spin around me.

I'd underestimated the battle-hardened prince warrior because he appeared stocky and didn't look very smart. And he was mostly straightforward, so I hadn't thought he could be good at deception. Now I knew he put on that dumb look to fool his opponents. He was Jerkface's second-in-command for a reason.

But before I fell over with my face down, I left a small gift for Going-gray. My prank magic could target only one victim at a time, or I'd have deployed it and made all the shifters jump when I'd first fallen from the wall.

Going-gray's eyes widened as his hands flew to his chest. And then he started frantically rubbing his itching nipples through his uniform.

"Pip girl, what the fuck did you do?" he yelled menacingly. "Stop this right now!"

I smirked at him. Black stars burst before my eyelids, then the world and I with it died around me.

CHAPTER TWENTY-EIGHT

I woke on a couch in a sparsely furnished room, my head throbbing like I had the worst hangover. I sat up slowly and noticed I was still wearing last night's clothes: a black shirt, a jacket, and a pair of slim jeans.

Someone had taken off my boots before putting me on the couch. And now I discovered a broad magical cuff around my left ankle.

I let out a curse, and my trembling hands tried to pry it off me, but instead of coming off, the magical band glowed and shocked me. It hurt more than I'd expected. The spells and runes etched along the rim of the cuff weren't something I could overcome this time.

Going-gray had been true to his word. He'd followed Jared's orders to the letter and put me under house arrest.

I rose to my feet and stared outside through a barred window. Soldiers milled around the military compound. There were guards outside my door as well. Even if I could endure the shock and pain caused by the cuff and make an escape, the shifters would track me down, drug me again, and drag me back.

I sank back into the couch in dismay while I simmered with fury at all the assholes who kept trying to control me.

Just then, the heavy door swung open, and Jerkface walked in.

It'd probably been three or four days now since I'd last seen him.

He wore a gray and blue uniform with red stripes and golden stars that indicated his high rank. The fucker probably wore the uniform better than any man. It fit him like a glove and highlighted his muscled chest and strong physique. His uniform slacks also showed off his powerful legs.

He appeared broader and taller than when I'd last seen him, alpha power rippling off him.

His dirty-blond hair was combed back. His gray eyes looked brighter.

He was a very handsome man in any setting, and the prick always carried an arrogant air, as if he owned everything in the universe.

And by the way he was staring at me right now, he thought he owned me.

Hate and heat coursed through me at once. Hatred for him seared my heart, but my body still craved his touch.

My ex-fated mate's gaze roved over me, lingering on my lips before it dipped toward my breasts. By sheer will, he lifted his eyes to my face again, yet they seared with raw male lust.

Emotionally, I was repulsed by his desire for me, especially when he was eye-fucking me and picturing me naked, but my body was more than eager to comply and please him, right here, right now.

If he commanded it to bend over for him to fuck it, it'd purr, "How low?"

I bit my inner cheek until it bled to stop my stupid body from cheapening itself.

"How are you holding up, Pip?" Jerkface asked softly as he pulled up a chair and sat down across from me. "Did you rest well?"

"You mean how do I feel after waking up from being drugged and dragged here against my will?"

He sighed. "It couldn't be helped. You shouldn't have run. You know the drill. It isn't safe for you to be alone outside Shifter City. You're being hunted."

"And I was attacked inside your city," I said coldly. "Then someone got into the Academy and slit my friend's throat that was meant for me."

His face hardened, rage pouring off him. "I'll make sure it won't happen again. I had a long meeting with High Mage Daeva. She promised to deliver the justice I demanded. Her team will cooperate and assist mine to hunt down the rogue mages who dared to attack us. In no time, we'll round them up. You're safe here."

"What a 'noble' excuse for keeping me prisoner here," I said. "I want to leave Shifter City and go my own way. I'll take the chance with my own safety."

He stared at me hard, not appreciating me always having my own opinions, yet desire still poured off him in waves. He couldn't control it any more than I could. The mating heat hit him harder since he didn't resent me as much as I did him.

"I can't allow that, Pip," he said, interweaving his fingers as he tried to be patient. "You're a shifter, so you're under the jurisdiction of shifter laws."

Everyone knew that the North American Shifter King and Alpha Heir ruled Shifter City with an iron fist. It was pointless to argue with Jerkface as to where I belonged. In his eyes, I was his subject and his to command.

And worse, he now believed he owned me after he'd fucked me, even though he'd cast me aside.

"What are you doing here exactly?" I sneered. "I'm but a lowly shifter. If you have any orders or news, including your new engagement, you could just send a messenger. You don't need to grace me with Your Highness's presence in person. I don't require it."

His eyes flashed with anger before he composed himself.

"You're special to me, no matter what you think, or how mad you are," he said. "Any other who talked to me disrespectfully would surely be punished, or might not see the light of day again. You're wild and undisciplined, and I get that it'll take time for you to learn all the rules." He sucked in a sharp breath before continuing. "Right now, you need to look at the big picture, which isn't all black and white. In case you're wondering, I haven't abandoned you. I'm merely preparing you, and you'll learn about shifter politics first, then world politics, including how vampires, mages, and humans run things. Your situation might not be ideal at the moment, but whatever I've done, I did it to protect you."

"Is this how you protect me—you fuck me, then propose to Princess Blow Job right away so you could get benefits from both of us? I already told Miss BJ she could have you in every way. I've bowed out already."

He growled, then stopped as he worked on controlling his anger.

"You'll drop the crude language, and that will be the first part of your education," he said. "I reached an agreement with the King of the Great

European Shifter Kingdom and his heir, for the greater good of the entire shifter species. As the future King of the North American Shifter Realm, I can't put my personal desires and needs above my duty. That's not how it works. One of the terms they signed at my demand is that they won't harm you. They won't target you. Even after I wed Princess Viviane and she becomes queen, you'll still be with me as my favorite concubine. And one day, you might just be my queen when you're ready. We have a future together, and you'll be sheltered and taken care of. With Princess Viviane, it's only a political arrangement. You're what really matters to me. As Fate deems it, you belong to me. You'll play your role, and I'll do everything in my power to protect you."

I roared with laughter.

Jared narrowed his eyes.

I laughed so hard that I had to wipe away a tear.

"I feel so sad for you because you don't even realize that you sound like a broken record." I said after I was no longer laughing. "You really think I want to climb any shifter social ladders? Do I look that desperate to want to be your bitch? Go ahead and claim your princess's deep throat. I hope you enjoy it every day. You two are a match made in Heaven or Hell, for all I fucking care. But know this: I don't belong to you. I never did and never will. That unfortunate fuck in the cabin was just one meaningless bang, driven by a moment of weakness and animal heat. It'll never happen again. I guarantee you. Fate can go fuck herself in the asshole."

A vein throbbed on Jerkface's temple and his fists clenched, as he tried to contain his rage.

"No woman ever says no to me," he hissed. "Neither will you."

"Bad news then," I snickered, jerking a thumb at myself. "Because this chick just rejected you, and she meant every word. Get used to it." I yawned, not bothering to cover my mouth, "Now I'd appreciate it if you fucked off. And if you need anything else in the future, send Shade. We're done here."

"We'll be done when I say we're fucking done," he snarled, his handsome features reddening and twisting in rage. "I understand you're angry and jealous so you aren't thinking straight. I'll forgive you this once for lashing out."

He shook his head. "You have no idea what I've been dealing with for your sake, but I won't explain further when you can't be rational. You'll accept things as they are, and you'll accept what's assigned to you quickly and respectfully."

I shook my head, a mocking smile hanging on my lips. The mating heat could no longer influence my mind, even though a spark of heat still simmered in my belly.

"And for a start, you'll remove the curse you

placed on Princess Viviane," Jared ordered in a hard voice.

I scowled. "What curse? You think I'm a witch now?"

"You know what curse. I'm fed up with your childish games!" he said harshly.

A realization slammed into me. Oh, that funny business. I'd forgotten. I'd wished for Viviane's pubic hair to grow around her thin, broad lips.

So my wish had turned into reality?

That would be a sight to behold.

I stared at Jerkface blankly, feigning innocence. "I don't know what you're talking about."

"Princess Viviane has to wear a mask at all times," Jared said, voice dripping with irritation. "And as soon as she shaves the strange whiskers, they sprout right back. A team of mixed mages and witches said only the original caster can lift the curse, or the curse will vanish once the spell caster is dead. You could have been tortured and punished to death for that had I not shielded you."

Had Jerkface just threatened me?

What kind of male would threaten his own fated mate? He really regarded me as dirt under the bottom of his shoes. And he held this power over me and locked me in here just because he could.

In a male-dominated shifter society under Jerkface's thumb, I'd never have a place of my own.

I'd never be my own woman. I'd be treated as his breeder, and nothing else.

"So you don't like her soft hair that tickles Your Highness's dick? I thought you two lovebirds were kinky," I snickered. I wanted to humiliate and hurt him back. "To tell you the truth, I'm not afraid of torture. I had plenty of that until a brave man freed me. I was on my way to find him before you and your minions dragged me to Shifter City. So, hells no. I won't stay here. I'll go find him and reunite with him."

I looked straight into his furious eyes. His alpha stare had the power to make every shifter weak at the knees. A weaker shifter would've rolled over to show him their belly. But it didn't do a thing to me. I, Pip, was a wild card. I did not let anyone dominate me. "You can't protect me, but he can. He's the only one who will."

A ring of crimson appeared around his gray eyes as a fit of jealous rage seized him.

"Enough!" he bellowed, his face turning beastly. "No other man will ever touch you. Try and they'll be dead. You're forever a member of my household. You want to be wild? Only when I allow you to be. You think I can't tame you? I'm the future king of all shifters. I'm the law in Shifter City, and my territory will expand across the sea. And you, my concubine mate, will learn to obey me unconditionally."

I shot to my feet and flipped him the bird with both of my hands. "Does this look submissive? You're more delusional than I thought if you really think you can make me your bitch."

Jerkface snarled viciously and stripped the leather belt off his pants.

I read his intentions loud and clear. He'd whip me to tame me, then rape me to show me who was in charge. He truly believed it was his right to fuck and claim me any time he wanted since he'd done it once already. He'd marked me as his mate. To him, that meant I was his property, aka sex slave.

"You want this, is that it?" He bared his teeth, his fangs showing. "You want the hard way when I tried to go easy on you? If you can't wait for me to teach you to learn your place, I don't mind showing you, right here, right now. I've tamed a good number of horses and beasts wilder than you."

The asshole stalked toward me, snapping his coiled belt straight. It made a hissing sound. His wolf let out a warning growl, but he ignored his beast. The brutal man was in control now, and he wanted to show me just that.

I wouldn't let that fucking whip land on me.

He slashed the belt in the air, the whooshing sound offering me one last warning. I unleashed my storm, even though I knew it could get me killed.

I no longer cared.

I kicked up a chair, and it flew toward him. He caught it and hurled it into the wall. It shattered into pieces.

He appeared in front of me and swung his belt toward my hip. My hand lashed out, faster than he expected, and grabbed its end. A burning sensation blossomed in my palm, blood dripping to the ground, but I didn't let go of the whip.

I swung my leg up to boot him in the jaw and scored. He stumbled, eyes wide with surprise, and took his belt with him. I threw up my hand, and the wind I didn't know I could command appeared, tossing him backward.

He got up in a blink and kicked the other chair toward me. I jumped at the right moment and landed on its top. Using the momentum, I hurled myself toward him, horizontally.

My feet rammed into his chest. He lost his balance and fell on his ass, as he hadn't expected that.

Then I was straddling him, my fist ramming toward his face.

His large hand caught my fist, and with a burst of strength, he threw me off him. He was much stronger than I remembered. Using his full weight, he pinned me beneath him, his knee digging into my rib.

I gave a roar and head butted him, smacking

my forehead against his mouth. I offered him a savage grin at his split lip.

I now hated him. I hated him with my entire being. Yet my body still whimpered with need for him and wanted to writhe as his large body caged me, his hard erection pressing against my stomach. For that, I loathed myself as much as that cunt Fate.

"Stop, Pip! Now!" Jerkface barked, shocked to see the undisguised hatred burning in my eyes. "Don't make me do things I'll regret!"

He'd done that already when he decided to whip then rape me.

As he grabbed my head and shoulder to completely lock me in place, I managed to bring up my knee and drive it into his crotch. Roaring in pain and rage, he half-rolled off me. I took the opportunity to shove him off me and straddled him again. Then I rammed my elbow toward his eye.

The door burst open. Several shifter sentinels charged in, led by Going-gray. Electric bars rammed into my ribs and neck.

The pain was nothing other than an irritation. I could take a shock or two.

I threw a hand toward the assaulting guards, a surge of my magical air tossing them into each other. More guards rushed in, one of them pulling out a gun to shoot me.

"Don't kill her!" Both Jerkface and Going-gray shouted.

Jerkface's alpha power lashed out before I could react, slamming into the trigger-happy guard and sending him crashing into the barred window. The glass shattered at the impact.

"Use darts!" Going-gray barked his instruction.

Darts flew at me from all directions. I had no shield. I roared for my wind to come, and it arrived, shoving some guards away and hurling away most of the darts. But several darts had pierced my flesh, the sedative coursing in my bloodstream.

My wind hadn't been strong enough. As devastated, bitter, and desperate as I was, cold clarity blasted me like an ice storm. It wasn't that I wasn't powerful enough. I knew it then. Something else was at play. A black spell, more potent and malicious than any spell ever woven, had been implanted inside me for who knew how long. I could feel the dark spell attached to my essence, and it had bound my natural magic.

I had a very powerful, lethal enemy whom I knew nothing about.

"That's enough!" Going-gray shouted, yet he dashed toward me and plunged a syringe into my arm while I was defenseless, swaying from vertigo.

I threw my fist up and back, ramming into his

face and breaking his nose. The fucker deserved more than that.

I tumbled to the ground, my face morphing into a wolf's. I had one last job to do before I blacked out.

"I reject you, Alpha Heir Jared!" my wolf's voice called out. "I renounce the mating bond between us. If I'm Death's daughter, I call for the power of my birthright. I command it to break the bond. It shall never fully form!" I roared. "Break it!"

Jared lunged at me to stop me, but he was too late.

Fueled by the storm raging inside me, my magic temporarily broke though the binding of the black spell, rose, and snapped the mating bond into three pieces. It would never be whole again.

Agony twisting Jared's face, he curled into a ball.

"What…have…you…done, Pip?" he cursed.

Soul-searing pain surged into me, threatening to shred me. Acid burned my insides, like nothing I'd ever experienced.

I rolled on the ground in agonized tears, but I laughed like a fiend.

I'd plucked the thorn out of my soul.

I'd shattered the link to my ex-fated mate.

CHAPTER TWENTY-NINE

*I*t felt like I was having another bad hangover on a cold, rainy day.

A flash of dreams, memories, or gritty reality jumbled through my head. I woke up in a sealed cell with three concrete walls and an iron door. I vaguely remembered a cell similar to this, which might have been my room for a decade while I had been held captive and experimented on. When I tried to search and dig further into that piece of my past, I got lost in the maze once again.

A bonfire of memories and dreams was long gone now, and I was left in this cold, dim cell where my ex-fated mate had thrown me.

I fought the urge to panic and pound on the iron door and scream, demanding to be released. I knew better. It'd be useless to cry to my enemies and beg for mercy. It would only give them power over me.

So I sat on the cold ground, letting ice fill my veins, letting fear pass though me. Clarity and sanity eventually replaced my panic.

I moved to the next step, reaching for my inner magic, to see if it was still there, and if it was, I'd see what it could do to help my current situation. But it didn't rise. I didn't feel an iota of it. I bet the cell had wards around it, which could nullify my magic.

They had locked me in the most secure prison inside the military compound.

Time crawled by. I couldn't perceive how long I'd been sitting on the ground, leaning against the wall, alone and cold. I told myself not to focus on my current situation and that I'd survive this.

Tomorrow, I'd come up with a plan. Today, I would not rush to act. I would not feel dismay. I would wait for the drugs in my system to fade.

I flexed my muscles and rose, practicing the martial arts moves Shade had taught me. I chose to practice Tai Chi, also called shadowboxing, which combined martial arts with meditation. I moved slowly, let the energy of yin and yang flow through me, and let Zen fill my chaotic head.

And that summed up day one in solitary confinement.

My jailor was waiting for me to make a move, so I made no move to counter him.

Silence was my weapon.

Then day two came. First, the sound of footfalls tapped on the corridor outside my cell. Then, the lock clicked, and Shade pushed open the iron door and stepped inside.

A guard outside the door closed it quickly, which meant I wasn't getting out of here.

Shade looked at me, his Adam's apple bobbing with thick emotions. I didn't want him to feel bad for me. I didn't want my friend to be sad.

"Hello, Canary," I said with a forced smile. "Once again, I'm in a cell. But don't worry. I'm getting used to this."

He sat on the ground across from me. "I only have half an hour."

"Then let's not waste it," I said, my smile lingering. "What do you want to do?"

"I'm sorry I haven't been around lately," he said. "It's just family business and shifter politics have got me all tangled up. Shit's going down everywhere. We have traitors among us. Mages are playing games, as they know we're worried that they might form an alliance with the vampires instead. Bloodsuckers are on the move. We've also had confirmation that a vampire force led by the Vampire God has come to North America. One moment, he was but a myth, the next, he's stepped out of it and become our new nightmare. If his force joins Lucian's army, they'll outnumber us greatly."

My heart pounded at Shade's mention of Marlowe. So I hadn't hallucinated when I'd encountered him on the Academy grounds.

"You say the Vampire God—" I started.

Shade ran a hand over his tired face. "That's not what I came to tell you. There's just too much shit going on now." He focused on me, his gaze darkening even more. "I never thought things would get this bad this fast. If I'd known it would be like this, I'd never have dragged you to Shifter City."

"You didn't drag me here," I said. "I came with you willingly. I don't regret it. If I hadn't come with you, I wouldn't have gotten to know you as a friend. I wouldn't have had a pack with Danielle, Paris, and," I swallowed a sob, "Summer."

Sorrow passed across his face as well.

"I'll have to tell you this quickly, Pip," he said. "I'm the only visitor you'll see as long as you're here, and I won't be allowed to visit again unless you do what my brother tells you to do."

"Does Jerkface have a list?" I asked. "I bet it's long. He can fold it and shove it up his ass, preferably sideways. Feel free to pass along the message."

"You two are locked into some kind of pissing contest," he said with a troubled sigh. "It has to stop, Pip. Attacking the Alpha Heir is punishable by death, but Jared prohibits anyone from executing you. However, he must show the entire shifter world that he can tame you. You won't get out of here unless you beg for forgiveness, surrender your will, and swear a blood vow to obey him. I pleaded to my father for you, but the king denied my petition."

Shades didn't approve of how things were run in Shifter City, but he didn't carry the same weight as his brother, the heir to the throne.

"Jared refused to be persuaded either," he said, a helpless look flitting through his cornflower-blue eyes and darkening them. "I've never seen him this agitated, and no woman has ever riled him up like you did. He completely lost his shit and threw a jealous fit when you declared that you'd pick another man over him. If he knew who the man was, he'd go on a killing spree and slay any of his rivals. The worst thing is that over a dozen guards saw you attack the Alpha Heir, so he had no choice but to put you in here. If he can't tame you, his reputation will be in jeopardy."

I shrugged a little. "He can kill me and be done with it."

"He'll never do that," Shade said. "What kind of man would harm his fated mate? If word gets out, no one will trust him."

He didn't know his own brother that well. I scratched the idea of telling him that Jerkface had planned to whip and rape me in a fit of rage. I didn't want Shade to get involved.

Shade handed me a walkie-talkie. "The Alpha Heir said when you've had enough, press the blue call button and say, 'Forgive me, Alpha Heir. I vow to obey you from now on,' and he'll let you out. He said it was the only way you'd ever be free of this cell. He won't negotiate, and he won't have it any other way. It's his idea for making sure you submit to him."

"It doesn't surprise me that Jerkface lacks an imagination." I let out a low, mirthless chuckle and licked my dry lips. They only gave me a small bottle of water for the whole day in order to crush my spirit yet keep me alive. "He thought he could break me, Shade. But he doesn't know shit about me, even though he screwed me once. I was a lab rat for over a decade. I've been cut open daily, and yet I didn't break. I hate to disappoint him, but I've long passed the point of ever being tamed by any motherfucker. And when I get out of here, he'll suffer my wrath."

Shade sucked in a breath. I'd just confessed to him a piece of my dark past.

I smiled at him sweetly and smashed the radio against the ground. Shade stared at the broken pieces of metal and plastic.

A guard knocked on the iron door. Our time was up.

"Shade," I said. "Could you tell Danielle and Paris that I'm sorry for bringing death among them? Also, please tell them not to worry about me. I want them to move on. Watch their six."

Shade leaned in to whisper to me. "This isn't a goodbye, Catnip. The true purpose of me coming to visit was to tell you to hang in there. We—Danielle, Paris, and I—won't abandon you. We're working on a plan to get you out of here."

"No! Please, no!" I whispered urgently. "You must forget about me, Canary. I can't let you and Danielle throw everything away for me. I don't mind staying here. I never had anything or anyone good until I met you guys. I have nothing to lose, but your whole life is in the shifters' world, as is Danielle's."

"You're not going to rot in here." Shade lowered his voice further. "Even if you claim freedom, Jared will never let you go. He thinks you're his, even though he doesn't deserve you, even though he hasn't taken care of you. That selfish, arrogant prick has no idea how. Whatever he wants, he gets, since he's the heir. He doesn't understand the concept of 'no' in his universe."

He let out a heavy breath. "The Alpha Heir has become stronger and gained power he never had before. He realized that the perks must come from the mating bond with you. But when you broke it two days ago, he suffered some drawbacks—the new power left him. He'll seek to reclaim you and fully form the mating bond to reap the additional power you gave him. But first, he has to put on a show to punish and tame you, despite his wolf being against him."

I clenched my fists, simmering with rage.

A knock sounded on the iron door again.

"Prince Shade, your visit is over," a guard's brusque voice called outside the door. "We'll have to come in if you don't leave now."

He straightened and walked backwards toward the door, his gaze never leaving mine. "Just hold on, Catnip. This isn't the end for you, not by a long shot."

CHAPTER THIRTY

*I*t could be day four or day six. I'd lost count. And since there was no window, I couldn't tell if it was night or day. But I didn't care anymore. My life force dulled as the days passed. The spells infused into the cell continued to nullify my magic. This was what magic users called a dead zone.

I hadn't had any food since I'd been thrown in here. The Alpha Heir's will was made of iron, and his fucking words were law.

That was what he was trying to show me. Too bad for him, since I didn't give a fuck.

I would escape one day. I wouldn't die here. I knew that in my gut. Other than that, I tried not to think about it too much. If the ground beneath me hadn't rumbled so violently, I'd still be napping, my way of escaping reality and preserving my energy so I wouldn't crack.

I bolted up and listened. Something was blowing up outside—explosions and rapid gunshots—not too close to this prison but not far either.

Had the shifter and vampire war started while I'd been slumbering?

Damn, I'd missed out on all the excitement. They should have given me a window.

Then, I felt a presence encroaching, predatory and powerful beyond measure.

Friend or foe? Let me roll the dice. If it was friends, I might just get out of this jail. If it was foes, I might die, but I'd try to gouge their eyes out first.

A strange energy strummed in my middle, and it had me singing to myself:

"Hush, little baby, don't say a word.

Mama's going to buy you a mockingbird.

And if that mockingbird won't sing.

Mama's going to buy you a diamond ring…"

I had no fucking idea why I sang this song or where I'd heard it before; it just came out.

Metal scratched, twisted, and collided, making a terrible sound. Then the iron door that locked me in bent at the middle. A half-second later, the warded door was torn off its hinges and flung away by a pair of large, pale hands.

A gorgeous, otherworldly male stood in the open doorway to my cell—tousled dark hair, sculpted face that only a dark god could possess, and sensual lips that had once given me unholy pleasure in my dream.

The Vampire God had stepped out of dreams, myths, and fantasy to come for me.

Menace and power rippled off him in searing waves.

My skin tingled, my pulse spiked, and my blood raced and heated for the dark god. A connection snapped into place between us, a different mating call, like a long-forgotten song drumming in my soul.

I parted my lips involuntarily, not sure if I was more terrified or aroused.

His formidable gaze raked over me inch by inch and settled on the shackles around my ankles. His sapphire eyes burned with unconceivable dark rage, and a terrifying shadow storm wheeled at his feet.

"*Bride*, I've found you," he whispered, his rich, foreign, and ancient voice brimming with possessive and vicious fire.

I sat up straighter. I wouldn't rise abruptly to meet him since I might fall from dizziness, hunger, and fatigue, and thus embarrass myself in front of such a magnificent male.

So I just sat on the cold ground, my lips tilting up in a smirk.

"Took you long enough, *Marlowe*," I purred.

~ The End ~

***

But the story is far from over!
Preorder VAMPIRE GOD, book 2 in the
Vampire Wars series today!
Coming May 2022
(Release date listed on Amazon is only a
placeholder.)

***

P.S. If you enjoyed this book, please consider leaving an honest review. They not only impact other readers' purchasing decisions, but also help determine the success of my novels. Plus your opinion matters to me as well. I want to give you the best reading experience possible!

***

DON'T FORGET to sign up to Meg's mailing list to receive new release notifications and to get your exclusive bonus scene!

ALSO JOIN Meg's Legion of Hellions on Facebook to chat about all of Meg's books.

AUTHOR'S NOTE

Dear Reader,

Many of you want the final book in the Underworld Bride Trials first. Your wish, my command. As soon as I deliver you Hidden Court, I'll be hard at work on the Vampire God.

The second book in the Shifter War, Vampire God series is about the dark history and dangerous romance between Marlowe and Pip. There'll be a lot more battles, and you'll probably meet War, one of the worst villains I'll soon give you.

~ Meg

"Dangerous talk, Baron," I purred as he made all sorts of demands and promises while kissing me deeply and setting my body ablaze.

He carried me to the curve of the cave that cradled the red mountain so we would have more privacy. It wasn't ideal to mate in the arena, but it had to be done.

My need for my mates burned hot and primal.

"Evie." Baron murmured my name against my lips. "I'm going to take you. But if you ever sense danger from me, gut me and run for safety."

"I always sense danger and menace from you, even when we're outside the Wild Hunt," I told him. "So it's no big deal."

"I'll gut you, Baron," Rydstrom offered from nearby. He stood guard, his magnificent wings unfurling and forming a wide span to shield us.

"I'll have to keep earning your trust, then, my Evie," Baron said, ignoring the Night King.

"I trust Ryds and you already," I said. "I know, it's shocking."

I'd given both of them my heart, and it was already too late to take it back. If they turned on me in the end, like Rowan had done, then so be it. We lived only once, and I wasn't going to choose to live in fear.

"But I can't trust myself with you," said Baron.

"Yeah?" I asked. "What do you mean by that?"

He trembled, his eyes feral and full of lust. He wanted to fuck me so badly. My lips parted, my breath warm against his mouth.

"I can't be gentle, baby," he said, kissing my jawline. "I'll try to go slow so I won't lose it."

"I didn't ask you to go slow," I moaned as his scorching kisses moved to the column of my neck. "And I don't need you to be gentle."

"You won't mind me fucking you like a beast?" he asked. "Evie, I hope you can think better of me, but all I want is to thrust inside you like a caveman fucking his female. I want to fuck you like a wild beast."

My heart pounded, his pure male need dominating me.

"Fuck me however you want," I offered.

His warm, firm lips that tasted of sunlight devoured mine. At his demand, I opened my mouth to him. His lust set me on fire and made me so ripe for him.

My pussy was soaked. I propelled my hips toward him to urge him to take me now. He roughly pulled my pants down to my knees and lifted my bare ass, positioning me just right for fucking.

We couldn't afford to get naked when anything could happen in the Wild Hunt. Baron kept his trousers on, opened the fly, and let his massive cock spring free.

I'd like to get down on all fours and have him fuck me from behind, but it might put us in a vulnerable situation, even with Rydstrom guarding us.

At least with us fucking upright, we could see threats when they were coming.

Baron nudged the thick crown of his granite-hard shaft against my entrance. I moaned at the sensation and wiggled my ass to urge him in. A low growl rumbled in his chest, like a warning and approval at the same time, which made my pussy clench in desperate need.

"Are you done yet, Baron?" Rydstrom asked impatiently from several paces away, his back to us, his massive ebony wings forming a shield in front of us.

"We're just about to start," Baron hissed. "This

is my first time with Evie. I must make it special for her."

"Bad news for you, Summer King," Rydstrom said. "This isn't the time or place to romance Ileana. Just get it over with. Are you so rusty you don't know how to do a quickie anymore?"

I narrowed my eyes. I hadn't known the Night King could be such a buzz kill. I knew we were running out of time, but he didn't need to spoil it for us while Baron was trying to make me more comfortable.

"If you hadn't interrupted us, I'd be fucking my mate right now," Baron growled, his cock still nestled between my folds. "And if you think you can ruin this great moment with my mate, you're severely mistaken."

I also had a hunch that Rydstrom didn't want Baron to enjoy the hell out of fucking me. This definitely wasn't the threesome I'd fantasized about.

"This is a sprint, Baron, not a marathon!" Rydstrom snapped.

Really?

"You two are arguing in a dire situation like this?" I shouted at them. If the mating fever wasn't raging within me, I'd just unclasp my legs from Baron's waist and kick both Fae kings in the jaw and see how they liked it. "You two are insufferable, and I've put up with you enough!" I might have exaggerated a bit, but I wanted them to see their error. "You want to ruin this for me, is that it?" I raised my voice a notch. "What kind of mates are you? Either you both shut up or I stop this altogether."

Rydstrom apologized to me instantly, then turned to Baron and added viciously, "Just get it done before you no longer have a chance. I'm sensing the approach of an enemy force."

Baron grumbled unintelligibly, probably throwing one last curse at Rydstrom, before he thrust into me with brutal force.

The feel of him entering me was divine. My eyes fluttered shut, and when I opened them again, I could see golden sunlight blazing in the Summer King's amber eyes, so brilliant it nearly melted me. The Summer King was used to dazzling a woman. Old habits die hard.

But I was taking in his whole package, good and bad, as I gazed at him with passion and shivering need.

"My mate, *mine*," he whispered.

His fingertips pressed hard into my hips, anchoring me in place. I arched my back as his steel rod sank deep inside me and brought me incredible pleasure.

When Rowan took me that day, ice and frost had burned in my bloodstream. When Rydstrom claimed me, midnight starlight lit my every fiber, filling me with dark fantasy. Now, as Baron fucked me, summer heat blossomed within me.

Baron pulled out and thrust back in, faster and harder, and every spot he hit sparked with pleasurable electricity. I moaned breathlessly and begged for him to never stop.

The erotic sound of flesh pounding into flesh echoed in my ears, and I rocked with the rhythm, knowing and accepting that I was at the mercy of the Summer King. He pounded into me, filling and stretching my tight passage.

Baron let out a rough groan, his lion peeking out at me possessively through his fiery eyes. If we made it out of the Wild Hunt, I would never waste time arguing with my mates again. I'd spend all my time fucking them.

"Fuck me harder, Baron!" I cried out. "Yes, just like that!"

He growled and thrust into me deeply and rapidly, stoking the mating flame higher.

Nothing felt better than fucking—the most primal, glorious thing between a man and a woman—but you needed to fuck the right man.

He heaved me up and down the impressive length of his cock. The task might be difficult for a human male, but my Fae mate was all strength and muscles and burning lust.

My pussy gloved every inch of him and milked his cock as I grasped his shoulders and pulled him flush against me. My fire joined his sunlight, fueling each other.

"Evie, baby." He threw his head back and groaned in intense pleasure. "Ride me hard. Take all you want from your male!"

We quickened our pace, pounding into each other. Our breath mingled, his minty scent intoxicating, as we fucked like two beasts.

"The best fuck I've ever had," Baron hissed, thrusting into me with bruising strength, driving in and out of my body at blinding speed.

My savage!

A cry of pleasure spilled out of my mouth, yet I demanded more.

"I'll give you more. I'll give you everything," he growled, a shudder rippling through him.

Waves of pleasure burst in me, so much it was almost unbearable. I arched my back, then I stilled and exploded around his cock.

He called my name like he lived and breathed for me.

In a long, glorious thrust, the Summer King emptied himself into me and roared.

The mating bond snapped into place. A thread of golden light looped around us in a rush of heat. Now, not even the ancient force of the Wild Hunt could overcome the forming of our mating bond.

"I've waited centuries for this," the Summer

King whispered, "to truly belong and bond to one woman, to my one true mate."

Tears shining in his eyes, he stared at the thread of light between us in awe. It glittered for a moment then sank into us, bonding us forever.

Rydstrom turned his head slowly and gazed at me while Baron and I were still joined. A riot of emotions wheeled in his sapphire eyes like a midnight storm. There was such desperate need and scorching desire in them that my heart ached for him and my body demanded to have him, too.

The Night King saw what I craved from him and let out a rasping, regretful breath. I wanted to extend my hand to him and invite him to join us, but we both knew we didn't have time for another mating. This moment belonged to the Summer King.

"I'd have mated with you differently and cherished you as you deserve under different circumstances," Baron said. "Love, I'll make it up to you once we're out of the hunt."

"You've cherished me," I told him. "But I'll hold you to your promise."

Rydstrom turned his back again, scanning for threats as he waited for Baron and me to have our final tender moment, his beautiful and terrifying wings unfurled.

Then suddenly, he doubled over, the hand that wasn't holding a sword bracing on the ground to support his collapsed weight. His agony ripped into me through our mating bond as a force beyond the power of this world rammed into him.

"Hurry," Rydstrom said, clenching his teeth and rising to his feet. "Our enemies are here!"

Then Baron's agony also rushed through me like hard waves, and I screamed in pain.

The revenge of the Wild Hunt had come for my mates.

Continue to read Dark Fae Kings

Book 4: Blood Fae

THE WAR OF GODS SERIES

A Court of Blood and Void

A Court of Fire and Metal

A Court of Ice and Wind

A Court of Earth and Ether

OF SHADOWS AND FIRE SERIES

The Burn of the Underworld

The Rise of the Underworld

The Dragonian's Witch

The Witch's Consort

SHIFTER'S WITCH

ABOUT THE AUTHOR

Meg Xuemei X is a USA Today and Amazon Charts bestselling author of paranormal and fantasy romance. She finds it delightful to be around drop-dead gorgeous alpha males who are forever tormented by her feisty heroines, unseelie fae, dark vampires, menacing demigods, demon A-holes and fallen angels, fun shifters, and cunning witches.